I0451700

Keep Her Contained

By Oscar Corral

A novel

Copyright © 2012 Oscar Corral
All rights reserved.

ISBN-13: 978-0-9882131-1-1

DEDICATION

This book is dedicated to the millions of immigrants who continue to come to the United States, seeking a better life. Their hope, determination and grit are the definition of the American character.

ACKNOWLEDGMENTS

I want to thank Newsday in New York for giving me the opportunity to pursue this story wherever it led, be it El Salvador or Manhattan. And my wife and fellow journalist, Cecile, for her support and invaluable editing input.

CHAPTER 1

By Long Island standards, the house at 97 Forest Drive was in full bloom. Built in 1957, it still retained its simplicity in architecture with clean angles, large windows, a low roof. Alterations over time had kept the structure modern looking. One family added a bay window overlooking the front yard. Another extended the living room 10 feet to the east. The second garage was added in the 1970s, by an owner who dug Starsky and Hutch and pampered his Camaro the way sports trainers pampered Joe Namath. Landscaping had spread over the years from a simple cherry bush hedge along the front window to islands of native perennials outlined by faux rocks. In the winter, patches of colorful cabbage along the path from the sidewalk to the front door lightened the ominous moods brought on by skeletal maple and oak trees.

The neighbors were fixtures. On the left, Harriet and John Finklestein anchored the neighborhood crime watch association. They had lived there since 1964. After raising four children and retiring recently, they spent their time walking their three dachtsunds around the block, scoping out strange cars and delivery trucks. They owned a CB radio donated to them by Citizens on Patrol with a direct link to the second precinct police dispatcher. No one took them seriously as watchdogs until they helped nab a burglar three days before Christmas at a house down the street in 1996. The house was empty at the time, abandoned for the winter. Like many other families in the neighborhood, the owners were snowbirds, seeking refuge from Long Island's blizzards and deep freezes in South Florida.

The neighbor on the right of 97 Forest Drive was as far from an activist and vigilante as they came, despite her 40-plus years living there. Rose Parker, widowed 14 years ago when her drunkard husband walked into the path of a Long Island Rail Road locomotive, seldom left her home. She spent most of her days reading true crime books, listening to Howard Stern and National Public Radio, and working her vegetable garden in her back yard accompanied by her trusty mut, Silver. Every now and then, Rose Parker's worthless drunkard son would stay with his mother for a few weeks stretch, laying low while bookies who wanted to break his legs cooled down.

Across the street, Jessica Goldfarb, wife of Marty Goldfarb and stay-at-home mom of two teenagers, was the information tornado. She sucked in all the gossip on the block with her three special tentacles: nosiness, brazenness, and pushiness. Anything that happened on Forest Drive was churned through the editor/publisher/distributor in Jessica's mind and wrapped in melodrama for proper telephone consumption.

Jericho was one of the older developments on the island, sprouting up in northeastern Nassau County only a decade after Levittown came on-line to accommodate World War II veterans looking for a tranquil suburban existence. But many of Jericho's homes were custom built, as opposed to the cookie-cutter like Levittown, which took just two years to complete. Jericho was maturing with grace. Tiny seedlings planted 40 years ago had swelled into stately trees that lined every block and arched over every street. Property values had exploded, and a house bought for $29,000 in 1960 could sell for $700,000 today. Wealthy Manhattanites with young children often relocated there, looking to trade in urban grit for a slice of suburban sod. Second mortgages pumped home improvement capital into the neighborhood. Luxurious landscaping, second garages and back yard hot tubs and swimming pools sprouted everywhere.

In this backdrop of permanence and maturity, 97 Forest Drive was the anomaly. Since it had been built, it had changed owners six times. No one seemed to consider it home for very long. And it was strange, because the house had been so intensely upgraded over the years by new owners that it outpaced most of the other homes in the neighborhood with elegance, charm and originality. So many families made their way through the house that

Rose Parker stopped baking cookies for children that lived there after the third family moved out in 1979 because she figured it wasn't worth being nice if the neighbors would just be moving on soon.

When the house would go up for sale, neighbors would drop in to lament the residents' decision, and ask why they were selling. Some of the owners said the house just didn't feel right. Some said they had outgrown it. Others, after closing on a deal, would admit that the house gave them the creeps.

CHAPTER 2

Eight homes in one day were too many. Real estate burnout prevented the Bazis from absorbing too much detail.

Their realtor pushed a crummy Levittown duplex on them. They nixed it from their list before getting off the car.

"I've had it on my listings forever," their realtor admitted.

The other houses on her list weren't much better: Three were too small. One was too isolated. Two were on blocks with too much traffic. Searching for a new home had been a nightmare: Bazi worked late. Seeing homes on weeknights was impossible. His wife didn't want to go without him. She had to bring their kids everywhere, ever since she snagged her teenage son smoking a cigarette in a neighborhood park with a hoodlum.

Eight years and four children into their Muslim-American matrimony, the Bazis had outgrown their three bedroom split level in East Meadow. Bazi had been burning the midnight oil at Computer Tekdom. Promotions were almost weekly. The inflating bubble on Wall Street's tech sector was pumping rich air into Bazi's pockets. No overtime, but a nice salary and $2.65 million in lush stock options were enough to catapult his family into Long Island high society.

97 Forest Drive was the last house on their list for the day. Nestled in a birch and oak-lined street, the lazy, shade-covered surroundings peaked their interest. They walked around the two-story house once, glancing inside for just a moment. They put a star next to it on their list and asked the realtor how much the owners were asking.

"A million," she said.

The sun was coming down and mosquitoes were feasting on their ankles. Hunger was making the kids irritable. They agreed to continue shopping another day.

A week later, the Bazis scouted 97 Forest Drive one more time. They split up, each of them to check out their preferred amenities. Mr. Bazi rounded a birch tree and entered the back yard. The wood deck triggered fantasies of barbeque paradise: lamb kabobs, date-stuffed chicken, maybe even burgers. Bushes provided privacy for the hot tub built into the deck. Mr. Bazi pictured himself splashing hot tub water onto the bed of roses sprouting nearby, a stogie dangling from his mouth.

Mrs. Bazi noticed how the afternoon light invaded the living room through the skylights. The future indoor garden was coming together in her mind. She saw herself sipping herbal tea by the eucalyptus sprouts. Outside, the empty tract of dirt near the back door was perfect for a summer vegetable garden. She loved the bay windows overlooking the porch garden.

The kids scoped out their future bedrooms: one for each. They shot hoops on the rim built into the driveway. The lush foliage was hide-and-go-seek paradise. They gave the game an early run. Big Samir counted down from 30. Little Noel and Sarah scurried into the crawl space under the house addition. There was a steal drum lying down against a corner. The children crawled behind it. After a few minutes, Samir gave up.

"You guys won, I can't find you!" Samir yelled. "Come out, come out wherever you are."

But the kids were stubborn. Their hiding place was too good. They'd outsmarted big brother. Mom and Dad soon joined the search. All three were yelling "Noel, Sarah, where are you?"

Mr. Bazi heard giggles coming from below. He crawled under the addition, toward the laughter. He noticed the barrel and grimaced. Two little heads popped out from behind it.

"There you are!" he said to his 7-year-old daughter and 4-year-old son. "Come on out of there, you little devils." The kids screamed and wailed with laughter.

The Bazi feedback to their realtor was unanimous: "We love the house. We'll take it. Let's sign the contract tomorrow. But just one thing, please make sure to tell Mr. Cohen that I want all the property removed from the house, especially that barrel in the crawl space."

"No problem," the realtor said. "It'll be gone."

CHAPTER 3

The movers were morons: They dropped a box of China, couldn't fit the couch through the door, stacked heavy books on top of glass painting frames. To make matters worse, one of them patted Cohen's wife's rear when she brought them a glass of lemonade. Cohen never imagined moving out would be such a fiasco. It had cost him hard-earned vacation time, prompted arguments with his wife, and forced him to take inventory of the fruits of his labor — nothing but a pile of boxes filled with tacky knick-knacks.

When the Bazi's came to look at the house one more time on August 31, they walked around the property, eyeing everything carefully. The Cohens, exhausted from packing, waited to give them the keys. Cohen was trying to beat the summer heat by standing in the shade of a tree.

"Is that it?" Cohen said as the Bazis rounded the corner.

"It looks great," Mr. Bazi said. "Just don't forget that barrel you've got down there under the crawl space."

"That thing down there?" Cohen said. "It's been here since I moved in, it's not mine."

"Well, it certainly isn't mine and I don't want it there," Bazi said. "The contract says you'll leave the house empty. And that's our final request."

"Fine," Cohen said. "I'll take it out."

After Bazi left, Cohen crawled under the house. A ring of crud on the concrete floor surrounded the barrel, as though it hadn't been moved in a decade. But the barrel wouldn't budge. Cohen pulled it, pushed it, clawed at it and kicked it, but the thing must have weighed half a ton.

Reluctantly, Cohen appealed to his moronic movers for help.

Two big guys went down there and rolled the barrel out. They came out sweating, wondering what the hell was inside. Together, the two movers and Cohen rolled it to the trash pickup and stood it up next to a pile of old toys, furniture and junk the Cohens were throwing out.

Early the next morning, a trash truck rumbled onto Forest Drive. The junk heap in front of number 97 intimidated the rookie hanging onto the back of the truck.

"This is a fucking abuse," the rook said. "They should charge these assholes extra."

"No use thinkin about it too much," said a veteran trash man.

He and the rookie dug in quick. They set up the pile so the mechanical claw could carry as much as possible in one grab. The steel hand lined up over the stack. It dropped open and clutched a load. Ten years worth of worthlessness disappeared into the truck: a couch, a table, a desk, an old mattress, boxes of clothes, hangers, an old computer, pots, magazines. The pile dwindled to scraps. The men gathered those into a small heap and the claw came down again.

The rookie lit up a cigarette. Just recently hired and he was already slacking. He walked to the green barrel standing on the curb and gave it a kick. The thing didn't budge. He dropped his shovel and pushed it, putting his shoulder into it. The barrel tilted to the side. The rookie held it there for a moment. Then the barrel tilted back onto its base with a thud. The rookie fidgeted with the sealed top. It was rusted on tight.

Trash men had rules. The rules were fresh in the rookie's mind. He slacked. He complained like a housewife about his job. But he knew the fucking rules. It said clearly on page 16 of their training manual: no container shall be loaded into a truck without examining the contents. If a trash man doesn't know what's in a container, they just won't take it away. He was going by the book.

"What do you think?" the rook asked the vet.

The veteran walked over. He eyed the drum, giving it a shove of his own.

"I think it's alright," the vet said.

"Alright!?" the rook said shocked. "Are you fucking crazy. It says in the rule book, man, we can't load shit up if we don't know what's in it."

"It's probably just dried up old tar," the vet said. Then he yelled at the driver, "Load it up."

"Hang on," the rookie yelled to the driver. "Hank, come here."

The veteran threw up his hands, obviously annoyed at the rookie's tenacity. The fat driver got off and came over.

"What the fuck is it now, junior?"

"That drum's sealed," the rookie said. "We ain't supposed to take sealed shit, right?"

The driver eyed the veteran.

"The kid's got a point," the fat driver said.

"Fuck it, then leave the shit right there," the veteran said. "I don't give a flying fuck."

The truck rumbled down to the next load two houses down.

A few minutes later, Cohen showed up to give the house a last glance before parting from it for good. Much to his disappointment, the steel drum was still on the curb, on the same spot where the movers had left it the day before. Cohen saw the trash truck turn the corner down the block and went after it in his car. The two trash men were loading a pile of yard waste into the truck when Cohen pulled up next to them.

"Hey, hey you two," Cohen yelled.

The veteran looked over.

"What's up?" he said.

"You guys just came down that block, right?" Cohen said.

"Yeah."

"Well you left that drum sitting on my curb," Cohen said. "That's trash too. I want you guys to take it."

The veteran glanced at the rookie angrily.

"I knew we'd have to go back, you fuck," the vet snapped at the rookie.

"Sir, we can't take that barrel cause we don't know what the hell's in it," the rookie said.

"Who cares what's in it," Cohen said. "I don't want it."

"Those are the rules sir," the rookie said.

"God dammit," Cohen said. "So if I open it up for you will

you take it?"

"If it weighs less than 300 pounds we'll take it," the rookie said.

The veteran, shocked at the rookie's harping over the rules, spoke up.

"Hey fuck your rules junior, I told you it would mean more work later," the veteran said, then turned to Cohen. "Look. If you open it up, we'll take it. We'll meet you over there as soon as we finish up here."

Cohen thanked the man and drove home. Back at the barrel with a tool box, he struggled to unscrew the sealed top. Time had rusted it shut. The trash men pulled up. The veteran asked Cohen for a monkey wrench. With brute strength, the trash man loosened the rusted screws.

They finally came off, loosening the steal belt around the lid. Cohen hammered a small pick into the crevice between the lid and the barrel. Using the pick as a wedge, he pushed down until a small section of the lid popped up. After doing this every three inches around the diameter of the lid, Cohen grabbed the top and yanked it off. The three men standing around the drum stumbled back.

It took just a moment for Cohen to identify the object in the barrel: it was an upside down red woman's shoe on what looked like a human foot. Next to the foot was a solidified human hand with a ring. Cohen gagged and leaned against a tree.

"It's a goddamned body," yelled the rookie.

The veteran covered his nose and walked closer. A woman's red pump on a rotting foot jutted out from the bottom of a second barrel that had rusted through. Next to the shoe, a shriveled hand attached to an arm could be seen. The veteran shook his head.

"You should be proud, junior," the veteran said. "I've been doing this for 21 years and I've never found a body. I used to hear stories about the mob dumping bodies in trash heaps, and I was always afraid I'd find one. I almost feel like I can fucking retire now."

"I guess we can't dump this, right?" the rookie asked.

The veteran only gave him stupid look. He called to Cohen: "Hey, hey you."

A ribbon of puke saliva stretched out of Cohen's mouth as he hunched next to the tree. He wiped it and looked at the trash man.

"You better call the cops," the trash man said.

Cohen nodded and walked back to his neighbor's house. The trash workers placed the lid loosely on the drum and backed off. But no matter how far they walked, they couldn't shake the stench emanating from the drum.

Cohen jilted the trash goons and sat in his car. The air conditioning quelled his nausea. His head swirled. That barrel hadn't budged from under his house in ten years. He and his wife had shared the last decade with a cadaver. Talk about lack of resting in peace: every time he had walked over his living room, it was like tap-dancing on an unholy grave. Dizziness replaced the nausea. He passed out with the engine running.

Cops responded en masse. In minutes they were everywhere. A trash guy tapped on Cohen's window, jolting him awake. Cohen opened his door. The smell from the barrel had intensified outside. Cohen walked out into a shifting scene.

About ten squad cars lined the block. A few neighbors had come out of their houses, all of them probing officers for answers. Cops herded them to either side of the house. They hung yellow police tape across the street, tying it to trees to hold it up. Three cops guarded the barrel. No one went near it. No one touched it. But everyone smelled it.

The trash guys were talking to a uniformed sergeant. They called over to Cohen. He ambled over, still shocked. The questions began: when did you find it? Who were you with? Did you know what was inside? The trash guys corroborated Cohen's account. They knew almost as much as he did.

A gold Crown Victoria cruised under the yellow tape and pulled up next to Cohen and company. A short, stumpy man in a light gray suit and a tall, hefty man in a blue suit got out. All the cops quieted down. The uniformed sergeant ceased his questions immediately.

"That's homicide," the sergeant said. "They'll want to talk to you guys."

The two suited investigators walked to Cohen and the others. The stumpy man adjusted his glasses. Every cop, every journalist, every crime news junky in New York knew Detective Sergeant Roger Connery. His name was almost synonymous with Amy Fisker, the Long Island Lolita arrested for attempted murder after shooting Joey Batanulu's wife. Connery himself had snapped the cuffs on Fisker, and paraded Batanulu before the video cameras after his interrogation at police headquarters. The problem was, he wasn't known for anything else. After a series of consultations for television movies, books and talk shows, Connery had entered a slump phase in his career that had yet to break.

"What's up?" the stumpy man said.

The uniformed sergeant filled him in: a body had been found by trash men and the homeowner inside the drum. The homeowner had been insistent that the trash men take the barrel. He seemed extremely eager to dispose of it. Nothing had been disturbed. The scene remained intact.

Connery waddled to the drum. A slight limp from a Vietnam shrapnel wound still plagued him. A crime scene investigator wearing rubber gloves lifted the drum cover. Connery bent over it, but snapped back when the stink hit. He pulled a handkerchief from his back pocket and held it over his mouth and nose while he briefly examined the contents. He turned to the witnesses waiting nearby.

"How you gentlemen doin? I'm Det. Sgt. Roger Connery and this is Det. Daniel Poppel, we're with homicide."

The trash men nodded hello. Cohen barely twitched. His mind was a loose wheel. Connery noticed Cohen's unease.

"We're going to need to talk to you guys one by one," Connery said. He pointed at a trash man. "You first."

They walked to a shady corner of the property, away from the glaring neighbors. The conversation didn't last long, maybe five minutes. Connery and Poppel finished up with the trash guys. The investigators absorbed all the information. Cohen was last. Cohen was the prized lamb, the homeowner, the ostensive owner of the barrel, their first suspect.

Connery paused for a moment in front of Cohen. The old

investigator let his stare do the initial testing. His blue eyes carved out a reaction. Cohen averted his look, first down at Connery's jacket, then toward the trees. Poppel watched. He was still learning, even after 8 years on homicide.

"Who's in that barrel?" Connery asked.

"I have no idea," Cohen said.

"We understand you tried to dispose of it today," Connery said.

"I didn't know what was in it," Cohen said. "I'm moving out and the guy moving in asked me to get rid it."

"Trash guys said you were pretty upset when they didn't take it," Connery said.

"I just wanted to finish moving out," Cohen said. "That thing has been down there since I moved in here ten years ago."

Connery glanced at Poppel.

"Really, ten years ago?" Connery said. "You never wondered what was in it?"

"It never got in my way," Cohen said. "The wife and I never go down there. So we just forgot about it."

"So you're telling me that you moved into this house ten years ago, you saw that barrel down there and you never bothered to throw it out or even check what was in it?" Connery said.

"Well, yeah. I never go down there. Call my wife at work and ask her if you want."

A breeze carried over a strong odor from the barrel. Cohen gagged.

"What's your wife's number?"

Cohen gave them the number. Poppel stepped away with his cellular phone. He called Cohen's wife and came back minutes later. He nodded at Connery. Cohen's story checked out.

"Your wife was pretty shocked," Poppel said. "She said she'd be happy to come in for further questioning."

Cohen shuddered. His face was whiter than a raw potato.

"Can you show us where the barrel has been all this time?" Connery said.

Cohen led them to the crawl space under the house. The old investigator crouched down to fit under the low ceiling. His bad leg acted up. He shook it off and continued to a niche by the stairs. Cohen pointed at a ring of crud on the concrete ground.

"That's where it was," Cohen said. "It hasn't moved from that spot since I've been here."

Connery sat down Indian style next to the ring of crud. Only musty, humid air circulated down there. He wiped his face with the handkerchief. For a little while, he just sat there, thinking.

The air smelled stank and humid. It was a distinct odor of earth and wood. It reminded Connery of a foxhole he crouched in for three straight days in Vietnam. Connery looked down at his hands, pudgy and hairy, trapping his wedding ring in a cushion of fat.

Cohen sat on the stairs, apparently exhausted. Detective Poppel looked around the area then approached Connery.

"Hey Bobbie," said Poppel. "We don't even know if it's a homicide yet. Let's let the Medical Examiner have a look, then we'll move forward, huh?"

Connery nodded. "Ok," he said. "But let's do some legwork. Let's face it, if someone died of natural causes, they wouldn't be put to rest this way."

"I'm thinking about pulling the property records on the house, finding out who's lived here," Poppel said.

"Good," Connery said. "And check the barrel for a manufacturer label and a serial number."

"What for?" Poppel said.

"We need to find out when the barrel was manufactured, so we can put a time frame on the body."

"And the media?" Poppel asked.

"No media," Connery said. "We still don't know if it's a homicide right? So they don't need to know."

Cohen stood up.

"Can I go?" he said.

"Not yet," Connery said.

Connery left the crawl space just as the Crime Scene Investigators crawled in. The woman who headed the team said hi to Connery.

"So what have we got here?" she said.

"A body in a drum," Connery said. "Possibly female due to

the shoe."

Connery knew it was a murder. The chips of logic began parachuting into place in his mind. It didn't take a medical examiner to tell him that whoever was in that barrel had been the victim of a homicide. Early indications signaled foul play. Someone had stashed the body. If it was merely a case of improper burial, the cadaver would never have been abandoned. Improper burials occur when someone can't part with the remains, when death sparks inability to act. The body becomes indispensable. The loved one keeps it close: in a chest, a bedroom, an attic, a crawl space, a closet.

Connery remembered the case three years ago when he walked into the master bedroom of a run-down North Shore mansion -- a handkerchief cupped over his nose -- and found the cadaver of a millionaire partially melted into the mattress. The old widow had never reported her husband's death. She still served him breakfast every morning, as evidenced by the tray with a croissant and jam on the nightstand. What had smelled putrid to Connery was a comfort to the widow that her husband was still near. That case was very different from this one. The only people close to this body, the Cohens, didn't know it was there. Someone wanted it hidden. They picked a steel drum and a luxury house to hide it under.

Connery cranked the A/C in his black Crown Victoria. His dashboard imitated a firebreathing dragon: hot air galore. He kept still until the air cooled down. It took a few minutes in September. He whipped out a notepad.

He brainstormed the early facts: Cohen discovers a body inside a steal drum. Trash guys are standing by when he opens it. Cohen seems innocent. The body is probably female, due to the shoe. It's been under the house at least as long as Cohen has lived there.

Connery stared out the windshield. This wasn't a typical gangland murder, or domestic homicide or drug killing, he thought.

Det. Daniel Poppel opened the passenger door and sat next to him. Poppel was Connery's lead dick. His instincts were only dwarfed by his appetite. The only thing he did at work without Connery's approval was eat. The passenger side of the car dipped.

"What do you think?" Poppel said.

"We don't have much," Connery said.

"M.E.'s office is sending the van."

"OK, good. Did you get pictures?"

"Yeah."

"I was just getting down some early facts," Connery said. "What do you think about the Cohen guy?"

Poppel chuckled.

"I think he needs a shrink," Poppel said.

Connery shot a sarcastic look at his lead detective.

"We need a time of death, at least a ballpark."

"The ME will have that for us in less than a day."

"I don't know about that," Connery said. "If that drum was airtight, the ME might not be able to pinpoint time of death."

"After I pull property records, at least we'll know who lived here and when," Poppel said.

"Right," Connery said. "When you get the records, check the building history. I want to know when the house was built and if and when any additions or alterations were made. If you find alterations, get me the name of the contractor, engineer, architect, everything."

"Right," Poppel said. "Anything and anyone that can build us a time frame."

"One more thing," Connery said. "Tell Cohen not to stray. He ain't a suspect but he's all we have right now."

"How about the neighborhood canvass?" Poppel said.

"Let's hold off on that until we know a little more about our victim," Connery said. "Once they open up the drum at the morgue and remove the contents, we may be able to paint a better picture."

"OK, I'm gonna go grab some lunch," Poppel said, and exited the car.

Connery glanced out the window. Neighbors were packed in behind the yellow police tape. They were waving at uniformed cops to ask them questions. Flashbacks hit Connery of the time he was invited to the David Elderman show a decade ago to talk about the Amy Fisker case and had to walk past a group of gawkers behind barricades to get into the studio. He never knew how to react when strangers waved at him. He usually ignored them. It was the easiest thing to do.

CHAPTER 4

Jessica: little housewife, PTA president, neighborhood information switchboard. She was the first neighbor on the scene outside the Cohen house. She had spotted the police scene on her way back home from her mother's house in her big Ford Expedition. Now she had the scoop. She had spent hours working the uniformed cops on duty. She had even brought them coffee and cookies. Now they were her buds. They called her Jessie. They confided in her with new info. Other neighbors gravitated toward her, scrounging for scraps of the tale. At first Jessie held back, the gossip tease, acting ignorant. The cops told her not to tell anyone else. It was "just between me and you" every time a blue uniform spilled facts to her.

Jessie center stage: queen of know. She parlayed the self-righteous act. Those cop secrets were only treasure as long as she kept them. Neighbors cajoled her, sweet talked her, enticed her with favors, but Jessica held still. She didn't tell what she knew. And by now she knew what the cops knew. Most people had heard there was a body involved. But only Jessica had it from a cop that it was probably murder.

The longer she stayed quiet the more she wanted to talk. It was like holding her breath underwater. It would be so easy to just surface and breathe. Keeping secrets was not her greatest strength, and spewing and soaking up gossip was as much a part of her existence as eating and sleeping.

The cops started breaking up the party. The undertaker's van drove off. Homicide unit sedans pulled away. Jessie stood there, waiting for more, surrounded by neighbors. She figured there had to be a punch line. The story had to have an end. There was no way the cops could just leave her hanging. The only thing she knew was the beginning of a mystery.

The cops were now keeping their distance, something had changed. They weren't coming up to her anymore. She noticed a high-level uniformed officer lurking in the middle of the scene. She waved at a couple cops, but they just waved back and ignored her. She felt the urge to purge information rising up inside her the way a bulimic feels lunch tickling her esophagus.

The cop who had told her the most got into his squad car and peeled off. That was the final straw. Jessica pulled aside a neighbor, Anne Hutchinson, and leaned in close to her ear. Others were watching. As Jessica spoke, Anne's eyes widened, then her mouth opened slightly, then she covered it with a hand. Jessica straightened up nodding matter-of-factly. Anne only said "in this neighborhood?"

Several people swarmed them. Anne repeated the story. Kyle Grimsley, a retired advertising executive who lived down the block, heard the whole thing.

Kyle Grimsley went home that night, had dinner with his wife, and told her about the crime scene in the neighborhood. He didn't say more than what he had heard. But he told the story in a somber way.

"Oh Jesus!" said his wife. "Have they caught the killer?"

Kyle Grimsley shook his head gravely. In seconds, his wife had the television on, scanning channel 12 and the networks for answers. It was still early. No news was on. She took to the phone with renewed energy. She called her sister in Connecticut, her son in Manhattan, her brother in Massapequa, her daughter in Fort Lauderdale. They all asked her the same question: have they caught the killer. But Ms. Grimsley didn't know. Before going to bed, she scanned the tv for news again, to no avail.

Her restlessness and curiosity compelled her to pick up the phone one more time before she turned out her lights and call her best friend, Rose Parker. Rose hadn't heard anything about a murder. Rose was a news hound who scoured the newspapers every morning and listened to the radio all day: Howard Stern, National Public Radio, The Eights. If anyone would know about a murder it was her. But it hadn't been in the news today, she told her friend.

"But it should be," Rose said. "Stay on the line."

"Who are you going to call?"

"Newstime."

"You can't just call Newstime. No one is supposed to know about this. Besides, how would you even know who to call there?"

"I do it all the time," Rose said. "Whenever I read the newspaper and have questions about a story, I call em."

The phone rang once before a clerk picked up the phone at Long Island's biggest newspaper. Both women giggled at first, but then Rose cleared her throat.

"I want to report a murder," she said.

"Who is this?" the clerk asked.

"It doesn't matter. But listen to what I'm going to tell you."

"Hang on, let me put you through to a reporter."

Muzac entertained the old ladies while on hold. They giggled like schoolgirls. Finally, a young man's voice appeared on the other end of the line. It was Michael Cervantes, the paper's crime reporter.

"Can I help you?" Michael said.

"I want to report a murder. It's been kept quiet by the police, but trust me."

"So what happened."

"Cops found a body today at 97 Forest Drive in Jericho. The body was stashed in a metal drum underneath the house. I think the cops want to keep it quiet, but it's got the whole neighborhood spooked."

"Ok, thank you, I'll check it out," Michael said. "By the way, can I get a name and number to call you back in case I have any questions?"

"It's an anonymous tip," Rose Parker said.

A technician rolled the drum down to the Medical Examiner's office in a dolly. People taking cigarette breaks outside cringed and turned away, the rancid stench slapping them as it passed. The descent to the morgue was cruel punishment for the technician. He tried to hold his breath.

The elevator opened in the autopsy room two floors down. Dr. Lesley Lancaster, chief medical examiner of Nassau County, was standing right there. The old doctor's bushy eyebrows were crimpled up over his eyes, his nose held high. The technician stopped in front of him, startled by the doctor's sudden appearance.

"I've been waiting for you," Lancaster said.

Lancaster was 80, as tall as a streetlamp with a beard that reached his chest, and he never parted with the boots he wore during the second World War. They had been re-soled seven times and half the leather had been reinforced by patches.

His mind was a bank of forensic files, a human library of the county's suspicious deaths. Some days, he couldn't remember where he parked his Lincoln Town Car at the pharmacy, but the details of autopsies he performed in 1965 were emblazoned in his memory like a database. It was safe to say he had seen it all in his career, which stretched back to 1942. Back then the government had him dissecting bodies of soldiers killed by Nazi chemical warfare, studying what mustard and nerve gas did to lungs. Sometimes he would take apart bodies burned to a crisp, only to discover their insides as moist and rosy as the next victims'.

The war triggered in Lancaster a fascination with death that never left him. He wanted to understand it so that he would not be afraid when it came for him. And during every single autopsy he performed or supervised over the course of his career, Lancaster looked for clues to bolster his theory that death was not the worst part of living. Sometimes he convinced himself. But sometimes he found himself staring into the battered mechanics of a murder victim's body, knowing that their last gasp was their most bitter.

Lancaster only spoke when he had something to say, and liked to joke that dead bodies held better conversations than most people. His rationale was that bodies, like organic diaries, revealed the deepest truths about people better than any oral confession. So many dead bodies had come before him, so many secrets hidden behind underwear, and sleeves and skin. He no longer saw corpses as former people, but as vehicles of riddles and tales.

A few times, Lancaster had submitted his retirement papers. But he always pulled them before the end date, worried that death would find him. He figured that as long as he was hiding out in the morgue, carrying on with his work, death would leave him alone another day to ponder its eternal question.

Dr. Lancaster stood over the barrel and rubbed his white beard. The smell in the room turned the heads of the two other pathologists in the morgue. The technician put his whole arm over his nose.

"If you don't mind, Dr., I'm just going to leave it where you want and go," the technician said.

Dr. Lancaster looked around and decided to conduct this autopsy at the farthest table. He signaled to his chief assistant, Dr. Maletzky, to follow him. Lancaster put his hand on the stainless steel table to feel the coldness of it. It always calmed him to think the metal was colder than any dead body.

"This is good," Dr. Maletzky said to the technician. "Just leave it here."

The technician slipped the dolly out from under the barrel and turned to walk away.

"One moment, son," the ancient Lancaster said. "How much does it weigh?"

"I didn't weigh it," the technician said.

The technician's ignorance annoyed Lancaster.

"How many men did it take to hoist the drum into the van?" Lancaster said, still bothered by the technician.

"It took three of us," the technician said.

Lancaster gave the drum a slight kick and nudged it. He pried off the lid with his fingers and glanced inside.

"We better weigh it before we get started," he said.

"What for?" said the technician.

"For the sake of science," Lancaster said.

Lancaster noticed that Dr. Maletzky and the technician were standing far away and holding their sleeves under their noses. They didn't budge.

"What's the matter with you two?" Lancaster said.

"It's the stench, Dr., the worst I've ever smelled," Dr. Maletzky said.

"I've smelled worse."

But Dr. Lancaster was only joking. It was common knowledge that he was good at his profession not only because of his abilities, but because of his inability to smell. His sense of smell had been a casualty of war, lost to Nazi chemicals used on American soldiers during combat. Since World War II, steaks grilling on a barbeque, wafts of perfume left by beautiful women, and rank decomposing flesh never again registered in his nose. Over the years he had examined bodies at their rancid worst: after weeks in a jungle or in the trunk of a car, after charring in a fire, after 3 days in the stomach of a great white shark. And not once did he wince at the smell.

Sometimes his wife or a colleague would get into his car and jump right back out because Lancaster had stepped on dog shit and had smeared it all over his floor mat without ever noticing. Lancaster did not like telling people he couldn't smell, and many times lived in denial of it. He even went as far as to ask some women what perfume they were wearing. A woman, Lancaster said, either had perfume or she didn't. And he could tell which was which without a sense of smell.

Lancaster's tolerance for stenches was an enormous irritation to his staff. When badly decomposing bodies were brought in, Lancaster would tease his colleagues for wearing scott packs, which resemble the oxygenated masks firefighters wear. Since he was so reluctant to wear protective equipment, his beard would sometimes absorb rancid smells and Lancaster would carry the scent around for hours.

"Here we go again," Dr. Maletzky muttered under his breath.

"It's really horrible, sir," the technician said.

"Well, alright, then gear up and let's get started," Lancaster said.

A few minutes later, Sgt. Connery and Det. Poppel from Homicide stepped out of the elevator. They were eager to meet the victim and establish a cause of death. They often observed Lancaster's autopsies when it involved a case.

"Christ, did a hippo crap in here?" Poppel said.

"I'd say it's more like fermented foot cheese," Connery said.

Dr. Maletzky handed them scott paks and protective suits. The technician, no longer needed, dashed out. Dr. Maletzky dollied the drum to the scale. It weighed 345 lbs. Lancaster made note of the weight on his clipboard. The technician rolled the barrel back next to the examining table. After a few minutes, Poppel and Connery walked out of the dressing room. They stood around the barrel, peering into its dark contents, looking like three astronauts in moonsuits.

CHAPTER 5

"This is going to be messy," Dr. Maletzky said.

He rocked the barrel. Fluid could be heard swishing at the bottom.

"Looks like a low heel shoe," Det. Connery said from behind his oxygenated facemask.

A spotlight shined directly over the open metal drum. Much of the barrel had been faded from its original dark green color to a rusted brown. Inside, the investigators could see a red, low-heel pump jutting out from what looked like the bottom of a second barrel that had been crammed inside the first one.

"Looks like there's a second drum," Dr. Maletzky said.

Lancaster grunted his acknowledgement.

"The bottom seems to be rusted out of the first one," Det. Poppel said.

"We could either flip the barrel or try to remove the second one, or we could cut the top off the second one using a power saw," Dr. Maletzky said.

"No cutting," Connery said. "We shouldn't risk damaging any evidence."

"Ok, then, let's just heave this thing upside down and dump everything out."

"Why don't you just try to pull that second barrel up?" Lancaster said. "Maybe it doesn't have a top and will slip right out."

Three of the men gripped the eroded bottom of the second drum near the low-heeled pump and yanked up. The barrel slipped right out. It had no top. They dropped it nearby and peered into the first barrel, eager to get a glimpse of the contents.

The investigators made out two clothed legs and an arm. The

rest of the contents were buried in a soggy heap of what looked like rice grains.

"It looks like risotto," said Poppel.

Dr. Lancaster swung the light from the examining table over the barrel. Bending down, he first touched, then grabbed the ankle sticking out from the bottom and shook it. The skin on the hand looked light brown and dry. The skin on the leg looked darker and more papery, a result of black stockings on the victim, Lancaster said. The limbs were stiff.

"Extraordinary," Lancaster whispered.

"What is it?" Sgt. Connery said.

"The preservation of this body," Lancaster said. "The barrel must have been completely airtight. I can still feel tissue under the skin."

"Let's get her out."

Lancaster glanced from the barrel to the examining counter.

"It'll take the four of us to lift the barrel onto the table," Lancaster said. "From there, we lay it on its side, and ease the body out. You ready? Ok, on three. One, two…"

They hoisted the barrel onto the examining table and slowly laid it on its side. Dr. Maletzky and Sgt. Connery grabbed the arm and ankle inside and tugged, but it wouldn't budge. Dr. Maletzky reached as deep inside the drum as he could, sinking his gloved arm into the soft pulp on the bottom half. Connery and Poppel pulled as Dr. Maletzky pushed from behind. As the body emerged onto the examining table, the other contents in the barrel slid out.

For a while, the men could only stand around and stare at the cadaver and debris. It was obviously a woman, folded carefully in a sitting position with her arms stretched out by her side. Her long, black hair was wrapped in sticky strands around her face and neck and she was dressed in winter clothes. Moisture from her bodily fluids had soaked into all her clothes, which were well preserved. Jewelry adorned her fingers, neck and ears.

Det. Poppel, breathing heavily in his scott pack, touched the face lightly.

"My God," he said.

Sgt. Connery's face was also in awe.

"She's a mummy," said the old Dr. Lancaster. "An honest-to-God American mummy. From her hair to her leathery skin right down to her clothes and jewelry. I believe we have just met Long Island's first genuine mummy."

Just then, Sgt. Connery received a call on his phone. But it was underneath the moon suit and he had no way to check the number. A minute later he received another call, then another. He pardoned himself and went into the locker to check it out.

"I fucking knew it," he said under his breath.

He dialed the number on his cell phone.

"Newstime, this is Michael Cervantes."

"You got no fucking patience you know that," Connery said.

"Hey Bobby, thanks for calling back, how's it going?" Michael said.

"It's going great, just great," Connery said. "So what's up?"

"What's this I hear about a murder in Jericho?"

Connery was surprised, but not shocked that word of the body in the barrel had made its way to Michael Cervantes.

"What murder? What are you talking about? I don't know of any murders in Jericho," Connery said.

"I heard it from neighborhood sources. You guys found a body in a house over there and it's murder," Michael said.

"Hang on, Mike, hang on, let's take a step back here. Who's the cop here, me or you?"

"Alright, alright, I'm sorry. So tell me, what's this I hear? I'm curious."

"Off the record…" Connery said.

"Why off the record? Is it something sensitive or secret?"

"Look, I'm in a hurry. If you let me talk – off the record – I'll tell you what's up,"

"I'm listening. And not typing. Go ahead."

"We got a call from Jericho today," Connery continued. "Apparently someone found a body in a metal drum under their house and inside there was a body. We are currently conducting an autopsy to determine the cause of death. Until we determine how the person died, I'm not calling it anything but a body."

Connery heard typing on the other end of the line.

"This is off the record, Mike," he said.

"Of course," he said. "But I won't be reading about this in other newspapers tomorrow morning or seeing it in the news tonight, right?"

"No, I promise. You're the only reporter who's called me on this so far."

"Any chance the examiner will determine cause of death before my deadline at 11," Cervantes said.

"No chance," Connery said. "We just got the thing on the examining table. But, I tell you what, when we're done, I think we might have a story that's going to knock your socks off."

"O yeah?" he said excitedly. "What is it?"

"I've never seen anything like it. And I'm sure you and most people on Long Island haven't either."

"You're killing me, Bobby," he said. "Come on."

"All I can tell you is that we found a mummy," Connery said.

"A mummy?"

"It's a perfectly preserved human body that's been dead for some time. Her hair, nails, skin, tissue, eyes – it's all intact."

"You've got to let me run something – anything – in tomorrow's paper. The neighbors in Jericho are talking. People want to know."

"Please don't," Connery said. "We have no idea how this mummy ended up there. Not yet. We need a few more hours to work this thing before it hits press."

"Alright, then can we make a deal? I promise not to run anything in Newstime tomorrow. But you gotta give me the address where you found the body. Throw me that little scrap. I'm good to you guys. Come on."

Bobby paused for a minute to think.

"Goddamnit. Fine. 97 Forest Drive, Jericho. The guy selling the house found the body. His name's Ronald Cohen. But I don't know the people moving in. So I'd rather if you didn't snoop too much tonight."

"Thanks Bobby," Cervantes said. "You're the best."

Dr. Maletzky turned the drum completely upside down and shook as much of the contents out of it as he could. A pile of weird plastic pellets and other clumps of trash accumulated near the cadaver's feet. It looked like dirty grains of rice in a dark fluid.

"What the hell is that stuff?" Det. Poppel said.

"I'm not sure," Dr. Maletzky said.

"It looks like Styrofoam, but it's too hard to be," Connery said.

"Styrofoam can turn solid if subjected to the right environment and chemicals," Dr. Lancaster said. "But just from looking at it, I'd say it's probably vermiculite, or some other moisture absorbing grain. Whoever put her in the barrel didn't want it to leak."

"Makes sense, Doc," Sgt. Connery said.

"Well, it's only a theory," Lancaster said. "The material should be tested to determine exactly what it is. Dr. Maletzky, can you get Lola to take a sample of this stuff and begin testing?"

"Right away, sir," Dr. Maletzky said.

Sgt. Connery sifted through the gooey pile with his gloved fingers. A purse protruded from it. He lifted it by the straps. It was heavy with moisture, and bits of the grain were pasted to it.

"Maybe we have an ID in here," Sgt. Connery said.

"Good," Det. Poppel said. "Let's open it up."

"Not here," Sgt. Connery said. "We should get forensics involved in this. Who knows what the hell's in there, or what condition it's in. Call Joan Bagley in Questionable Documents and get her to come here and pick it up."

"Bobby, just open it up and take a look inside before Forensics gets it, just to have an idea," Det. Poppel said.

Sgt. Connery placed the purse between himself and Poppel and opened it up. It was made of black leather, which had hardened like the skin of the cadaver. It wasn't a large purse, maybe six inches long and four inches deep. The inside was a mix of slush and tarnished cosmetic cases. The two men hunched over it to look inside, like two aliens staring into a crevice.

"Oh, the hell with it," Ewards said, and dumped the contents onto the table.

A pocket book, an eyelash curler, a compact, lipstick, and blush tumbled out. In the mix with all the pellets were what looked like two little plastic flowers. Everything was separated, catalogued and placed in plastic bags. Moisture from the body permeated the entire purse and its contents. There was no wallet. The pocketbook was soaked and sealed shut.

"Forensics should really get this pocketbook into their lab," Connery said. "It looks like that's all we got. There's no wallet, which means probably no I.D. either."

Dr. Lancaster placed his hand on Connery's shoulder.

"I'll be damned," the old doctor said. "I can smell this thing."

"I bet," Connery said. "The smell is seeping right into these scottpacks. It's the worst I've ever experienced."

Lancaster whiffed the air.

"It smells like Bavarian Lynburger cheese," Dr. Lancaster said. "I remember I ate a lot of that stuff during the war. What we're seeing here is years worth of decomposition in a small amount of time. This flesh hasn't seen oxygen in God knows how long. It's accelerated toxicity."

Lancaster gave the body a closer look. The clothes was stained dark with bodily fluids. But the uncovered parts -- the head and face, the hands and wrists -- were extremely well preserved, if a bit dry-looking. The fingers had shriveled but the little rings still fit. The natural wrinkles on the knuckles were still there. Lancaster cleared some of the wet hair from the face, revealing an intact nose, a slightly open mouth, and a set of front teeth with gold bridgework. A locket – he couldn't make out the metal because it was stained -- hung around the neck. The eyes, which had slightly desiccated and lost their color, were still framed by eyelashes and eyebrows.

"First things first," Lancaster straightened up. "We have to remove the clothes. It won't be easy because the body is in an awkward position. But we'll try to cut as little as possible. Dr. Maletzky, get Samson to clear a good size space in the ionized evidence locker. That's where we'll store the attire."

Sgt. Connery ordered Det. Poppel to get an update on the manufacture date of the barrel. Poppel left the autopsy room and did not return.

The remaining investigators meticulously stripped the clothes off the mummified corpse. The limbs were stiff, and they had to be careful not to damage the skin. Dr. Lancaster didn't want to mistake a fresh injury with an old one. It was like changing the clothes on a big doll. Her arms were stiff and locked down by her side. Her legs were extended. In some parts of the body, such as the thighs and torso, layers of tissue were still intact under the skin. But on the arm and lower legs, the tissue had withered and they felt like bone surrounded by cardboard.

The first thing to come off were her pumps. She was wearing stockings. Next, they removed the waist-length faux leopard fur coat. Connery carefully laid it on the floor next to the examining table.

They removed the rest of her clothes: a black wool skirt, a button-down pink cardigan, warm undergarments, and a religious scapular around her neck.

"This is a goddamn fashion show straight out of the 1960s," Sgt. Connery said.

They also removed the jewelry, artifacts from a life lived long ago. The locket around her neck was inscribed with the words, "Patrice, Love Uncle Phil." A gold wedding band, with the inscription, M.H.R. XII-59, came off her left hand. Another green-stoned ring also was on that hand.

"What do you think, Dr.? Gold bridgework on the teeth, cheap-looking clothes," Sgt. Connery said. "She could be a hooker."

"Maybe," Dr. Lancaster said. "But then you also have a wedding ring, a religious scapular, and a locket with an affectionate inscription. I'm not so sure we're dealing with a streetwalker here."

With the entire corpse naked on the examining table, the investigators had a better perception of their victim. The body, while well preserved, had withered. The leathery skin clearly outlined ribs, the pelvic structure, a spinal column and leg muscles. Her hair reached halfway down her back. And the nails on her hands had grown long.

"It looks like the body released many of its fluids in the airtight drum," Dr. Lancaster said. "I believe that's what the slush at the bottom was."

"I can't figure out the ethnicity, Dr.," Sgt. Connery said. "The skin just looks like lightly tanned leather. Could it be stained, or is that the original color?"

"Even if it's stained, we can rule out a black woman," Dr. Lancaster said. "Skin usually stains to a darker shade, and if the victim had been black, the skin would be much darker."

Dr. Lancaster walked to the head and held up some of the sticky locks.

"She also has straight hair," he said. "The hair is black, but it's definitely not an African-American woman's. Judging from the shape of her eyes, she may have an element of Asian, but the eyes could also be Native American. I'd say the color of her skin perhaps darkened slightly, but not much."

The skin underneath the formerly clothed areas was slightly less pruned. Dr. Lancaster tried to pry back one of the arms, but it wouldn't budge. He walked slowly around the corpse, analyzing its contours, occasionally pressing a finger or two into the skin. He passed his hand over the legs and arms, feeling for any possible signs of broken bones or skin damage. After he and Dr. Maletzky had visually examined one side, they flipped the body onto its right side. They repeated the visual inspection. Sgt. Connery stood nearby, waiting patiently for a cause of death.

"It's an old body," Lancaster said. "But I can't pinpoint the exact time of death. It's difficult to know how long it's been in the drum. The container was just so airtight. She may have been in there two years, ten years or fifty years. She doesn't have any visible injuries. No bullet holes or knife cuts. Her neck isn't broken, and it doesn't look like it was badly bruised, so I'd rule out strangulation for now. Her body doesn't look beaten."

"So what the hell happened? Did they stick her in there alive?" Sgt. Connery said.

"Alive, perhaps, but not conscious," Lancaster said. "If they put her in there conscious, she'd probably have bruised fingertips from trying to claw her way out. Her arms would not be frozen down by her side. They'd be up around her head."

Sgt. Connery looked closely at the hands, which were outstretched and unbruised. Dr. Lancaster massaged the head carefully.

"The skull doesn't feel right," Lancaster said. "Let's open it up."

Dr. Maletzky fetched a small wheel saw. They pulled the body to the end of the table, so that the top of the head jutted over the end of it. Dr. Lancaster placed a plastic container on the floor under the head. With a whirring sound, Dr. Maletzky carved into the skull at the line where the hair meets the forehead, continued over the right ear, down along the hairline, and around the other side. Lancaster grabbed the edge of the cut marks and gently tugged. The top of the head popped off like a helmet, revealing the well-preserved brain inside. Lancaster shined a light inside the top of the skull in his hand. The bone was shattered inward at the crown. The area of the brain underneath the facture was stained dark and swollen.

"It's murder," Dr. Lancaster said. "I'm tentatively ruling it blunt force trauma pending the toxicology report. Someone smashed this girl's skull with a blunt object."

Sgt. Connery jotted down notes. He nodded his head as he scribbled down the words "blunt force trauma." He noted the time, 12:45 a.m.

"Like what, Dr., a bat, a hammer,?" Sgt. Connery said.

"I can't tell, Sergeant. It's possible," Dr. Lancaster said.

"What else can you give me?" Connery said. "How old is she? Can you tell me her ethnicity?"

"There's still a lot left to do," Dr. Lancaster said, as he placed the skull on the examining table. "We will conduct a full autopsy, run every test available, study stomach, intestinal and blood contents. I'll get as much as I can for you. For now, I can tell you that the woman looks relatively young, between, say, the ages of 25 and 30. I want to say her ethnicity is Native American, because her eyes just don't quite reach the narrowness of Asians. I saw enough japs during World War II to spot Asian eyes. But her skin is light enough to be considered a mix. She may be Hispanic, from Latin America with mestizo populations, perhaps."

The phone call summoning Det. Joan Bagley to the medical examiner's office to pick up evidence in a murder case seemed like routine business. But the moment she set foot in the elevator to descend to the morgue, something didn't smell right.

"What the hell is that stench?" she asked one of the technicians sharing the elevator with her.

"That's our latest case, the mummy," the technician said.

"Mummy?" Det. Bagley asked.

The odor intensified as the elevator door opened. Bagley plugged her nose tightly, but still couldn't avoid the smell. Sgt. Connery spotted Bagley across the room, walked over and handed her a sealed ziplock bag with what looked like a little address book inside.

"Ok, Joan, here's the deal," Connery said.

"Good to see you too, Bobby," Det. Bagley said.

"We have one victim, sans ID," Connery said. "Her wallet produced no drivers license, credit cards, ID cards, nada. I'm hoping we can use this little address book to identify her. She had it in her purse, along with some other stuff. I tried opening it but it's very delicate. It almost fell apart in my hands. It's been soaking in bodily fluids for, hell, I don't know, decades."

"So you want me to take this thing back to headquarters and examine it," Det. Bagley said.

"Right away," Connery said. "This one's real high profile."

"Just like this? In this little bag?" Det. Bagley asked.

"Yeah, just like that. What do you want, a freaking shipping crate?"

"A cooler or something would be nice."

"There's no time. We need this ASAP."

Det. Bagley drove an old jeep. The windows were zipped up and the roof was raised because it had been raining. She climbed in, placed the bag with the book on the passenger seat and took off. Suddenly her head swam as she shifted into first gear. The smell from the book permeated every square inch of air in the jeep. Now she was at a traffic light and couldn't pull over to lower the windows. Her arm covered her nose again. It stayed that way the rest of the trip. The smell clung to her so viciously that her dog ran away from her when she got home, her husband refused to sleep in the same room with her that night, and her co-workers declined to share an elevator with her for two days after.

As she carried the bag down the hallway to the Questioned Documents Unit Laboratory, colleagues grimaced and turned away from her. Her boss, Sgt. Dennis, immediately placed the book in an ionized locker and fetched full breathing regalia. The two of them stood in front of the locker, which had a see-through glass door, staring at the address book with masks on.

"Can't we just burn it?" Det. Bagley joked.

"You think they'd notice if we did?" Sgt. Dennis said.

Bagley laughed.

"I've done wet documents before," Det. Bagley said. "But nothing like this."

"I guess we should examine the thing."

They took the book out of the locker and placed it on a table in the middle of the room. It was black, about 3 inches wide and 4 inches tall, and covered in slime. It weighed a whole pound, much of it from liquids that had seeped into the pages. Det. Bagley tried to open it, but with the thick rubber gloves she was wearing it was impossible to handle the delicate pages. She switched to latex gloves, the type used by surgeons, and tried again. She opened the front cover, but a piece of a page—as delicate as wet toilet paper—tore.

"We have to let it dry a bit," Det. Dennis said. "Maybe if we leave it in the locker overnight, it'll lose some of the moisture."

She stared at it for a few more minutes.

"I can smell the answers inside that thing," she said.

CHAPTER 6

Michael Cervantes pulled up in front of 97 Forest Drive early in the morning. There were no cars parked it the driveway. He knocked on the door but no one answered. The neighborhood was quiet. Children were at school. Adults were working.

He jotted down notes: "White, split level ranch, tony landscaping, basketball poll on the two-car driveway, tree-lined street, large houses, quiet neighborhood."

One of the neighbors was pulling into their driveway. It was John Finkelstein, the crime watch retiree. Cervantes walked over.

"Hello there," he said.

John Finklestein, always suspicious of strangers, gave him the evil eye.

"May I help you," he asked suspiciously.

"I'm Michael Cervantes. A reporter at Newstime."

"Newstime, huh? What's Newstime doing here?"

"I'm writing a story about the body that was discovered in your neighbor's house yesterday."

"No comment."

"Oh, no, no, of course not, that's not what I came over here for. What I'm doing is trying to understand the neighborhood a little better. See, I've never been to this part of Long Island, and I have to write an article that really explains the location. I don't want to write anything that misleads people into thinking this is a dangerous or crime-ridden neighborhood."

Finkelstein bristled at the thought of having his neighborhood portrayed as anything but an example of suburban tranquility. He strolled over to Cervantes.

"This is not a dangerous neighborhood, sir," he said.

"Please, call me Mike."

"Well, Mike, this really is a model neighborhood. All the neighbors know each other. It's a beautiful block. We have a great crime watch program, and we haven't seen any crimes here in a long time. That's what you should write in your article."

"Of course."

Cervantes took a notebook from his back pocket and started taking notes.

"You're not quoting me, are you?"

"Not if you don't want me to. But I'm just writing down some of your insight as an education. What if I don't find anyone else to describe the area so accurately? Then the only thing I have to write is that there was a murder on this block. But I'd really hate the neighborhood to be stereotyped for the next few years as a place where there was a gruesome murder. I need people such as yourself, real neighborhood mainstays, to tell me what this place is all about."

Finkelstein eyed Cervantes for a few seconds.

"So what exactly have you heard?" Finkelstein asked.

"I heard that the man who lives there pulled a drum out from his house. Then the garbage man wouldn't take it unless he opened it. So when he opened it up, there was a woman's body inside. The medical examiner's office did an autopsy and determined she had been murdered. So here I am."

"Wow, you know more than I do," Finkelstein said. "Do they know who did it?"

"Nope, but they're investigating."

Cervantes stood next to him and gazed over at # 97.

"So, who lives there now?" he said.

"A guy named Cohen. He and his wife are old hippie types. Two dogs. No kids."

Cervantes scribbled.

"How long have they lived there?"

"Five, seven, ten years. You lose track. The house has a high turnover rate. It's just one of those buildings that lots of people have lived in, but no one seems to call home."

"Do you remember ever seeing a drum in the crawl space?"

"Naw, I was never really friends with anyone there, except for the first owners, but I forgot their names. It was a long time ago. I remember my kids used to crawl around in that crawl space. That I do remember."

A Lexus pulled into the driveway at Forest Drive.

"Those are the new owners there," Finkelstein said. "I wonder if they know about this."

"I'm going to go say hi," Cervantes said. "Thanks Mr..."

"Finkelstein. John Finkelstein. That's F-I-N-K-E-L-S-T-E-I-N."

"Thanks, nice meeting you."

The Bazis were getting out of their car. Cervantes called to Mr. Bazi from the sidewalk.

"Hi there," he said. "I'm Michael Cervantes from Newstime. It's a beautiful house."

"Thank you," said Mr. Bazi. "We are very excited. We just got the key from our realtor."

Mrs. Bazi, a thin woman with curly brown hair, told her children to go play and joined the conversation.

"Newstime, did you say? We are already subscribers. I will make sure to change the address as soon as we move in."

"Oh, I'm not trying to sell you a newspaper subscription. I'm writing an article about an incident that occurred here yesterday. I'm a reporter."

"What incident?" Mr. Bazi asked.

"You haven't heard anything?" Cervantes said.

"Anything about what?" Mrs. Bazi said.

Cervantes glanced to Bazi's wife, who was now paying close attention.

"Mr. Cohen, do you know him?" Cervantes asked.

"Of course, he sold us the house," Mrs. Bazi said.

"Of course," Mr. Bazi echoed.

"Well, yesterday, he removed a barrel that was underneath the house," Cervantes said.

"Ah, yes, I remember, I asked him to take it away," Bazi said, eagerly following Cervantes's every word.

"Inside the barrel, they found the body of a woman. She had been murdered."

"No!" Mrs. Bazi said.

Cervantes could see the blood rushing away from Mrs. Bazi's face. She steadied herself by gripping her husband's arm. Her other hand covered her mouth. The Bazi's teenage son, Hamid, took a basketball from the trunk of his parent's car and started shooting hoops, oblivious to the news.

"I'm sorry to be the one to tell you," Cervantes said.

"Are you joking?" Mr. Bazi said.

"No. I thought you would know."

"This is, just, I don't know what to say," Bazi said as he rubbed his forehead, his face stunned.

"No one said anything to us," he said. "Someone should have told us."

"You're right, someone should have."

Bazi took the loose key from his pocket and walked to the front door. He unlocked it and went inside. His wife stayed outside.

"Well, come on, Hadi," Bazi said.

"I don't want to go inside that house," Bazi's wife said.

"Why not, we have to move in?"

"Move in? You must be joking. I am not moving into that house. And neither are you or our children."

Bazi must have realized that it did no good to have this conversation in front of a Newstime reporter. He grabbed his wife by the arm and yanked her into the house. Cervantes heard arguing inside. A few seconds later, Bazi's wife stormed out of the house, jumped in the car with her children and peeled off. Bazi watched her from the doorway.

"Look what you have done," Bazi yelled at Cervantes. "Now my wife doesn't want to live here."

Cervantes stayed quiet. He sheepishly kicked a rock near the front porch.

"Why didn't anyone tell us?" Bazi said. "We should have known."

"The investigators only determined early this morning that the woman had been murdered. Would you have changed your mind about the house if you had known?"

"Yes," Bazi said. "There are many houses to choose from. Why choose one with such an ugly history?"

Bazi sat on his front steps. He was restless. He stood up again, pulled out a cell phone and called his realtor.

"Hello, Sandy, this is Mohamad Bazi. I am standing in front of my house here with a reporter from Newstime. Yes, a reporter from the Newspaper. He tells me that police found a dead body under my new house. Did you know about this? Did you?"

Then Bazi snapped.

"Stupid woman. Don't lie to me. This is shit. This shit about a body. My wife won't set foot in the house. I'm calling my lawyer. I'm going to sue you, sue everybody. This is shit. You are shit. Hello, HELLO!"

The line went dead.

With his best imitation of a Major Leagues pitcher, Bazi cocked back his arm and beamed his cell phone at the front door, shattering it to pieces. Cervantes took the hint and walked quietly away. He continued his neighborhood canvass, asking residents on the block what they knew, or how they felt. No one knew much. They all said the same thing. Owners of that house never stuck around too long. Turnover was pervasive. Attachments and friendships with neighbors were fleeting.

When Cervantes returned to his office, he called Sgt. Connery for extra details. Connery cooperated until Cervantes told him that he had broken the news to Bazi about the body. Connery flipped, accusing him of violating his trust.

"I told you not to go over there!" Connery said.

"I never agreed to that," Cervantes said. "How am I supposed to write a story without talking to neighbors?"

"Goddamnit," Connery said. "Next thing I know, I'll be reading a story about the Long Island Mummy."

The cops held a press conference to announce the investigation of a murder. By then, buzz had spread around the media that it involved some sort of mummified body. More media than anticipated showed up, including all the New York City television stations and newspapers. Reporters bombarded cops with mummy questions. How long was she in the barrel? How did she die? Is she Egyptian?

Long Island, land of Amy Fisker and The Hamptons, was back in the national spotlight for a crime investigation: the mystery of the mummy in the barrel. Newstime assigned several reporters to cover the story.

The media devoured it. It hit the front pages of every newspaper in the area, Newstime, The New York Daily News, The New York Post, The New York Times. The wires carried it across the nation. Newspapers around the country picked it up. Nightly newscasts spiced it up by interviewing Egyptologists at the Museum of Natural History who had worked with mummies their whole careers. They said mummies were like time capsules, freezing a moment in time for future generations to better understand the past.

But journalists suffered from the same setbacks as the police: few new developments kept the story in hibernation. After the talking heads and Egyptologists had their say, angles dwindled and facts were few and far between. Only Newstime's Michael Cervantes followed the daily twists and turns in the investigation.

One big headliner was that the autopsy had revealed that the woman in the barrel had been nine months pregnant at the time of her death. Dr. Lancaster was trying to lift samples of the fetus tissues for DNA testing. Sgt. Connery told Newstime that a pregnant dead woman was always a potential motive if the father did not want to be discovered. Good DNA samples from the baby could be compared with DNA from suspects.

Investigators found limited information on Melrose Plastics, the company that had apparently purchased the barrel in the mid 1960s. The company had been sold in 1972, and records so old at the state division of corporations were incomplete. The company once operated in Manhattan's lower east side. It made plastic plants. The file from the company lay under a pile of paperwork in the Homicide unit's warroom.

Lancaster ventured that the woman died at some point in the late 1960s, guessing from the style of clothes. The dead woman's skin tone, gold bridgework on her teeth and the religious scapular around her neck led Lancaster to officially declare her Hispanic. Even though this deduction clashed with investigator's other clues. Based on the locket she wore, investigators assumed early on that the victim's name was Patrice, a name that sounded Irish, not Latino. This prompted them to delve deeper and check the missing person files in the New York metropolitan area from the mid 1960s until the mid 1970s. The only two Patrices reported missing during that time were old women who had disappeared from nursing homes in New Jersey and White Plains. Both were too old to be the victims.

M.H.R. XII-59, the inscription in the ring the woman was wearing, led detectives to a high-school in New Jersey, Mary's Holy Rosary. Detectives pored over the school's yearbook archives, looking for pictures of Hispanics. There were none. They asked the school if any of their alumni had ever been reported missing. There weren't. The ring was another dead end.

The investigation hit a wall. The few clues went stale. Pressure built up inside the police department to crack the case. The county manager pushed the new police commissioner, Gilford Cooper, to come up with a suspect. It had been years since the county received this kind of attention for a criminal case. Not since Amy Fisker shot Joey Batanulu's wife in Massapequa had the Nassau County Police Department been so inundated with cameras, reporters and photographers.

Commissioner Cooper responded to the pressure. As the department's first and only black commissioner, the media held strong interest in his progress and leadership. In daily morning meetings, Commissioner Cooper grilled Sgt. Connery and the top staff in Homicide. The sessions were progressively unpleasant. Cooper began to question Connery's commitment to the case. He had Connery's record pulled. He pointed out that Connery worked on fewer cases every year, insinuating that Connery was washed up. The old cop ground his teeth and pledged his dedication to his job and the case.

Sgt. Connery took it out on his detectives. "Fuck this" and "fuck that" and "fuck you too". He snarled and sneered and snapped. He worked them round the clock on nothing, wild goose chases to appease his appetite for progress. Desperate for leads, Connery combed the mummy and her clothes for missed evidence several times.

The old cop lost sleep and his appetite. The doughnut boxes in the brainstorm room went untouched. His wife noticed his weight loss.

Back at headquarters, Dennis and Bagley spent four days wearing charcoal-filtered respirators, goggles, rubber gloves and lab coats as a precaution against potential toxins from the victim's address book. It was difficult for them to be with it in the same room for more than a few minutes because of the unavoidable stench. The smell seeped into their hair, their clothes, their skin. They resorted to sealing the book in plastic every time they handled it.

Two days after they first put the book in the evidence locker, Det. Dennis took another crack at opening it. He delicately slid the blunt corner of a plastic ruler between the pages, which were stuck together. He tried to catch an open spot on the book and slide the ruler through the page, but nothing could be read at that point.

The next day, Det. Bagley picked up where Dennis left off, and separated more pages, placing pieces of paper towels between them to absorb excess moisture. She placed the book under the green light of a VSC 2000 machine that scanned it with high-resolution light rays. The VSC 2000 exposes a document to a variety of light sources and light filters covering various wavelengths of the light spectrum to aid in visualizing marks and writings that the naked eye can't see.

Every time Bagley wanted to flip a page, she had to return to the forensic evidence room, gear up in full breathing regalia, take the book out of the plastic, flip the page, and seal it again to walk the book back to the VSC 2000 in her office. It was about a 30 minute process each time.

Four days after Bagley took possession of the book, she began to make out names and numbers. The leads were passed on to detectives, who fanned out around the New York area and beyond to other parts of the country to check them out.

But it wasn't until a week later that Bagley stumbled upon the identifying information. She noticed something on the screen that looked like cursive handwriting, in the front page, where the name of the address book owner is supposed to be. As she tweaked the machine to try to get a clearer picture, Sgt. Connery walked into the room.

"Any luck yet on a name?" he said.

"Look at this," Bagley said. "You're luck may have just taken a turn."

Connery peered at the screen.

"I don't see anything."

Bagley taped a piece of clear acetate over the VSC 2000 computer screen above the handwriting. With a magic marker, she traced the name and information as it appeared on the book: Karina Angelica Fuentes; immigration number 2256-9674; country of origin: El Salvador.

It took the U.S. Department of Immigration and Naturalization Service two days to dig up the immigration file on Karina Fuentes. Connery sent Poppel to Washington D.C. to pick it up and bring it back to Nassau County. The cops held off on a press conference until Connery had the file in his hand.

Poppel delivered it early in the morning to Connery, who pored over the papers and photo with enthusiasm. Also in the Homicide brainstorm room were Detectives Spinner and Vasquez, who was Puerto Rican.

"She's pretty good-looking," said Connery. "Kind of looks like that actress, what's her name?"

Poppel shrugged.

"She sure doesn't look like your regular Salvi chick," Poppel said, using cop slang for Salvadoran.

Long Island's Salvadoran community had burgeoned over the last few decades to become the second largest in the United States outside of Los Angeles. Poverty and a language barrier had turned the community inward, making it ripe for gang activity. The largest street gangs on Long Island, MS-13 and Salvadorans with Pride, hailed straight from Central America.

"She must have been the first Salvi on Long Island," Connery said. "We're talking more than 30 years ago. Salvis didn't really come to Long Island until the civil war started there in the early 80s."

"They sure fucked this place up," Poppel said. "Paradise lost."

"Right," Vasquez said sarcastically. "And you Irish really spruced up New York with intellect and culture."

"The Irish assimilated," Poppel said. "These Salvadorans don't give a fuck about the system here. There are no laws here as far as they're concerned."

Vasquez shook his head.

"You're full of shit," Vasquez said. "Yeah the Irish assimilated-- after a century of gang and mob warfare. You guys didn't even have to deal with a language barrier. But the Irish still settled for menial jobs like cooking, custodial service and window washing before moving on to the prestigious professions of beat cop and firefighter."

The department's public information office put out a press release calling a press conference to reveal the identity of the woman in the barrel. The commissioner congratulated Connery and the Questioned Documents Unit on good forensic work. With an identity and a photograph, holes in the case could be closed and questioning of suspects could be more specific.

Connery didn't expect a big turnout at the press conference. With new developments scarce, most of the media had started to lose interest in the case after a couple of days. But when he walked into the department's press room, he could barely reach the podium. The room was jammed with radio reporters with cassette cases dangling from a strap, cameramen holding up white papers to measure the white balance in the room, newspaper reporters gossiping in the corner, young women aspiring to be the next Barbara Walters primping with compact mirrors.

Connery turned his head to Poppel, who was standing behind him.

"Do I have anything in my teeth?" Connery said.

"No, not unless you count the yellow everywhere."

"Wise guy," Connery said.

A few reporters came over to say hello.

"Ok, people, is everyone ready?"

People shushed each other. A rookie yelled out.

"Can you please tell us your name and spell it for the record?"

"I am Homicide Det. Sgt. Roger Connery. This is Det. Poppel. As you know, for the past two weeks or so, we have been investigating the case that has become known as the woman in the barrel. Today we have a confirmation on the woman's identity."

Connery pulled an 8 by 10 black and white photograph out of a file and held it up for the cameras. Flashes sparkled all over the room.

"She is Karina Angelica Fuentes. A native of El Salvador who came to New York in 1965."

Someone yelled out, "can you spell her name?"

Another reporter answered: "It's on the press release."

"Go on sarge," said another.

"Ms. Fuentes came to New York in 1965 at the age of 22. She came legally, staying with a host family in Nassau County when she got here. According to her immigration papers, she came from a town called Tonaca...tonakee...tunaku...anyways, it's on the press release, in El Salvador. Apparently, she was married in her home country and had no children."

Newspaper reporters scribbled notes. Connery adjusted his eyeglasses.

"How did you identify her?" asked John Jiraff from the New York Daily News.

"We were able to restore an address book that was found inside the drum with the victim. That book has yielded several numbers and leads, which we are now investigating."

A woman TV reporter with bleach-blond hair raised her pen: "It sounds like that book really propelled the case forward."

Connery nodded.

"Obviously, identifying the victim was a big obstacle in the investigation. There were several false leads in the case such as the jewelry she was wearing that led us down the wrong road. The address book is an important break. I believe it has provided us with the information we need to solve this case."

"What else can you tell us about her," someone asked.

"About the victim. Has her family been contacted? Does she have any kin?"

"So far the address book has not produced any names of kin or family, but we are still looking."

Then a reporter asked him a question that really pissed him off.

"Is the investigation receiving less than top priority because the victim is Hispanic?"

Before answering, Connery glared for five full seconds at the reporter, sleazebag Kirk Grimly from the sensationalist New York Post. Connery's jaw bulged.

"That's offensive to me, to this department and to the memory of this victim," Connery said.

"But is it true?" Grimly insisted. "That's what some sources are saying."

"What sources, your mutha? No, wait, I bet it was her garbage can," Connery said.

The room erupted in laughter. Kirk Grimly, who always dressed in the same black suit and was known to rummage garbage cans for information, scribbled the response into his notebook.

After the press conference, Cervantes pulled Connery aside, knowing that the proud detective's sentiments against his rival reporter could compel him to throw Cervantes a bone. Indeed, Connery passed Karina's immigration number to the reporter, and leaked some key information about her life in El Salvador.

CHAPTER 7

"I want you on the next flight to El Salvador."

Michael Cervantes looked up from his computer. Dan Larkin, the Long Island Desk editor, was standing next to his desk. Larkin was Mercy Hirshfeld's underling and whipping boy. Few orders came from Larkin that didn't originate with Hirshfeld. Larkin had coffee breath and coffee nervousness, typical morning personality traits for any first class newsman. There was an unusual brightness in his tone and a pleased smirk on his face.

"Are you serious?" Cervantes said.

"Yes indeed."

Cervantes looked at him like he was crazy.

"What for?"

Larkin shook his head in disappointment as though he were talking to a 3-year-old. Like any good editor, Larkin's consideration for the personal life of his staff was non-existent.

"We should try to track down her family," Larkin said.

"We? You mean me."

"You got it," Larkin said, snapping his fingers.

Cervantes laughed loudly. Several reporters turned to stare at him.

"You're nuts," he said. "That was decades ago. The house probably doesn't even exist anymore. Her family is probably all dead or something."

"We won't know unless we try. Even if you don't find anything. It would make a good story. You know, the origins of the mummy in the barrel, her life living in a mud hut, the river where she and her family took a dump and bathed. Whatever comes of it, it'll be a great story."

"When do I leave, tomorrow morning?"

"Actually, we'd like you to leave today if possible. But I guess tomorrow morning is acceptable. We don't want to read in the Times or the Daily News that they've gone there and tracked down her family. I want to read it on page 1 of Newstime. So come on. What do you say?"

Cervantes looked around the newsroom. Cheryl Hodges, a black reporter sitting next to him nodded enthusiastically.

"Fine, I'll go," Cervantes said.

Dan Larkin nodded too, patted him on the back, and said, "Better get ready. And ask the photo department to give you a digital camera so you can send us some good art with your story."

Although he didn't regularly cover Latin America, the fact that Cervantes was one of the only reporters at the paper that spoke fluent Spanish got him recruited for his fair share of stories in the Americas. Over the years, he had covered a hurricane in Nicaragua, a coup de etat in Ecuador, elections in Venezuela, and an earthquake in Mexico City, among other big events. But this assignment was not as clear cut.

"This is the weirdest fucking travel assignment I've ever had," Cervantes complained in whispers to Hodges.

"At least your getting out of this shithole for a while," Hodges said. "I'd take a trip to Bosnia if I could to get the fuck out of this dump for a few days."

Cervantes booked a morning flight to San Salvador on Grupo Taca Airlines. Early the next morning, he drove to John F. Kennedy Airport and ditched his car in the long-term parking garage. The plane was full of Salvadoran immigrants from Long Island. Each one of them seemed to have packed everything they owned in huge taped-up boxes to make the trip. Many of Long Island's Salvadorans only stayed in the New York area as long as they needed to earn some dollars to help their families back home. Others with the intention of staying long term in the U.S. traveled periodically between the two countries with box-fulls of supplies and goods – blending machines, computers, shoes, food and even pharmaceuticals -- that they'd sell on the Salvadoran black market for a profit or give to friends and family members as gifts.

Cervantes had never been to El Salvador, but he figured it couldn't be much different than Nicaragua and Guatemala. He was right.

It was a similar scene at the airport, with countless unlicensed taxi drivers soliciting arriving passengers, family members reuniting after months or years apart, lazy attendants at the car rental agencies. He considered renting a car, but he didn't know his way around El Salvador, and had had learned long ago not to trust maps of Third World countries. Sometimes roads were misnamed, or main arteries were closed because of flooding or mudslides, or criminal activity. Instead, he approached the scrawniest taxi driver he could find.

The driver, a skinny dark Indian man named Isaac, sported gold-framed front teeth, and a pair of gold-framed sunglasses straight out of Top Gun. He was dressed in black from head to toe, including black boots.

"Do you know how to get to Tonacatepeque?" Cervantes asked him in Spanish.

He responded with a long "chi!", the way Salvadorans pronounced *sí*, which is Spanish for yes. "Of course I know how to get there. I am a professional."

He grabbed Cervantes' bag, which weighed barely 10 pounds with his computer inside, and led him to his cab, a black 1980s style Mazda pickup truck the size of a Honda Civic. The pickup was decked out with tinted windows, chrome rims, and a comic-book like drawing on the hood of a bikini-clad goddess with flowing blue hair and spiked heels.

Isaac popped a cassette of Johnny Cash into his tape deck and cranked the volume. Cervantes took a long, patient breath. Isaac explained that living in Los Angeles for 9 years had given him a real sense of style and an appreciation for real American music. He had left El Salvador in the 1980s to flee the nation's bloody civil war and had returned after it was over. They passed dozens, if not hundreds of roadside stands, selling fruit, tires, chickens, just about anything. In El Salvador, roadside stands were the equivalent to American convenience stores.

The drive to Tonacatepeque led them through the heart of

San Salvador, which was about 30 minutes north of the airport. Isaac took a couple of wrong turns while trying to find the road that led to northern towns, but quickly found his way. The roadside stands faded out in the capital's more upscale neighborhoods, but sprouted up again on the northern outskirts. From the moment they left the airport, Cervantes had noticed a certain smell in the air, the unmistakable signature scent of burning wood and garbage that characterized any visit to the Central America countryside.

North of the capital, as Isaac drove along the right face of a hill, the drop-off to the right overlooked an informal, smoldering garbage dump. Smoke billowed into the green hills and mutts scampered about the pile, searching for discarded chicken bones and other scraps. Shacks made of crate wood, chopped down trees and corrugated metal were scattered on the hillsides.

The entrance to Tonacatepeque was non-descript. No signs identified it as such, and many of the concrete houses that were leveled during the war remained collapsed above their foundations. Once inside the town, Isaac said he would have to ask directions to get to the exact address Cervantes had for Karina's family. They passed the town center, a dusty plaza surrounding a tree, where a soccer team was kicking a ball around as they waited for a bus to take them to the next town. Nearby, vendors had pitched a small market under a tree-lined street. Skinny mutts with pronounced rib cages hovered in the periphery, constantly alert to any scrap that may hit the ground or any whistle from a generous merchant.

Isaac parked next to the market. He and Cervantes asked a couple of the vendors for directions to Karina's address. The first couple of people didn't know. But an older, pot-bellied man said he knew exactly where it was, and volunteered to lead them. The man climbed into the back of Isaac's pickup, slid open the window that separated the cabin from the bed of the truck, and directed them up an unpaved street filled with potholes, and lined with mostly whitewashed concrete houses and fruit trees. As the street curved left, the man told them to stop. They were about 200 yards from the main plaza.

"That's the address you're looking for," the man said, pointing at a pile of demolished concrete bricks and pilings. The debris had been neglected so long that plants were growing through the pile.

"It looks like a Mayan ruin," Cervantes said. He took the digital camera from his bag and snapped a couple of shots.

The potbellied man said. "During the war, the guerrillas used the strongest houses like this one as bases, and they were eventually attacked by the army. Most of them were leveled."

The fence around the house was partially demolished as well. The lot took up a large tract of land, about an acre, and old, stately trees still stood as sentinels around the yard, which was overrun with bushes and weeds. Three mutts hovered near the visitors, searching for food. Cervantes looked at Karina's address in the immigration file that she brought with her. In El Salvador, houses usually didn't have numbers. You had to count houses on a street to guess which one was *Casa Numero* 4 or *Casa Numero* 8.

"I knew it," Cervantes said. "This is a wild goose chase."

"A what, *Señor?*"

"A lost cause," Cervantes said. "I am trying to find the family that lived here, *la familia Fuentes.*"

Isaac pondered Cervantes' mission.

"*Bueno, señor,*" he said. "Maybe someone in the village knows what happened to them. Many families moved around during the war. But many stayed."

Cervantes was hesitant to comb the neighborhood house to house in a country where former soldiers had turned in vast numbers to g a n g lifestyles and crime. But Tonacatepeque seemed mellow, off the beaten path and a bit old fashioned. The graffiti that had tarnished the benches and walls of San Salvador – an obvious sign of gang presence -- were missing in this town. Cervantes decided to visit the immediate neighbors around the demolished Fuentes house. Several other houses had also been destroyed. None of the families in the immediate vicinity knew the Fuentes family. Cervantes was carrying the copy of Newstime with Karina's picture on the front page, showing it to neighbors in the hope that it would jog their memory. No one knew her.

Dusk approached, and the mosquitoes began their nightly massacre. Michael asked Isaac to take him back to Tonacatepeque's plaza. He entered a house that had an open front door and had a picnic table set up outside, a clear sign in Central America of an informal restaurant. Inside, the foyer had been converted into a convenience shop. Coca Cola, potato chips, rum, and even a couple of live chickens prancing around inside were for sale. On the other side of the room, a ramshackle addition harbored what looked in the dim light like a vast collection of wooden statues.

A shirtless man with short-cropped gray hair turned from the soccer match he was watching on television to welcome Cervantes.

"*Buenas noches,*" he said, putting down a cigar he had been smoking. "How can I assist you?"

The man stood up, revealing a thin chest and abdomen, all hairless, as with many Indians. His arms were well built, but also thin, outlining the striations of the muscles that stretched down his forearm to his wrists. His cheeks were hollowed out like a hunger-ravaged African's, making his age difficult to assume. But his green eyes, framed in a nest of wrinkles, still beamed with genuine emotion.

"Hello, *señor,*" Cervantes said. "I am a journalist here from New York. I came to Tonacatepeque to try to find some people, but I haven't had any luck, and I'm looking for a place to spend the night around here. Are there any inns in Town?"

The man shook his head.

"No," he said. "We used to have an inn, but, well, the war…"

He didn't have to explain any further.

"Yes, it sounds like this area was very affected by it," Michael said. "Everywhere I've been, I've seen its aftermath."

"This is nothing," the shopkeeper said. "We have already cleaned up much of it. But people don't have money to rebuild. Neither does the government. So, what people are you looking for?"

Cervantes reached inside his bag for the copy of Newstime with Karina's picture on the front cover.

"I'm trying to find the Fuentes family, relatives of Karina Fuentes," Cervantes said as she showed the man the newspaper cover.

All the muscles in the man's face suddenly contracted, bringing his eyebrows down and his lips up so that everything crowded against his nose. He took the newspaper from Michael and held it under a bare light bulb in the center of the room. For about a minute he stared at the picture. "I can't believe it," he repeated over and over again. "I can't believe it."

"You know her?" Cervantes asked.

The man nodded without taking his eyes off the picture.

"*Chi*," he said. "*Chi*, I know her."

Cervantes took a notebook from his bag and quickly started jotting down notes. The man finally looked up.

"Where is she?" he said.

Cervantes made a wounded face.

"I'm so sorry to say this, *lo siento*, but, she's dead," Cervantes said. "She was murdered in New York many years ago. Were you a friend of hers?"

"Yes," the man said. "I am Hector Elias. I remember Karina very well."

"How did you meet her?" Cervantes asked.

"We just met one day. I am a sculptor, as you can see. She liked my work. And she used to visit me."

The man offered Cervantes and his taxi driver, Isaac, a cold Coca Cola and asked them to come into his private quarters, where an old, faded couch and two wooden chairs offered a comfortable place to sit. The sculptor told Cervantes everything he knew about Karina: how they met, how long they knew each other, how she was unhappily married and her husband was abusive. Hector seemed to be telling a story that had swollen up inside him for decades.

"Karina always had big plans," he said. "She always wanted to be remembered for something great. So I sculpted her. Would you like to see it?"

Cervantes nodded. Hector disappeared into a hallway and a few minutes later, using an old dolly, hauled out a 4-foot cedar statue of a robed woman. The woman in the statue was in a contra-posto stance with curvy hips, large breasts. One arm was relaxing down her side, and the other was held up across her chest, just under her breasts, as though the woman was covering herself just enough to seem enticing. Her hair was straight and long, and a sly, insinuative smile was frozen on her lips. The cedar had dried and darkened over the years, but Hector had done his best to preserve it. Cervantes snapped a few photos of Hector with the statue.

"This is Karina," Hector said proudly. "She had no idea how beautiful she was. I made a statue of her because there was no other woman like her around here. She had a kind heart. She was worried about her family, her sisters, never herself. She sacrificed everything for them. She went to El Norte for them."

"It's a wonderful piece," Cervantes said. "Do you know how I can find Karina's family?"

Hector scratched his head.

"The only person I ever knew from her family was her husband. He and his friends paid me a visit once while I was sculpting this piece. He was very violent. He almost smashed it. He still lives down *Avenida G*, the third house on the left. But he is a drunk. I think he is very sick. Maybe he knows where Karina's family is."

By the time Cervantes wrapped up his visit with Hector, it was almost 9 p.m. He phoned Newstime to let his editors know he was ok, and tell them he would file a story the next day. Hector offered to let him and Isaac sleep in hammocks. They accepted, having nowhere else to go. Isaac slept in the living room, and Cervantes in a second bedroom with an old, creaky ceiling fan. Isaac, who Cervantes had officially hired as his driver for the remainder of his trip, borrowed Cervantes cell phone to call his wife and tell her he wouldn't be home for the night. It took him a few minutes to convince his wife that he was not cheating on her. "I'll show you the money [la plata] I made tomorrow," he said.

After an uncomfortable night, Cervantes woke up early and had a banana and a Coca Cola for breakfast. He walked around the village alone for a while. Taller and more light-skinned than most of the men in the village, he stood out. He approached some of the older men walking around, showed them Karina's picture and asked if they knew her. A couple of men smiled and nodded, but none of them said much except a comment regarding her beauty.

Isaaac met up with Cervantes in the plaza and they walked to the house where Hector said Karina's husband lived. A middle aged woman was sitting on the front porch with a teenage girl and a baby. Cervantes identified himself as a journalist from New York.

"I'm looking for Carlos Conejo," he said. "Is he here?"

"I don't know. What do you want?" The woman said.

"I want to talk to him," Cervantes said. "I have news about his wife."

"I am his wife," the woman said.

"Then it's about his ex-wife, Karina Fuentes."

"I remember that name," the woman said.

"Do you think Carlos remembers her?" Cervantes said.

"Carlos is very sick. He can't see any visitors," the woman said. She ordered the younger girl to take the baby inside.

"Can I just see him for a moment, I've traveled a long way, and I need his help," Cervantes said.

The woman shook her head with a bashful smile. She wouldn't budge. Carlos Conejo was off limits.

"*Lo siento*," the woman said. "I'm sorry but he's very sick. Come back in a couple of days."

Cervantes thanked her and moved on. He vented to Isaac.

"God damnit," he said. "We're so close."

"In El Salvador, the women are very jealous," Isaac said. "They guard their men."

As Cervantes approached Hector's convenience store in the plaza, a short, pudgy man with a bushy black mustache walked toward them.

"Are you the journalist looking for the Fuentes family?" the man said. "A friend of mine told me he met you this morning in the plaza."

"Yes," Cervantes said. "Can you help me find them?"

"I know where they live." the man said.

"You know where the Fuentes family is?!" he said. "I can't believe it. *Al fin.* That's what I came here for. Please take me to them. I have to see them. How do you know them?"

"I am Mario Delgado," he said. "Karina Fuentes was my older cousin. My mother, Maite Duarte, was Emilia Fuentes's sister."

"And who is Emilia Fuentes?" Cervantes said.

"Karina's mother," Mario said. "She is still alive, at least as far as I know. She is living nearby in San Martin."

Karina's mother? Still alive? But she must be ancient.

Cervantes couldn't believe his good fortune.

"Can you guide us there?" he said.

"Of course," Mario said. "I'll help you in any way I can."

Mario led them to a pink, one story house in the middle of a residential block in San Martin, a market town about 7 miles from Tonacatepeque. A wrought iron gate with a heavy door formed the façade of an enclosed garden in the front porch. Cervantes banged on the metal door, and a menopause-aged woman with almond shaped eyes and short hair greeted them. She immediately kissed Mario and scolded him for not visiting more often.

Cervantes identified himself as a journalist from New York and asked the woman if she was a member of the Fuentes family.

"Yes. I am Camila Fuentes. You must be here for my mother's 95th birthday. Everyone in town knows about it. I just got in from Los Angeles myself yesterday."

"Really, well happy birthday to her," Cervantes said. "But actually, I didn't know it was your mother's birthday. I'm here for another reason."

"Well, come inside," Camila said.

Camila Fuentes led Cervantes and Isaac past the garden, where several empty birdcages hung shrouded in violet bougainvillea.

Inside was a very old woman with a back so severely curved it seemed to prevent her from ever seeing the sky. Sitting across from the old woman was a younger woman wearing a bandana in the colors of the Salvadoran flag. Much to Cervantes' surprise, the hunched old woman stood up and walked with grace toward the visitors. She looked charming in her lightly tinted bluish hair combed neatly into a small bun.

"Welcome. *Bienvenidos*," the old woman said, leaning in to kiss her new guests. "Thank you for coming."

Cervantes quickly creased his copy of the Newstime cover and tucked it under his arm so as to conceal it.

"Thank you so much. My name is Michael Cervantes. Happy Birthday, and I'm happy to meet you. Are you Emilia Fuentes?"

"You have to speak up. She doesn't hear very well," Camila said.

Cervantes repeated a shorter version, but raised his voice for the last part.

"*Si, Si,*" said the old woman. "I am Emilia. Today is my 95th birthday."

Suddenly, a wave of nervous nausea crept up in Cervantes' throat. It wasn't part of his job to inform "next of kin" as Connery would have called them, of their dead loved ones. So consumed had Cervantes been in trying to find the Fuentes clan that he hadn't even considered how he would break the news to the family about the discovery of Karina's battered and mummified body. He hesitated for a moment, disappointed in the Nassau cops for not making the same effort to find Karina's family.

"Did you have a daughter called Karina Fuentes?" Cervantes asked.

Cervantes should have asked her to sit down first. He should have softened the blow somehow. But there was no easy way to tell a woman her child had been murdered, even if it was decades after the fact. The old woman raised her head, as though perking up her ears.

"Que?" Emilia said.

Cervantes drew closer to the old woman. He could smell the violet-smelling perfume on her. "Karina Fuentes!" Cervantes yelled.

"Karina?" the old lady said, clearly taken aback. "My daughter?"

"I am Karina's sister," Camila Fuentes said, jumping in. "What can you tell us about her? We have not heard from her in more than 30 years."

"I am afraid I have some bad news," Cervantes said, speaking loudly and slowly. "Police in New York have found Karina's body. She was murdered many years ago."

Cervantes unfolded the newspaper cover and showed it to the old woman and her daughter. A trembling, wrinkled hand slowly ascended to Emilia's mouth as she focused on the photograph. She teetered, and almost fell, but the other women quickly stabilized her.

"Karina," the old woman said, touching the newspaper cover with her dry, papery fingers. "Oh My Lord. My Sweet dear Lord God in heaven. My Karina."

Emilia broke down into sobs. Cervantes wanted to comfort her, but knew this moment had to be preserved for his article. He hugged the old woman with one arm and with his free arm, he rifled through his bag for his camera, hurrying to get a clear shot of the family's initial reaction to the bad news. He loosened himself from Emilia Fuentes and started snapping pictures. Camila Fuentes, overwhelmed and annoyed, held her hand up to block the lens.

"Not now, please sir," Camila said, crying. "This is too much for my mother, for me."

Camila led her mother back to the couch. The other woman in the house brought her a handkerchief and consoled her.

"How can you shoot pictures now?" Camila continued. "Do you know how long we have been waiting to know what happened to Karina? My mother still has nightmares about it."

"I'm so sorry," Cervantes said, putting his camera away.

Cervantes stood aside while the family gasped and sobbed for a few minutes. Then Camila invited Cervantes to sit down.

"Tell us what happened."

"Let me tell you everything I know."

Cervantes filled them in on the criminal case. Emilia held her head down, wiping her eyes with a handkerchief. After collecting herself, she told Cervantes that she still had nightmares about her daughter. One recurring dream was of Karina stuffed in a barrel that crashes down on a waterfall. The story sounded bizarre. Cervantes asked the old woman to please repeat the dream to be sure she was in her right mind. The old woman did so.

"Emilia, tell me about Karina?" Cervantes asked. "What kind of a person was she."

The old woman glanced at a framed photograph on a shelf near the front door. It was a picture of Karina standing on the sidewalk next to Central Park in a red sweater and a trench coat with two friends. A big smile on her face revealed gold bridgework on her front teeth, which could only be made out by the glint from the glass-wrapped high rises that flanked the edge of the picture.

"Karina was my oldest daughter," the old lady said as she removed her glasses and rubbed her eyes. She spoke with a lucidity that surprised Cervantes. "She was very close to her father, Antonio. He was the mayor of Tonacatepeque. She wanted to be like him. She wanted to be a leader. I remember when she told me she wanted to leave to El Norte, I said to her, 'daughter, you don't have to leave. We love you here, and your family is here. We can make due.' But she didn't listen. She was like her father in that way. She always did what she wanted to do."

The old woman broke down crying again. Cervantes waited for her to regain composure. Camila hugged her and rubbed her back and shoulders. A few minutes later, the old woman went on talking.

"I never wanted to die without knowing what happened to my daughter," she said. "That's why I'm so old."

The old woman stood up again. Camila tried to dissuade her. But the old lady was hard-headed. She approached Cervantes, who was scribbling notes. The journalist stood up as the old woman approached. Emilia embraced him as tightly as her 95-year-old bones would allow.

"Thank you," Emilia said. "Thank you so much. *Por fin.* Finally, we know what happened to Karina. I knew something bad had happened. Karina used to write letters all the time. It wasn't like her to stop writing. But since we didn't know anything for sure, I always had hope that she was alive but hiding somewhere. At first, that hope is good. But after so many years, it just eats away at you from the inside. Maybe now I won't have any more nightmares."

Camila helped her mother back to the couch. A few other guests showed up to celebrate Emilia's 95th Birthday. The front room became too crowded, and Camila asked Cervantes to join her in the back terrace, where a bench and two chairs had been set up under a wooden trellis at the edge of a bougainvillea-filled garden.

"It's such a relief to me to find you," Cervantes said. "For many days I worried that Karina was one of these lonely souls that every once in a while turns up in the United States, unaccompanied by relatives, left to fend for themselves."

Camila interrupted him.

"Karina never broke ties with her family. She always kept in close touch with us. We loved her very much. Karina was the type of person that always thought of herself last. Everything she did, her marriage, her political work with my father, her trip to El Norte, everything, she did it for the people she loved. At night, when we were young, she was always the last to fall asleep, reading. I'd find her at night sometimes just staring out the window, thinking. When she left, I lost my idol."

"Of course," Cervantes said. "In the United States, and especially in New York, the people are trying to understand Karina a bit better. And as a journalist, it's my job to honor your sister's memory, and write the truth about her and her life. There are people I can interview in New York who may or may not have known your sister well. And these are the people who will end up providing the information that your sister will be remembered by. They can know half truths, they can invent things about your sister, they can even lie, just so their names will appear in the newspaper…

Camila shook her head.

"But you can stop that. You are here."

"Exactly. I am here to find out the truth from the people who knew her and loved her most."

"What do you want to know. It has been a long time, but I remember her very well."

Camila motioned toward the bench and sat on a chair in the garden. Cervantes sat next to her, notebook at the ready.

"Well, I guess I should begin at the beginning," Michael said. "Why did Karina go to El Norte?"

Camila took a deep breath…

CHAPTER 8

Turbulent days of preparation wore Karina Fuentes down to her core. Her father wanted things done one way. She would often suggest an alternative. Bickering over strategies often led to shouting matches. She had come on board as his helper and secretary two years ago, and had hijacked the day to day operations of his infant political machine, unwittingly become the gatekeeper and face of the Socialist movement in their area.

Either way, intense absorption in work lately had caused her to overlook the constant primping that had typified her image. She was 19, scholarly, commanding in her knowledge of leftist subterfuge.

Unfortunately her intelligence, at times condescending to the simple peasants and farmhands in Tonacatepeque, was often sabotaged by her looks. Men in her village who needed motivation to rebel politically, were more often motivated by her to propose marriage. A vicious cycle resulted. The more they told her she was beautiful, the meaner she would treat them, and the more she would study. The more she would study, the more intelligent she seemed to the men, who in turn found her even more alluring for the sharp wit she delivered with stinging efficiency. The bag of American makeup she had bought on a trip to the capital had been retired to the mysterious box she harbored in her closet. Her hair, even when tied in a messy bun behind her head, delivered a teasing hint of her femininity. The long, loose dresses she wore could not conceal her figure. There were days she wished she was hideous just so the men in her village would treat her as a leader instead of a potential lover.

Among the people in her village, she was only one of a handful that spoke English. Her fluidity in *El Norte's* language was the irony of Tonacatepeque. In his fiery political discourse, Karina's father, Antonio, identified no greater oppressor than the United

States of America. But yet he insisted that Karina spend two summers learning English at an elite bilingual boarding school in San Salvador. She hated the language. It sounded boorish to her. It seemed to lack punch. And there was no one in Tonacatepeque to practice it with. On the rare occasion she spoke English in front of her father, he would scold her immediately. Then she'd accuse him of insanity for making her learn it.

Antonio's attitude toward Karina's coming of age was equally contradictory. He knew her looks were an asset at his political rallies. Young men, the coveted herd of socialist rebellion, flocked to the meetings to see Karina. Yet Antonio criticized every man who ever showed interest in her. In his opinion, they were all too poor, too stupid, too violent, or too womanizing for his daughter. His intention as a father was to teach Karina to aim high in choosing a mate. But the consequence was unforeseen. A frustrated Karina responded by masquerading as a hag with ugly clothes so that no men would look at her. The tactic failed. As it turned out, her simple prettiness could only be enhanced, not disguised. She adopted a rigid checklist of what she wanted in a man, scripted in part under the influence of romance novels. As it turned out, there was no man like that in Tonacatepeque.

The latest spat between Karina and her father had been over whether Antonio should reach out to neighboring villages in his endeavor to spread socialist doctrine. Karina, eager with the energetic zeal of *juventud*, had for weeks tried to convince her father to advertise his rallies in neighboring San Martin. She told him that he had already enlisted many of the men in Tonacatepeque, and that it was time for people in other villages to hear his message. Antonio, whose caution reflected the wisdom that comes with a lifetime of dissidence, told his daughter that spreading the movement too far too soon could have disastrous consequences. It was better to limit the scope at first, then spread gradually. But Karina persisted. She brought men from Tonacatepeque and San Martin to tell her father that the mood was ripe for change in both villages. She made dozens of extra carbon copies of enlistment forms and contribution sheets. Antonio, facing a daughter with a far deeper reserve of motivation, finally relented.

To promote the next rally, Karina spent two weeks riding a bus between the two towns either with her younger sister, Camila, who was 13 at the time, or with Antonio's handpicked protégé, Amado, a twig-thin student in political science imported from the Autonomous University in the capital. Amado, a follower of Ernest "Che" Guevara, was apparently oblivious to any thoughts that deviated from communist dogma. Love, lust and laziness were not part of his language. His aloofness to Karina's good looks and his rigid, cold demeanor earned Antonio's trust.

With a pouch of rusted nails and an old hammer, Karina walked from tree to tree in Tonacatepeque and San Martin tacking on hand-written pamphlets promoting the rally. Men constantly harassed her. Amado's presence did little to curtail the catcalls. His reaction to the constant whistling and air kisses that showered Karina was to put on an indignant face, tug Karina by the arm and walk in the opposite direction. Karina simply ignored them, or shot a cold stare in their direction. A few times, she walked right up to the disrespectful *cabrones* and jammed a pamphlet into their hands. "If you're a real *macho*, then you'll be at this rally," she'd say.

Only one man glazed Karina Fuentes' eyes over when he spoke. And that was her father. His sense of virtue, his boldness when speaking to a crowd, even his straight posture were signs that pointed to his infallibility. As far as she was concerned, her father never sinned. He never conspired, for his sense of honesty seemed to forbid him from leaning toward the cryptic. Since girlhood, she had cultivated a deep admiration for him. With every lecture he gave in public that Karina heard, with every course he taught at the local university, she added a floor to the castle of sand she built in honor of her father.

The Saturday before the meeting, Karina delivered her oral report to Antonio: dozens, if not hundreds of pamphlets had been posted. Some had been torn down from trees, but most of them were still there. The rally should be one of the biggest ever. Her and Amado would have their hands full at the meeting.

On Sunday, Karina woke up early and checked to make sure everything was ready. She scanned the checklist in her head: notebooks - check; pencils - check; membership forms - check; files -

check; pamphlets – check. Her father had already left the house to walk to the makeshift auditorium added to the east end of the Tonacatepeque school house. As Karina walked past the kitchen, she grabbed a slice of papaya and headed out the door, her arms wrapped around the bundle of supplies. Men were congregating near the hall. Karina, who never wore a wristwatch, realized she was running late.

She hurried through the front door, glancing around momentarily. A stranger – an unusually tall, well dressed man – caught her attention. Their eyes met and her mind wandered for just a split second – long enough for her to trip over an electric cable and tumble to the ground. Men rushed to help her. As she stood up and brushed herself off, she flipped her hair to the right and gave the stranger a steady, three-second stare. He returned her stare and smiled.

The stranger's gaze made her feel ashamed. Standing alone without speaking to anyone, he seemed different than all the other men in the room. His skin tone was lighter than everyone else's. He was taller, hairier, more mysterious looking. Other men stepped out of his way.

When the crowd waiting to hear Karina's father speak thickened between Karina and her admirer, a shade of gloom washed over her usually professional personality. She lost sight of the stranger, and strained her neck to try to catch another glimpse. But the crowd only grew denser in the hall. The sun grilled the tin ceiling, trapping the heat inside. Every time someone entered the auditorium, the temperature seemed to rise another degree. The two ceiling fans hanging from the rafters circulated the hot air. The few women in the room began to fan themselves with *abanicos*. Some of the campesinos had sparked up hand-rolled stogies from surplus tobacco plucked from a neighboring farm. The few florescent lights on the ceiling illuminated the cigar smoke climbing into the rafters.

Above several heads, Karina noticed the stranger remove his straw hat and fan himself with it. Others in the room cast suspicious glances at him, including Karina's father. It was obvious to Karina that everyone was looking at him because he stood out physically, not because he was unknown. There were many unknown men at these rallies. Suddenly, the buzz in the room quieted down as Karina's father took the stage at the front of the hall.

Antonio nodded his head at the crowd and held up a hand. Karina perked up, proud of her father's impeccable stage presence. He thanked the crowd for gathering on a Sunday, usually the only day of the week when the *campesinos* didn't work. Most of them were in their Sunday bests -- slacks, ironed short-sleeved shirts, hair slicked back. There was no microphone so Antonio had to speak up so his audience of 200 could hear him.

"You know," Antonio said in Spanish. "I see it in all your faces today that El Salvador has a good future. If our little El Salvador ever looks as good as Mr. Rodriguez here in front of me, we're sure to be alright."

The Indians in the crowd smiled, as did Rodriguez, whose gold-framed front teeth glinted nearly as brightly as his dapper slicked hair. Karina knew that her father used the country's name early in a speech for effect. *El Salvador.* The Savior, a beacon of hope. A tiny country with big ideas. Antonio took a deep breath and continued.

"As we read in the papers and hear in the radio every week, our brothers in Cuba are making excellent progress in land reform, health care, education. Just five years ago, they overthrew that corrupt and greedy regime of Fulgencio Batista."

The crowd grunted their approval. Karina had watched her father's admiration for the 1959 Cuban revolution grow every year. He was an open admirer of Fidel Castro.

"I know I ask you to come here every Sunday," Antonio continued. "And I'm seeing the crowd grow every week. That's very good. Because what I have to say is important and it concerns every one of you. The Salvadoran *sociedad*, those 15 families that own 80 percent of our country, feel they are not obliged to give anything back to you through agrarian reform or other socialist policies."

Antonio took a handkerchief from his back pocket and wiped his forehead. Sweat was now seeping through his blue guayabera.

"According to them," he continued. "They created whatever resources our poor people have to go around. They feel that they are above the law, by virtue of their social and economic positions. They feel that they can dispose of people with very few legal, moral or cultural restrictions."

The last remarks seemed to shake the crowd. Some of the men yelled "No, *señor*! It can't go on!" Antonio nodded his head, challenging the peasants to accept the truth.

"But my people, we don't have to tolerate this is if we don't want to," Antonio said, shaking his head side to side. "We can do something about it. Our people need unity to overcome this inequality in our society. Are we all together on this? Then let's unite and change our nation. Let's bring in social justice, like in Cuba."

The men yelled their approval. Karina, jumping up and down, yelled louder than anyone at her father's words and clapped with her hands held high. Amado, who had been standing on the stage a few feet away from Antonio, clapped enthusiastically, his stoic face unmoved.

Karina pushed forward in the crowd to get closer to the stage and ran into the stranger who had been eyeing her before. He was taking notes on a small notebook, not smiling, not cheering. A drop of sweat fell from the tip of the man's nose onto the notebook when Karina bumped him.

"Pardon me," Karina said.

The man smiled and bowed his head in a regal gesture of approval. The man was about to speak when Karina's father once again proclaimed the need for change. Her attention snapped back to her Antonio.

"We need social and political change," Antonio said. "To stick together, we must be organized. That is why I am asking those of you who are wondering how you can contribute to join the local Christian base community, the CEB. Here in Tonacatepeque, we are all in agreement that the CEB can serve as a strong political force to give us a voice. You may feel that you will never be heard as individuals, but I guarantee you that our government, and even the rich cannot ignore us if we continue to grow as a mass."

The crowd cheered. Some of the peasants whistled and raised their right hands in the air. Antonio, now sweating more profusely, ended his speech on a charismatic note, citing Fidel Castro's success as a reformer and encouraging the peasants to follow in his footsteps. Karina noticed the stranger turn away from her to jot down some notes. She had the urge to ask him what he was writing, but again, her father stole her attention.

"*Solo toma voluntad!* (All it takes is will!)" Antonio said. "You have to be willing to sacrifice for change. You have to be willing to commit yourselves to this cause. It is your only alternative to the unjust poverty and strife that confront you every day. I will ask my assistant to pass around membership forms. For those of you who can't read or write, form a line in front of that table and someone will take your information down."

Karina reached into a bag she was carrying and yelled "over here." The entire crowd, mostly male, turned to her, including the handsome newcomer, who seemed surprised to see a woman break out in such a bold gesture. Karina held up a bunch of leaflets. Hands shot toward her. The paper forms disappeared from her hands. Using her elbows, she nudged her way to a table on the far side of the room. The men dumbly followed her. She sat down behind the table, took a pen from her bag, and ordered the men to make a single line behind the chair. Amado and Antonio sat beside her on the table, but the men all lined up in front of Karina.

"If you can't read and write, I'll take down your information, but keep things in order or I'll leave," she warned, glancing around. The illiterate men, and even some who were literate, formed a perfect line behind the chair, waiting patiently in the heat to be able to sit for a moment with her.

The stranger got at the back of the line. Antonio and Amado announced that they were also available for assistance, but few heeded their call. Rodriguez, the gold-toothed peasant, politely asked Antonio for permission to come over to visit his daughter.

"I don't make those decisions for her," Antonio said. "You have to ask her."

Antonio, the light-skinned son of a Spanish father and an Indian mother, nurtured some of his father's European traditions, including allowing his daughter to choose and screen the suitors who visited her at their home, so long as the rendezvous were chaperoned.

The man looked over at Karina imploringly and asked her if he could visit her.

"*Esta bien,*" she said. "Someone else is visiting me at 4 this afternoon and then another one at 5, right, father?"

Antonio nodded.

"I think I can squeeze you in at 4:30," she said, grabbing her father's arm and glancing at his wristwatch.

"Thank you, *señorita*," Rodriguez said, and moved on.

After an hour of taking names, meager contributions and compliments from the peasants, the handsome stranger sat down in front of Karina. She became flushed and ran a handkerchief over her bare neck. She and the stranger just stared at each other for a few seconds. She knew he could read and write because she had seen him taking notes. The man placed his straw hat on the table and introduced himself to Karina's father.

"Buenas, señor, I am Tomas Hernandez," he said in a Spanish accent that did not sound local. The man was cutting off the last vowel of his words, like the s in *buenas*. And he spoke loudly and exuded confidence, as though he had known Antonio for years.

"Ah, I recognize your accent, you must be Cuban," Antonio said. "I am Antonio. Good to meet you."

Tomas looked at Karina eagerly.

"This is my daughter, Karina," said Antonio.

Karina's face was serious. She nodded to him. Even though Tomas was sitting at arms length from her, he stood up courteously and extended his hand. She offered her own delicate-looking brown hand. When Tomas grabbed it, she squeezed his hand firmly and smiled.

"Nice to meet you," she said.

"A pleasure," he said. "I am here on behalf of Fidel Castro's government."

Antonio's head cocked up and his eyes widened with pleasure. He stood up and spread his arms, as though inviting this stranger to hug him. Tomas smiled. Antonio had often told Karina that Cuba was trying to spread socialist revolution across the world, funded with Soviet subsidies, and that they would eventually aid Salvadorans in their own Marxist struggles.

"I admire Mr. Castro very much," Antonio said. "It is wonderful to have one of his people here with us."

"We have learned in Cuba that El Salvador is ripe for change, that the masses are restless. I am here as an…" Tomas stalled. "As an unofficial emissary, let's say. I heard your speech today. I must say, you remind me of *El Comandante* himself inspiring those peasants to rise up."

"Thank you, *señor*," Antonio said. "After watching the success you've had in Cuba, we feel that we can follow in your footsteps."

"Are you willing to commit yourself, as you asked your men to do?" Tomas said. "It is a serious undertaking, one that even requires a commitment to violence if you really want to bring about change."

"Violence is always a last resort," Antonio said. "But we are committed to change, just as Mr. Castro was, and we won't stop until we get it."

Tomas leaned forward on the table. Through the neck slit in his *guayabera*, Karina could see a mat of black hair on his chest. She checked herself for being so uncouth and turned away. But just as quickly, she glanced at it again.

"So, I can see you are the leader here," Tomas said.

"I'm just one of many local leaders across El Salvador," Antonio said. 'Our movement is strong, and getting stronger."

"So what is your background?"

"Well, I am a University professor, but I moved out here from San Salvador 15 years ago to educate peasants," Antonio said. "Five years ago, I was elected mayor of my town, Tonacatepeque. I'm a local leader of the CEB and a member of the Salvadoran General Association of University Students, a leftist organization started in 1927."

"That's very impressive," Tomas said. "But elected mayor? Doesn't it seem strange to people that an elected official is preaching communism?"

"By electing me, the peasants felt that I should be the one to speak for them," Antonio said. "So how does this work between us? Are you here to help, or observe, or what?"

"Just observe for now," Tomas said. "Until I can judge how serious the movement is. But listen, you mustn't tell anyone about me. If it gets out to the Americans that Fidel has advisors in El Salvador, your movement could be crushed. You know how the Americans admire El Salvador. They have held it up as a regional model for progress and stability. In part, your movement is strong because the Americans have overlooked the eminent threat your grassroots movement poses. But that could all change."

"Okay," Antonio said. "I won't tell anyone about you. I wouldn't want the Americans to interfere. So when did you arrive here? How did you hear about me?"

"I heard about you from a colleague of yours at the university, Fernando Lamas," Tomas said.

"Really?" Antonio said, suddenly becoming suspicious of the Cuban. "The last time I spoke with him, Fernando did not seem very supportive of our cause."

"Oh, that has changed," Tomas said. "Anyways, I am staying at the Hotel San Salvador. I'd like you and your daughter to join me and a few associates for dinner next Saturday."

"That sounds fine to me," Antonio said, still harboring caution. "But Karina doesn't really need to come along."

"I want to, Papá," Karina said. "I've never seen the inside of the Hotel San Salvador."

Antonio paused, caught in an awkward moment. But then he flashed a grand smile, and his words came out easy.

"Well, there you have it," Antonio said. "We'd be glad to join you."

"Great," Tomas said, standing up. "It was good to meet you. I'll contact you this week to arrange a time and date for our meeting."

CHAPTER 9

When Karina met Tomas at her father's rally on Sunday, dormant musings came flooding back. His exotic, elegant look, his charm and manners, his style of dress, all epitomized the dark horse lover that Karina had cooked up in her daydreams. He had polish. There was no dirt under his nails. He came from somewhere she had never been to.

All week Karina had been anticipating her trip to San Salvador with her father to dine with Tomas in one of the finest hotels in the city. A kind of warmth entered the pit of her stomach when the rooster crowed near her window at dawn Saturday, a feeling akin to the one she experienced as a child on the morning of her birthday, when she knew her family would gather in her house to surprise her with knick-knacks.

She sprang out of the sheets, and noticed her little sisters, Camila and Gladys, were already awake. Camila was fumbling through a drawer, looking for something.

"Karina," Camila said. "Can we go with you tonight?"

Karina was standing in front of an old Spanish mirror hanging on the wall, running her fingers through her long black hair. She put on a long green dress and sandals.

"I'm on official business," Karina said. "No *zipotes* allowed."

"You're not on official business," Camila said. "You haven't stopped talking about that guy Tomas all week. That's why you're so excited."

Karina winked at her little sister and walked to the kitchen. Her mother, Emilia, was making fresh tortillas on the stove. Refried black beans were heating up nearby. Sliced papaya on a plate enticed Karina. She grabbed a chunk and ate it.

"That's all there is for everyone, so don't eat it all," Emilia said.

Camila had followed her sister out of the room.

"She doesn't care, mama," Camila said. "She only thinks about herself, and that guy she met last week, Tomas. She's in love with him, mama. She keeps talking about the hair on his chest."

Emilia banged the wooden spoon on the stove and turned around. Karina pinched her sister's arm. The little girl ran behind her mother.

"Camila, go help your aunt feed the animals," Emilia said, pushing the little girl out of the kitchen.

"But she's already done, mama," Camila said.

"Go!" Emilia said.

Karina's little sister left with her head hanging. Emilia wiped her hands and turned to look at Karina.

"Karina, you're father and I talked about it, and we decided that you're not going tonight," Emilia said.

"Don't joke with me, mama," Karina said. "Papa and I have been preparing for this the whole week."

"I'm sorry Karina, but you're not going," Emilia said.

"Yes I am," Karina said. "Papa needs me to go."

"You're father is the one who decided not to take you," Emilia said.

"That's a lie," Karina said. "You just don't want me to enjoy myself and see something new."

Emilia sighed and went back to her kitchen work.

"I'm sorry, *hija*, but that's the way it has to be," Emilia said. "There will be other opportunities for you to go to the capital with your father."

Karina stormed out of the house without saying another word. Her little mutt, Seco, scampered beside her. She decided to go find her father at the Church, where he said he went every Saturday morning to meet with the priest. Her father was always more reasonable. If he gave Karina permission to come along tonight, it would overrule her mother. Karina had a way of convincing her father, the way only daughters can. On the way to the church, Karina passed the village square, where she kicked up dust in front of the benches surrounding the center fountain.

During the past week, Karina's father had praised Tomas for his interest in the socialist cause, and for his apparent insight into the movement. Her father had never before spoken highly of a man Karina was attracted to. She pretended to ignore him when he spoke of Tomas, but she didn't interrupt him. Reluctantly, she wanted to hear what her father had to say.

He still wielded that influence over Karina. His opinions annoyed her, but she engraved them into her decision-making. And she had absorbed his words like a canvass soaks in paint.

Passing a home where the owners had set up two tables outside to sell meals, Karina spotted her cousin, Carlos Conejos, sitting on one of the tables with another woman and a child.

Carlos had asked for Karina's hand in marriage recently, but informed by gossip that the Conejos had begun an illegitimate family, Karina had turned him down.

Carlos saw Karina and ran to greet her. As far as Tonacatepeque was concerned, Carlos was well-off. He was the only person in the village who made bricks, which everyone bought off him when they had saved enough money to fortify their wood shacks. His business had done so well that he had bought a truck to transport the bricks.

"Hello, Karina," Carlos said. "You look more beautiful than ever."

"What do you want, Carlos?" she said speeding up her pace. "Isn't your girlfriend going to get jealous that you're talking to me?"

"Who? Her?" Carlos said tilting his head toward the woman at the table, who turned away indignantly. "She means nothing to me. You're the one I want. Can I give you a lift somewhere? Where are you going? I'll take you."

"Nowhere, Carlos," Karina said. "I think your girlfriend is leaving."

The woman at the table was walking away with the baby.

"Mamita!" Carlos yelled at the woman. He grabbed Karina's hand and kissed it, telling her "I'll do anything for you." Then turned to go after his girlfriend.

The Church was empty when Karina arrived. She walked

around the back, but the rectory door was locked. She sat on a bench and petted Seco. After a few strokes, Seco ran off down the street, barking as though greeting someone he knew. Karina called after him and followed the mutt down a dirt road that led away from church. The mutt stopped in front of a concrete house and serenaded it with a barrage of barking.

Karina grabbed the dog by the back of the neck. But just as she was about to start dragging the dog away, her father stepped out of the house with another woman on his arm. Karina was partly covered by some bushes. Before she could speak out, she watched as her father kissed the other woman on the mouth.

"Papa!" Karina yelled.

Antonio gave a start when he heard his daughter's voice. The other woman, who had thick black curly hair and huge breasts, patted Antonio on the shoulder and ducked into her house. The shocked father approached his daughter with his hands out and shaking his head.

"Karina, listen, it's nothing, dear," Antonio said.

Karina couldn't look at her father. She retreated from him, walking backwards, until she just started running away. Her father caught up to her and grabbed her by the shoulder. She couldn't look him in the eye.

"I can't believe you," she cried out.

"You're misunderstanding," the father said. "That woman wanted to join our cause and I went there to sign her up. That's all. Really."

Karina pushed her father away, shaking her head. Her skinny little dog pushed up against her leg. She walked away without saying anything. She felt disgusted, as though her father had suddenly turned into a capitalist.

"Karina, Karina please," Antonio called out after her. "Please, don't say anything to your mother."

For those who lived away from the glow of the capital, night in El Salvador was an enchanting spectacle. The stars powdering the sky seemed to cool the land like bits of ice. During the dry season, when the mosquito population dwindled, Karina would lie on the awning in her back yard and watch shooting stars. But on Saturday night, after Tomas picked up her father to take him to dinner in the capital, leaving Karina behind, the stars provided little peace. All week she had looked forward to seeing Tomas in the capital. When her father rode away without her, she felt like killing herself just to get even with her parents.

Karina refused to sew her grandmother's shawl, as her mother had asked. Anger oozed from her scowling face when her mother talked to her. After a dinner of tortillas and chicken, Karina locked herself in her bedroom. At first, Emilia and her sisters ignored her. But when Emilia ordered the two younger girls to go to bed, they started banging on their bedroom door, and yelling at Karina to let them in. Emilia, annoyed at the banging, walked outside to Karina's bedroom window. The white curtains swayed in the breeze. Emilia pushed them apart and glanced inside the room. Karina was gone.

By then, Karina was standing on the dark dirt road in front of Carlos Conejos' house, debating whether to involve him in her plan. Clutching a bag with lipstick, a dress and her mother's expensive shoes, Karina finally knocked on Carlos' door. His girlfriend, an older woman with dark Indian skin, opened the door.

"What the hell do you want, you little slut?" the woman said.

"Is Carlos here?" Karina said. "I need to talk to him."

"No, he went out," said the woman, and she slammed the door in Karina's face. But in El Salvador, windows were mere holes in the wall, and Carlos, who was sitting at his kitchen table, had heard Karina's voice. Karina had turned to walk away when the door opened again.

"Karina, what a nice surprise," Carlos said. "What brings you here tonight?"

Carlos' jealous girlfriend threw a fit. Karina could hear her yelling inside. It was the same woman who snubbed Karina whenever they passed each other in the town. Carlos darted back into his house to control his girlfriend. Karina walked closer to the door and heard the sounds of an argument. The girlfriend was referring to Karina as a "Puta." Karina heard what sounded like a smack and then a sack of potatoes fall to the ground. The screaming stopped suddenly. A frightened little boy ran out the front door past Karina, into the dark night. After a few minutes, a panting Carlos, his hair a mess, came out again and apologized to Karina.

"I'm sorry she's so rude," Carlos said. "So what can I do for you."

"You said you'd do anything for me, right Carlos?" Karina said, giving him a flirtatious glance.

"Anything for you, Karina," he said.

Karina grabbed his strong forearm and squeezed it tightly. She noticed the near-orgasmic breath he let out of his mouth. When she was convinced Carlos was under her spell, and would do her bidding, she leaned close to his face.

"I need you to give me a ride, Carlos," she whispered. "Tonight."

Carlos nodded, dumbfounded. "Yes, sure, right now?"

"Right now, Carlos," Karina said. "Take me into the capital."

"Into the capital?" Carlos said. "That's almost an hour away."

"I know it's kind of far, but I know you will help me," she said.

"Why do you have to go to the capital now?" he said.

"It's a long story, I'll tell you on the way," she said.

"Well, um let me get my keys," Carlos said. "Are we staying in the capital together? Should I bring some clothes?"

"No, no, no," she said. "I'm meeting up with my father there. You're leaving me there and coming back here. The drive there will be nice, just me and you."

The cab in Carlos Conejos' truck was as big as a couch. With one arm hanging out of the passenger window, Karina sat as far as she could from Carlos. The truck grumbled noisily over the dirt road leading to the highway. The roadway was dead. They had encountered only a handful of cars. Carlos asked Karina to sit closer to him, but she just smiled and stayed where she was. Carlos told Karina his girlfriend meant nothing to him, that he was looking for a clean, good woman, a virgin with whom to make a fresh start. The word "virgin" echoed in Karina's ear.

Halfway to San Salvador, Carlos pulled over to urinate. Karina told him to stay outside while she changed into her dress. While Carlos was outside peeing, Karina flipped on the cab light, took off her blouse and her pants, and slipped the dress on in the truck. Carlos watched her strip. After peeing into the bushes, he climbed back into the truck and slid closer to Karina with a wicked look in his face. Without warning, he yanked Karina by the elbow and wrapped his arm around her waist.

"What the hell do you think you're doing?" she said. "You're going to wrinkle my dress."

Carlos moved in for the aggressive advance, trying to kiss her on the mouth. But Karina turned her head at the last second, and Carlos' tongue slid up and down her cheek. Karina pulled back and slapped him, wiping her face with her arm. Apparently shocked, Carlos pushed her away and pulled the truck into the highway again.

It was the first time a man had tried to kiss Karina like that. Kisses in the movies she had seen and in books she had read were usually superseded by feelings of love, which she did not feel for Carlos.

She began to doubt her plan. Maybe bumming a ride to the capital to meet her father and see Tomas wasn't the best idea. Maybe her mother was right to scold and punish her for feeling sexual urges. Glancing over to Carlos, Karina put on a disgusted face, "The nerve of him," she thought, incensed. "If I was a man I'd knock his teeth out."

But at the same time, she was proud of her judgment for picking a dress she thought no man could resist her in. Carlos' advances were merely a successful test of her plan, she thought. Karina smiled as she imagined herself making a glamorous entrance into the lobby of the Hotel San Salvador. She leaned her head out the window, letting the wind blow back her long hair.

The last leg of Karina's road trip went by quietly. Conejo kept caressing the spot on his cheek where Karina slapped him. Karina touched up her lipstick and combed her hair with a brush. Even as they pulled into the capital, Karina didn't say much. She loved the crowds on the sidewalk and the cars rushing through the streets. Carlos pulled up to the hotel in his rumbling, dusty truck, and dropped Karina off at the front steps. The doorman eyed his jalopy closely and called security. But before two guards came out, he drove off, leaving Karina standing on the front steps, gazing at the crystal chandelier.

Mixed emotions flooded her as she stood there. Karina's father had always criticized the luxury hotels in the capital. To him, they were a symbol of imperialism. In the midst of a city of poverty, indigenous existence and growing unrest, the pristine grounds of the Hotel San Salvador touted to the masses of El Salvador exactly what the United States represented to the tiny nation on an international scale: exclusivity.

Two guards broke Karina's concentration. They were armed with shotguns, and approached her quickly. The look of awe on her face turned quickly to fright. The young sentries, staring at Karina in her red dress, eased down their arms.

"Are you a guest here?" one of the guards asked her.

"I am a guest of Tomas Hernandez," Karina said.

"It's late," said the other guard. "Is he expecting you?"

The question confused Karina. During the entire time she plotted her romantic escapade, she never once considered hotel security. She figured this must be routine treatment for all guests.

"I believe so," she said.

"Either he is or he isn't expecting you, which one is it," said the other guard, taking a suspicious, condescending tone with her.

"I was invited as a guest to his gathering here tonight, but I arrived late," she said.

A limousine was pulling up to the front of the hotel.

"Let's continue our conversation inside," said one of the guards, taking Karina by the elbow and leading her inside.

They guided her into the bright marble lobby, past regal

chandeliers, Persian rugs and luxury chairs. Three musicians in tuxedos playing Chopin by the bar turned to look at her. Karina had never seen three indigenous men dressed so elegantly, and she waved at them excitedly.

The guards took Karina to a seat next to the front desk. One of them pulled up a chair next to her, resting his shotgun on the floor.

"What is the name again of the guest you are visiting?" the guard said.

"Tomas Hernandez," she said.

The guard glanced behind the counter at a man in a suit, who shook his head.

"Senorita, we have no guest by that name here," the guard said.

"He invited my father and I to dinner here," Karina said. "My father is already here with him."

"They are here now?" the guard said condescendingly. "Where?"

Karina looked around the lobby.

"They must be in the restaurant," she said. "Can we check there?"

The guard suddenly put on a serious tone.

"Don't play games with me," he said. "I know exactly what you're doing here. We get women like you by the dozen in here. You go into the bar and try to hustle the rich men."

"What do you mean women like me?" Karina said innocently. "My father is Antonio Fuentes. He is the mayor of our town, Tonacatepeque."

"You little idiot," the guard said, standing up. He grabbed Karina by the arm. "We don't allow prostitutes in our hotel."

Karina's face went slack. It took a few moments for the full blow of the insult to kick in. By the time she came to her senses, the guard was leading her back to the front door to throw her back into the night. She stopped and yanked her arm away.

"I can't believe this," she yelled. "How dare you even think that I am a prostitute?"

A group of well-dressed couples walking into the hotel

stopped to stare at the commotion. The outraged guard smiled to conceal his embarrassment.

"Come on, *señorita*, time to go," the guard said.

"I am not leaving," she said. "I came here all the way from Tonacatepeque as an invited guest. How dare you call me a prostitute?"

Everyone stared at her. The band by the bar stopped playing. The manager walked over. If she had a gun, she thought, she would certainly open fire on this bastard guard.

At that moment, Tomas walked out of the elevator with two other men. They seemed to be discussing something intensely. He spotted Karina, said goodbye to the other men, and walked to her excitedly. As he neared her, she turned to him and said only "Tomas."

Tomas put his arm around her and kissed her on the cheek, running his hand over her hair. The guard gave a start.

"What's the matter?" Tomas asked Karina.

"This man insulted me," Karina said. "I came here to meet with you and my father and he called me a prostitute."

Tomas turned to the guard and raised a clenched fist, ready to strike the little man. But his hard stare was enough to send the guard away apologizing profusely. The manager came over and apologized too.

"We're very sorry, Mr. Robaina," the manager said, "but she told us she was here to visit a guest by the name of Tomas Hernandez, and I don't have anyone registered in the hotel under that name."

"I should have you all arrested right now for insulting my girlfriend," Tomas said.

This proclamation sent a wave of romantic dizziness through Karina. Tomas, who was dressed in a graceful white suit, extended his arm to her. As she took it, Tomas leaned over and whispered "you look beautiful" in Karina's ear. In response, she squeezed his arm and pulled herself closer to him, smelling the mixture of cologne and cigar smoke on his jacket. As though she had checked in her feistiness at the lobby, Karina strolled with Tomas, feeling safety in his presence. The romance and adventure that had drawn her to sneak away from her home now transformed into a sacrificial love. She felt she would do anything Tomas asked.

As they walked, Karina didn't even wonder where they were going. She was exactly where she wanted to be. Tomas escorted her to the terrace overlooking the pool. The wind blowing up from the San Salvador hills shuffled her hair. She leaned closer to Tomas, resting the side of her head on his shoulder. There was another couple smooching at another section of the terrace. The stars peeked out between clouds.

"Your father told me you weren't coming," Tomas said. "I was very disappointed."

"The truth is, I'm not supposed to be here," she said.

"Your father is upstairs talking business with some associates," Tomas said. "He seems to be managing okay by himself, but we can go upstairs if you like. Or, since your father has already eaten, we can sit down and have a nice dinner. And forget about politics for a little while."

Karina nodded. She raised her eyes to look at his. Tomas lowered his head and they locked gazes. Karina's heart thumped madly in her chest. Every second their eyes remained connected seemed to raise her pulse tenfold. Lightheadedness practically blinded her. To steady herself, she placed her right hand on his chest, feeling the mat of hair beneath. A stray breeze brushed a strand of hair across her face. Tomas gently removed the strand from her face and with a quick dip that gave her no chance of denying the motion, he kissed her mouth.

Not knowing what to do, Karina relaxed her jaw. Tomas placed a hand behind her head and ran his fingers through her dark, soft hair. Her legs felt like brittle twigs. To keep from collapsing, Karina threw her arms around Tomas' neck. She found herself kissing him back, sucking in his lower lip. She parted her mouth to accept his tongue, which tasted like coffee and cognac.

Karina always imagined kissing a man on the mouth would feel itchy and bristly, like when her mustached father kissed her good night on the cheek. But when she felt the softness of Tomas' lips, and the eel-like lubrication of Tomas' mouth, an unfamiliar craving arose inside of her. A sizzling flash shot through her face, her breasts and between her legs.

Tomas pressed her so close to him that she had trouble breathing. But it wasn't close enough. She didn't want the moment to end.

A group of people ambled onto the terrace talking loudly, and Tomas pulled himself away from Karina, leaving a vacant look in her eyes. That look was the only expression Karina's mind could permit as she signed a contract in her soul handing herself completely to Tomas. In those moments, her crush became a full blown love, powerful and convincing. She figured this was the feeling her father always told her was required to marry happily. It took a few seconds for her to respond to Tomas's question.

"Shall we eat?" he said.

Eating was the last thing on her mind.

"*Esta Bien*," she said.

Tomas took her by the hand and escorted her to the hotel's restaurant. The menu confused her. Everything was written in Spanish, but she didn't recognize any of the dishes: Rabo Encendido, Moros y Cristianos, Mero en Salsa de Mango, Ropa Vieja. Where were the pupusas? Where were the chicken tortillas? Where was the papaya juice?

"I'm not really hungry," she said, putting down the menu.

"This is Caribbean food," Tomas said.

"I'm happy with lemonade," she said.

"No problem," Tomas said. "Waiter!"

A short man hurried over.

"Yes, senor Robaina?" the waiter said.

"Bring her lemonade, and make sure it's freshly squeezed," Tomas said. "And please prepare us a plate of pupusas and white cheese."

"Yes, Mr. Robaina," the waiter said.

When the waiter walked away, Karina put on a confused face.

"Why do they call you Robaina?" she said. "Isn't your name Tomas Hernandez?"

Tomas leaned across the table, slowly glancing around.

"Robaina is just an alias," he said. "I have to cover my tracks, so that our enemies can't track me down."

"So your real name is Tomas Hernandez?"

"Yes," he said. "I only tell it to the people I trust."

"So you feel you are in danger?" she said.

"Because there are powerful people who would like to stop people like me and your father. What your father is proposing is very radical in the views of the United States. There are a lot of people who want to prevent any upheaval in El Salvador."

"I've always known that my father's activism wasn't sanctioned by the government, but most people want the changes he is talking about."

Tomas reached across the table and grabbed Karina's hand.

"I was very attracted to you when I first saw you," Tomas said. "I think you are a beautiful, intelligent woman."

Karina smiled and squeezed his hand. This was the moment, she thought. She was waiting for him to ask for her hand in marriage. But the waiter came back quickly and laid a plate of pupusas with white cheese and a lemonade in front of her. Tomas asked the waiter for a mojito, a drink made with rum, lime juice, mint and sugar.

Karina picked at her food, ate a pupusa, drank some of her juice. Eyeing Tomas' mojito, she asked for a sip. Tomas handed her his glass and she tasted it.

"It tastes like lemonade," she said.

"That's more or less what it is," he said. "Would you like one?"

"Yes," she said.

Tomas ordered the waiter to bring Karina a mojito. They raised their glasses for a toast.

"To your beauty," he said.

They drank gulps and squeezed each other's hands.

"This reminds me of a movie," she said.

"Which movie?" Tomas said.

"Breakfast at Tiffany"'s," she said.

"I've heard of it but never seen it," Tomas said.

"It's about a girl who lives a glamorous life in New York City."

"Sounds interesting," Tomas said. "Do you like your mojito?"

"Yes, it's delicious," she said.

"Would you like another?"

"Sure," she said.

"Your father is a real socialist," Tomas said.

"He believes in what he talks about," she said, already a little drunk. "But I don't always understand him. He criticizes the United States so much, but then he encourages me to learn English. He promotes communism, but then he wants his children to undergo the Catholic sacraments. He talks about the proletariat, but he's an elected mayor. I want to ask him about those things. Maybe I should go see him. Is he upstairs?"

"Yes, but I don't think we should bother him," Tomas said. "Besides, he may get upset that you're here. He may want to take you home, then our night would end."

"That's true," she said.

"So tell me about your father?" Tomas said. "How many people are in his group?"

"I'm not sure," Karina said.

"Aren't you his secretary?" Tomas said.

"Yes, it's just that there are so many people who say they are part of it, but they don't all give their names or pay their dues. It's probably about 200 farmers and poor people."

"Of course," Tomas said. "Is your father always with large groups of people? Is he always working?"

The thought of seeing her father kiss another woman earlier that day distracted her.

"Almost always," she said.

"Almost?" Tomas said. "Does he ever do anything alone. Is he religious?"

"We go to mass on Sunday afternoons. On Sunday mornings, he tells us that he goes to the church by himself, but I don't know."

"You don't know what?" Tomas said.

Karina didn't immediately answer.

"Let's toast again," Tomas said, changing into a more cheerful tone. "This time you choose what to toast to."

Karina thought for a moment, then raised her glass.

"To my father and to socialism," she said.

"Cheers," Tomas said, watching her gulp down her drink.

CHAPTER 10

For an hour, the conversation was all about Karina's father. Tomas grilled her on Antonio's daily routine, membership lists, recruitment strategies, ideological backing. All the while, Karina sipped on mojitos, letting the lightning lemonade carry her higher into the clouds. The drunker she got, the bolder Tomas' questions seemed to come out. He asked her about her father's bad habits, whether he ever lied about anything, his secrets. Then he touched a nerve in her that even alcohol couldn't dull.

"Does he cheat on your mother?" Tomas said.

Karina sat back on her chair, narrowing her eyes. She put down the glass without taking a sip. The whole morning came back to her now, interpreted through the numbing booze. It seemed like weeks ago that she caught her father leaving another woman's home. Every detail came back without mercy: the way Antonio had kissed the other woman, his arm wrapped around her waist; the way he tenderly passed his hand over her matted hair; the stunned look on his face when he saw Karina watching them.

"Why are you asking me all these questions about my father," she said. "All night I've been waiting for another kind of question from you."

"I'm curious," he said. "I want to know about your family."

"I saw him coming out of a woman's house this morning."

"A woman from your town?" Tomas said. "Who is she?"

"She is a hideous bag," Karina said, remembering with disgust how the woman looked. "Pilar Chicas. She is always at my father's rallies. You probably saw her there last week. You couldn't forget a face that ugly, believe me."

"You know, when I was a little younger than you are now, I came home early from school one afternoon and found my mother in her room with her cousin, Anselmo Bonilla. They were lying naked in my parent's bed. I just walked in without knocking and saw them. It really affected me."

"Why do men do those things?" Karina asked.

"Women do them too," Tomas said. "Sometimes people can't help it."

"I work so closely with my father," she said. "I see all the hard work, all the devotion. I hate that there are things about him that I don't know."

Karina's voice broke. Then just as suddenly she broke into a fit of uncontrollable laughter.

Tomas pulled his chair closer and put his arm around her. That gesture of tenderness felt strangely seductive to Karina. A revelation came over her at the moment: her virginity would end tonight. It occurred to Karina that a woman is free to choose with calculation the man to whom she first gives herself.

Karina had a whole week to think about Tomas. Skimming all the sensual passages from her old novels, she had pictured to the last detail the way she'd act around him. Surely, all her words during moments of intimacy would come out perfect. She would know for sure why she'd chosen Tomas over all her other suitors.

As a Catholic, she feared that God would damn her to hell, convict her of shamelessness and sentence her to be forever seen as a harlot if she had sex outside of marriage. But then she mulled the flip side of sexual restraint: waiting for one man to come along, not knowing what kind of husband he would turn out to be. She knew she had to go after what she wanted. In her village, the suitors all looked the same—as though they worked all day with their hands, washed themselves in a hurry and put on a half-clean shirt before visiting the woman they wanted to enslave.

Tomas settled the dinner bill and slipped his arm around Karina. She liked how it felt around her waist. It made her feel secure.

"We can go upstairs and see your father if you like," Tomas said. "Or we can go to my room and continue our conversation, just the two of us."

Karina didn't answer. But she looked at him in such a way that no response was necessary. Tomas escorted her to the elevator. As it ascended to his room, he pushed her hair behind her ear.

They walked off the elevator holding hands, and ambled together through the dim hallway. Tomas opened the door to his room. Then just as Karina was beginning to feel hesitant, Tomas whispered, "I'm falling in love with you. I want to be with you."

The words shot through her like electricity. But insecurity gripped her. Karina didn't know whether she should lay her bag on the antique couch, the matching chair, or the desk. Tomas took it from her and put it on a chair in the bedroom. When he returned to the living room, she noticed he had removed his white jacket.

"Can I get you a drink?" he asked her.

She shook her head.

"You can sit down if you like," he said.

She couldn't stand the tension. She wanted him to take control. Tomas turned on the radio, located a frequency playing scratchy mambo music and sashayed to Karina.

"Do you like to dance?" he said, taking her hand and pulling her closer.

"Yes," she said.

The strumming guitars made her nervous. She had never danced to mambo. But Tomas' smooth rhythmic jerks set her at ease. Soon her hips also began to sway. With every beat, Tomas drew a bit closer, clutching his arm around her back. She felt his gaze on her face, but fought the impulse to look him in the eye. Instead, she turned her head, exposing her neck. Tomas bent down and kissed her gently on the nape. They stopped dancing, although the music continued to pulsate. Tomas bent down and kissed her. Both her arms slithered around his neck like erotic snakes.

His fingers gently traced the curves of her body, from her shoulder blades to her lower back to her hips. When his hands passed over her back, she flinched. But instead of pulling back respectfully, Tomas squeezed Karina's bottom together, pressing her close to his groin. Not knowing how to react, she reached behind him and did the same. The kissing paused just long enough for Tomas to say:

"I'm going to make love to you."

"Yes," she said.

Tomas took Karina's hand and led her into the bedroom. The fluffy queen-sized bed was bigger than any she had ever seen. As the bedroom door clicked shut, her heartbeat seemingly accelerated tenfold. She felt lost, as though she had entered a country where she didn't speak the language. All her illusions of how she should act faded into clumsiness. She wanted Tomas to tell her what to do and how to do it. He gingerly pushed Karina onto the bed and stood in front of her.

"Unbutton my shirt," he told her.

With her fingers trembling, she reached for the top button. She stumbled with it awkwardly. It dawned on her that she wasn't the sexy starlet she had envisioned earlier. She felt like a clumsy kid trying to open a gift that was really meant for her mother. Tomas grabbed her hands and undid the buttons himself. As he revealed his hairy chest, Karina placed her hand on the wiry patch and ran her fingers through it. For some reason, she wanted to bury her face in his chest and smell him. He flung his shirt over the chair in the corner of the room and sat to the right of Karina on the bed.

"I've never seen a man so hairy before," she said timidly.

These weren't the sexy words she had dreamed of uttering at this most tender moment. She wondered if Tomas knew that he was going to be her first lover. She hadn't told him anything about her virginity. The way she looked, he may have thought she had experience in these things. But she didn't. She had never even kissed a man with tongue until tonight.

Tomas seemed to have sensed her nervousness.

"Do you want me to turn off the light?" he asked her.

In the dark, she wouldn't be able to see the hairy chest. That was unacceptable to her. She shook her head.

Any notions Karina harbored of how to act with a man in a sexual situation, she had learned from reading insinuative romance novels. She remembered a heroine in a book she read letting loose her hair before making love. She reached for the pins holding her hairdo in place and pulled them out. Her black Indian hair fell around her shoulders.

Tomas began kissing her again. The smell of his breath was an aphrodisiac. His hand cupped her knee and slowly slid up her thigh. It was colder than she expected and she gave a start. But like before, the inhibitive gesture only encouraged him. He eased her legs apart with his thumb and forefinger and rubbed her panties. The warmth between her thighs quickly heated up his fingers.

His lips drifted from her mouth to her neck, where he buried his face under her hair. A sucking sound filled the still air. Only the distant hum of mambo provided a background.

The longer her legs were apart, the more comfortable she felt. She barely knew Tomas, but she had no fear of what he was doing to her. The more he touched her, the more he quelled the doubts that remained in her Catholic conscious.

Tomas pulled back and reached behind Karina, unzipping her red dress. She stood up to make it easy for him to undress her. Her arms hung limply by her sides. She locked her eyes on his as he inched the dress up from her knees, pushed it past her hips, then held it suspended as it passed over her breasts. Holding the entire dress in a wrinkled bundle between her neck and chest, Tomas closed in and kissed each cup of her bra. Karina bit her lip and lifted her arms so he could slip the dress over her head. As soon as the dress came off, she blushed. But it was a hot feeling that came over her cheeks: more like excitement than shame.

Tomas sat Karina on the bed and knelt down on the carpeted floor in front of her. Slowly, so as not to frighten her, he slipped the white bra straps off her shoulders. Pulling down the bra, he kissed the soft mound of flesh. Karina grabbed the back of his head with both hands and rubbed his hair.

She lost all feelings of inhibition. A moan escaped her mouth. She wanted his hairy chest to rub against her nipples. Funny needles seemed to prod every inch of her skin.

When she looked again at Tomas, he had unbuttoned his pants and pushed them down. The moment was nearing. Thomas pulled her panties off and stood up in front of her. He grabbed her under the arms and pushed her toward the middle of the bed. She hadn't felt so manipulated since she was a little girl. But it fascinated her. Instinctively, her legs closed and tilted to the side. But Tomas grabbed her knees and pushed her legs apart.

He knelt between her, ready to take her. Then the look in her eyes changed completely from allurement to a child-like, last second fear, as though she were standing 100 feet above the sea ready to plunge off a cliff that millions had jumped off before her. Every bit of self consciousness and insecurity she had felt when she first entered the room came back now, amplified by a million. She wondered if she looked stupid, lying there helplessly, ready to please a man who was practically a stranger. This wasn't right. Was her father in a nearby bedroom? What if he saw her right now?

She shouldn't be doing this. She changed her mind. She wanted to call the whole thing off. But her legs stayed apart. She wished she were married to Tomas, so she wouldn't feel so devious: so God could nod his approval from a crucifix above the bed.

Tomas' leaned forward. He poised himself on his arms next to her shoulders. She looked at his face. He licked his lips.

"You are very sexy, Karina," he told her. "You're the most beautiful girl I have ever seen. Tell me if this hurts."

His hips eased down between her. She pushed up on his chest and he pulled back. But he entered her again, this time more deeply. The pain was worse, but she didn't push him off again. She expected – no, wanted -- the pain as punishment. She spread her legs as far apart as she could. Thomas worked up a rhythm. To stop herself from screaming and moaning, she bit down on his flesh.

Something was happening inside her. The burning pain turned into a jolting pressure inside her belly, as though she had to urinate badly. All the muscles in her body seemed to be contracting to keep what seemed like a huge flood of urine from easing out of her bladder. She clenched her teeth. The pressure built to a crescendo. A hot flush swept over her cheeks. Thomas jabbed and jabbed: a steady rhythm now. Everything tensed up. She could barely move.

Just when Karina thought the pressure would kill her, a blissful tingle shot up to her belly and her breasts. The pressure suddenly lifted from all her muscles.

Tomas collapsed next to her on the bed. She looked at him, but he didn't seem to notice her. She grabbed the sheets and wiped herself clean. A rose-colored stain on the sheet was the last trace of her virginity. She glanced around the room. It was so quiet now: only the radio squeaked outside. For the first time she noticed the splendid décor in the room: carved wood trimmings, antique mahogany furniture, satin curtains. Her gaze drifted to the bedroom door and rested on a crucifix hanging above the door. She quickly looked away.

No one would ever find out about this, she thought. No one she knew even ventured into the capital. But what about her father? Was he in a nearby bedroom? Did he hear her screams? Her mother would know for sure the second she laid eyes on her. Such a profound experience would surely make her unrecognizable. There was no way she could possibly still look like the same girl. What was she going to do?

She hoped Tomas would ask her to marry her soon. Karina looked over at him and nudged him. He groaned.

"Tomas," she said. "Are we going to get married?"

His head snapped up. He leaned on his elbow and ran his hand through his hair, smiling. She was expecting to hear good news. Instead, he lay back on the bed.

"Thomas?" Karina asked, waiting for a response.

"I could really use a drink of water," he said. "Go get me some, would you?"

Thomas never answered Karina's question about marriage. He didn't have to. A few minutes after the sex, Karina passed out on his queen size bed in the Hotel San Salvador. It was a heavy sleep, aided by the gravity of alcohol.

At about 10 a.m., a housekeeping maid entered the room after knocking several times and found Karina wrapped in the sheets. The maid woke her up. Karina's head throbbed as she turned over, her mouth dry.

The maid spread open the curtains, letting the harsh sunlight pour into the room. She told Karina she had to leave. The guest who rented the room had checked out. Karina looked around disoriented. It took her a moment to remember where she was and what she had done. It was her first hangover. She sat up in bed. The sheets slipped down. The maid looked away, grabbed Karina's dress from the floor and threw it at her.

"Get dressed," the maid said.

"Where is Tomas?" Karina said, looking around confused as her mind tried to peel away the hangover cobwebs.

"Who?" the maid said as she straightened out the items on the desk.

"The man who the room belongs to."

"He checked out, now you have to leave immediately before I call security."

"Where is he?"

"I don't know. Come on. You have to go. It's past checkout time."

Karina stood up dumbfounded and got dressed. The room looked different in the daylight, so common and unromantic. The harsh daylight amplified her headache. As she slipped on her shoes, her eyes darted around the room, looking for a message from Tomas.

"Did you find a letter or a note?" Karina asked the maid.

"No, I just walked in here."

Karina staggered out of the bedroom. Maybe this was a trick by Tomas. Maybe he was out looking for a church to get married in. Maybe he was waiting for her to join him for breakfast in the restaurant. Yes, she thought, that must be it. She hurried to the restaurant, excited to give Tomas a good morning kiss.

The maitre d looked at her funny when she walked inside. Her hair was a mess. Her makeup had smeared. San Salvador high society packed the restaurant for brunch. Women in bright Sunday dresses gave her the eye and shook their heads when she walked by. She walked from table to table, waiting to see Tomas at any moment. Rich men ogled her. Halfway into the restaurant, the maitre d asked her what she wanted. She told him she was looking for Tomas, then she remembered his alias and told the maitre d she was looking for Mr. Robaina.

"Mr. Robaina checked out early this morning, mam," the maitre d said. "He has left."

"Did he leave anything for me, a message, a note, anything?" she said, building up a dose of hysteria.

The maitre d' leaned close and whispered in her ear, "like an envelope with money?"

Karina pulled back and stared at the maitre d. Her eyes saddened. A clerk at the front desk confirmed Tomas' check out. She walked backward and collapsed on an antique chair in the lobby. In her mind, she tried to rationalize Tomas' departure. He was probably out shopping for a wedding ring, she thought. He seemed to be a busy man. Maybe he had a morning meeting in the capital and didn't want to wake her. Tomas would probably appear at any moment.

A morning kiss from him, even a quick hug, would reassure her that her immoral actions of the previous night were justified. Sitting there in the chair in the middle of the lobby, she felt a chill run down her bare arms and she wished she had a shawl to wrap around her shoulders. Thoughts of Tomas abandoning her made her nauseous, sucked the air out of her stomach – *Ay Dios!*

Tomas was never coming back. The reality sank into her slowly: so much intimacy the night before, and nothing to show for it in the morning. She couldn't understand it. She must have done something terribly wrong with Tomas in the hotel room. Maybe she had yelled too loud. Maybe she smelled bad. Maybe she said the wrong thing.

She blamed Antonio.

How could her father have used such bad judgment. Now she couldn't wait to see her father again to scold him for his ignorant observations of Tomas. It was her father's fault that she was in this situation. He's the one who told her Tomas was a visionary, that Tomas was a young man with his act straight, that the future of El Salvador and Latin America rested on the shoulders of men like Tomas. What an ass her father was! The image she had of him at this moment was no better than the one she had of Tomas. Her father was a worthless shit. A two-timing prick. It takes one to know one, she thought. That's why he liked Tomas.

She wanted so badly to give her father a piece of her mind.

But the concierge stared at her with a suspicious face when she asked if her father had spent the night there.

As hatred swam in her head, she glanced around the lobby. The dirty looks returned. She had gone from hooker to esteemed guest and back to hooker in the eyes of hotel staff. A security guard approached. She walked outside, into the steaming capital heat.

Instead of worrying about how she would get back home to Tonacatepeque, she wondered for the first time in her life what she could do to keep from ever going home again. She felt like wandering through the capital's streets forever.

Her mind kept turning: it was SHE who chose to run away from home and seek Tomas in the capital. It was SHE who executed poor judgment the previous night.

Karina's books had warned her about situations like these, the woman forsaken by a ruthless player. Such stories never ended well for the heroine. She usually died of a broken heart or threw herself in front of a train or some such nonsense. But that wasn't Karina. She wished she could throw Tomas in front of a train. That bastard had really played her for a fool. He never really loved her. It must have been a lie. But he was so convincing. He did it so well, sounded so honest.

The day drew on. Karina's feet throbbed. She wanted to buy some fruit, but she had no money. She finally persuaded a taxi driver to take here to Tonacatepeque. Karina expected to catch hell from her parents upon her return. But when she came to the corner of her block, she stopped dead in her tracks. A huge crowd – it seemed like the whole village – was gathered in front of her house.

Curiosity made Karina forget she was still wearing the red dress. People turned to stare at her as she passed neighbors on the edge of the throng. A murmur of whispers arose around her. Karina wiped below her eyes and her face, thinking she must look strange. For a moment Karina thought her escapade into the capital had triggered a search party, that the village had come together in grief because of her mysterious departure. But her appearance didn't seem to be cheering anybody up.

As she neared her house, her aunt Luz darted out and yelled "Karina!" at the top of her lungs. Tears were streaming down her face. She didn't soften the blow.

"You're father has been killed!"

Karina glanced around. No one was laughing. This did not seem like a joke. A neighbor stepped forward and placed her arm around Karina's shoulder sympathetically.

"It's horrible," said the neighbor. "It's so horrible."

Karina broke free of the woman's grip and stormed into the house. Her father's body was lying on the kitchen table beneath a white sheet. Karina yanked the sheet away and grabbed her father's arms, which were already cool to the touch.

"Papa!" she yelled in horror, her eyes filling with tears. "Papa! Wake up! Wake up, papa."

She shook her father's body and caressed his face lightly. She collapsed on his chest in heaving sobs. Her uncle, who was one of several people sitting on chairs around the table, got up and gently pried her off the body, hugging her firmly. Karina buried her head in his shoulder and cried for a long time. She eventually pushed herself free of her uncle's grip and returned to the body, this time taking a closer look.

Her father's eyes were closed. A gaping hole was visible on one side of his head, a smaller hole on the other side. His face was swollen and bruised. He had cuts on his cheek and over his eyes. Someone had wiped his face clean of blood, but his long sleeve shirt was still stained crimson. His face was so battered that it didn't look like her father. She looked down at his hands. Some of his fingernails had been torn off. But his wedding ring was still there. Karina put her hand over her mouth and took a deep breath. The smell of Antonio's cologne still lingered over the steel-scent of blood. He was dressed exactly as he had been when he left the house the previous night to visit Tomas in the capital: a white, long sleeve shirt, dark gray slacks, leather shoes. The skin on his face had slackened and gravity was making it sag.

A heartbreaking noise was coming from another room. Karina perked up, controlling her own whimpers long enough to make out the sound. It was her mother and siblings crying in her parent's bedroom. She walked over and opened the door. Her mother was sitting on the edge of her bed, with her arms around her two younger sisters and her brother, all of whom were crying. Her mother, who was dressed in a robe, looked up at Karina, a blank stare on her red eyes. The two little sisters, Camila and Gladys, were wearing dresses. Karina's younger brother, Julio, was dressed in a shirt tucked into shorts.

Karina rushed to them.

"Mama, I'm here?" Karina said.

Her mother could barely talk. She shook her head repeatedly, saying *"Dios Mio. Dios Mio."*

The younger siblings didn't want to let go of their mother. They all sat on the bed for a few minutes. Her mother continued her appeals to God. Suddenly Camila sprang free of her mother and yelled at the top of her lungs to Karina: "Where were you?! Where were you?! You don't care about anybody! I hate you!"

Karina sat next to them on the bed dejected. Her other siblings gave her dirty looks. She didn't say anything. A nauseating wave of guilt flushed through her throat down to her stomach. A few minutes later, her mother, with a trembling voice, instructed Karina:

"*Hija,*" she said calmly. "I'm not angry at you. But please go to your room and take off the dress. Put on your black gown and a veil. Tell the people outside to make themselves comfortable. It's going to be a long day.

Karina reached for her mother: "Mama, I'm sorry. I just wanted to go to the capital to help Papa. I didn't mean any harm."

The mother put her hand over her daughter's mouth. "It's okay. It's okay. Please go change and help me."

It was custom in El Salvador to hold an all-night vigil before the funeral. Karina looked toward her father's body, which had once again been covered with the sheet, and felt angry.

"*Que paso?!*" she said. "I need someone to explain to me what happened."

The aunt tried to soothe her, but Karina raised her arm

calmly. "I'm fine," she said. "I'm not hysterical. I want to know what the hell happened to my father."

The aunt looked toward her husband, who shrugged and stood up. He took Karina gently by the arm and led her to the back yard, where the dog, *Seco*, was sitting under a shade tree.

"Tell me everything," Karina said. "I want to know."

"Very well," her uncle said. "I'll tell you everything I know. At about 6 in the morning, Chiche, you know Chiche, right?"

Karina nodded.

"Chiche was walking by the plaza to prepare the church for morning mass. He was with his son, Ramiro, and Father Henriquez. Chiche said that while they were walking by the square, a green jeep that looked like it was from the military came down the street and stopped next to the tree in the plaza. Chiche said the car was going very fast. Two men got out of the jeep, one from the front seat and one from the back seat. Chiche said they had rifles. Chiche and the others were scared, but didn't run, because they didn't know what was happening. One of the men pulled your father out of the back seat. He was blindfolded."

"Blindfolded?" Karina said. Her uncle nodded.

"At first, Chiche didn't recognize your father because his face was covered. But one of the men took the blindfold off. Chiche realized it was your father, but his face was very beaten. One of the men kicked him in the knee, knocking him to the ground. Your father yelled to Chiche for help. Chiche and his son ran to him, but one of the men pointed the rifle at them and they stopped. Then Chiche said the other man took a gun from his waist."

Karina grabbed her uncle's arm. "Chiche didn't help him?" Karina said. "How could Chiche not help him. Is he some kind of coward?"

The uncle shook his head. "They would have all been killed," he said. "The man with the gun looked at Chiche and his son and the priest and said 'This is so you will all learn.' Then he shot your father in the head. He aimed the gun at Chiche, but he didn't shoot. They jumped in the jeep and sped off. That's it."

Karina shook her head. "This is so you will all learn?" she repeated. "What is that supposed to mean. What are we supposed to learn?"

"They killed him because of his political beliefs, Karina. They killed him because of his socialism."

"Who killed him?" Karina said. "Who was it?"

"I don't know," said the uncle. "I don't know. I still haven't talked to the priest or Chiche's son. But Chiche said he didn't recognize any of the men."

"What were the men wearing. What did they look like?" Karina said. "Has anyone called the police. Are the authorities out looking for the killers?"

The uncle sighed. "We don't know who to trust," he said. "We don't know if the police or the authorities were involved. We just don't know."

"But someone has to catch these men," Karina said. "Someone has to pay for this murder."

The uncle put his arm around her.

"God will avenge us," the uncle said.

"God?" Karina yelled. "That's what cowards say. They hide behind God. This is wrong. We have to find these killers and avenge my father's death. My father is the mayor of this town. My father is the leader of the socialist movement. People respect and love my father. He is a man of integrity, a man of ideals."

The uncle shook his head.

"You're father *was* the mayor," the uncle said. "You're father *was* the leader of the socialist movement. Let's bury your father and mourn his death first. Then we will decide what to do."

Karina could barely contain her anger. The crowd parted for her. "Where's Chiche?" she yelled. One of her neighbors pointed to a bench in the front yard. Chiche was sitting there, his straw hat in his hands, fanning himself. Karina marched to him, hatred in her eyes.

"Coward!" she said. "You're a damn coward. My father asked you to help him and you did nothing."

Chiche stood up. "There was nothing we could do," he said meekly.

As word spread around Tonacatepeque about Antonio's assassination, the crowd swelled outside the Fuentes house. Before long, the tree-lined dirt road that led from the house to the village square was so crammed that people had to wait in line to enter the Fuentes property.

Antonio had for years been considered not only the city's elected policymaker, but its master of ceremonies, its representative in labor negotiations with farm owners, its chief architect and engineer, its schoolmaster and its defender. His legacy was the topic in the streets.

Antonio's ideas on socialism and political organization were born during his college years, when he and other students tried to petition the government for better representation and land redistribution, and the government responded by sending armed soldiers and shooting innocent civilians. The slaughter coalesced a radical student movement known as El Movimiento de la Masacre (the Massacre Movement). That movement's success in organizing protests and presenting petitions to the government led to a reform in the university system. To appease the movement's leaders, the government allowed the university to hire several of them, including Antonio, as professors.

Antonio taught there for 15 years, during which he met his wife, Emilia, who was studying to be a teacher. By the time he started his 15th year teaching history and political science, the government had taken a turn toward the more conservative, and pressured Antonio and several other professors to resign, albeit with a healthy pension. Antonio decided to move to the countryside with his wife and start a family. They chose Tonacatepeque because Antonio's wife, Emilia, had relatives there, and it was only an hour from the capital.

What started off for Antonio as volunteer activism in Tonacatepque turned into an unprecedented success with rural organizing. He encouraged literacy among the poor farmers, and taught a course three nights a week to teach adults to read and write. After two years, Antonio had opened and ran the biggest school in the village. He and Emilia had four children, and he encouraged them to read from an early age.

Although the town had never had a mayor, the former village priest, Father Chamorro, had encouraged Antonio to run for the post in a Democratic election, even if it was unopposed, to give him a greater mandate to lead the town through the changes it was undergoing. Antonio used his candidacy to sound off on socialism and political organizing. More and more people were turning out at his speeches and rallies. He was elected to a two-year term, and was reelected three times after that, each time unopposed.

Meanwhile, Tonacatepeque's socialist movement had been gaining national attention. Antonio's former colleagues at the university visited him in the village to study his methods. He also visited the capital often to brush up on the latest political treatises and establish ties with other socialist organizers around El Salvador. During one of his visits, a newspaper reporter from El Nuevo Dia, El Salvador's largest daily, interviewed him for a story on the growing socialist movement in the country. Antonio had clipped the article, in which he was quoted, and had it proudly framed in the school building.

By the time he was murdered about a year after that, Antonio had become the most popular, if not the most important, person in Tonacatepeque.

The word on the streets was that the government was involved somehow in Antonio's death. *El Gobierno* didn't want socialism to catch on in the rural countryside. Chiche's account of Antonio's murder had widely circulated, and people were quick to recognize the mortal repercussions of political dissidence. Men on the streets asked each other if there was any word on a rally in response to Antonio's shooting, but all of them shook their heads, weary of committing to anything that might represent a danger to them or their families. Antonio's assassination would end the socialist movement.

Later in the day, Karina marched to Chiche's house. Chiche was sitting on his porch flanked by two of his sons and his daughter in law. They were all dressed in black. Chiche stood when he saw Karina. No one spoke for a few awkward seconds. Then Karina broke the silence.

"I need to know what you and your son saw," she said with her arms crossed. "I want to know what happened to my father."

Chiche looked back at his son, Tonio, who had been with him in the morning and had also witnessed the murder. Tonio nodded his consent. Chiche's other son and daughter-in-law went into the house. With his arm, Chiche gestured toward a chair for Karina to sit.

"There was nothing we could do, *senorita*," Chiche said.

Karina raised her hand, cutting him off. "Just tell me what happened," she said.

Chiche repeated the account that Karina's uncle had told her earlier. His son listened intently, occasionally nodding his head.

"I thought they were going to shoot us too," the son said.

"What did they look like?" Karina said.

"They were dressed in normal clothes, actually nicely dressed, like they were from the capital," Chiche said.

"I didn't recognize the two men who shot him," said Chiche's son, "But the man driving the jeep looked familiar."

Chiche gave his son a surprised look. "You never told me that today," Chiche said.

The son nodded. "Yes, I recognized him. He looked like a man who was at our meeting last week."

"Chiche, are you sure? I think you must be mistaken," the father said.

"No, I remember him very well. At the meeting, he had been wearing a white guayabera. He was light skinned and tall. I remember him because he was the last man to sit at the enlistment table with you and your father. It's vivid in my mind because I wanted very badly to be the last one to speak to you at the meeting but he waited until we all had our turn. That was the man driving the jeep."

Karina's eyes almost jumped out of her face. Her breathing quickened. Her chest heaved with a tidal wave of nausea. She knew Chiche's son was talking about Tomas. The change in Karina's countenance was so profound that Chiche, afraid that she may faint, stood up and reached for her.

"I know my words may embarrass you," continued Chiche's

son. "But it's true. I have always wanted to be near you. Please don't be offended."

Karina didn't hear a word he was saying. Pulsing through her mind were her memories of the previous night. She shook her head.

"No, no, no," she said in what seemed like a trance. "You must be mistaken. Tomas wanted to help my father. He was not involved. Tomas is a socialist. He is a personal friend of Fidel Castro."

Chiche and his son were confused.

"Who is Tomas?" Chiche said. "Is that the man who my son is describing?"

Karina was convinced Chiche's son was mistaken.

"No, there must be some mistake," Karina said more desperately. "Tomas wanted to help my father's cause, not hurt him."

"I'm only telling you what I saw," Chiche's son said. "Maybe I am mistaken. I only saw the man in the jeep for an instant. But I'm pretty sure it was him."

Karina returned to her house. The kitchen looked like a feeding trough for wolves. Freshly killed chickens were scattered over the counter, their feathers still on. Her aunt and some of her friends were patting down maiz for pupusas. The oven was already packed. Just outside the back door, water was coming to a boil in a cauldron over a fire fueled by wood from her yard. It would be used for coffee. Everywhere Karina looked there were people, neighbors, cousins, friends, strangers.

Toward the back of the living room stood Karina's cousin, Carlos Conejo, the man who had given her a ride to the capital the previous night. He was dressed in a black suit and was blatantly staring at Karina. As she passed him, he grabbed her arm and hugged her.

"I am here to serve you," he said. "Marry me."

After the funeral the next day, as Karina's aunt and several other family members cleaned up the Fuentes house, two men dressed in military fatigues pulled up in a jeep. They wanted to question the family about Antonio's death. Emilia greeted them in the living room and answered whatever questions she could.

"You should not have buried the body yet, it could have served as evidence," said one of the men.

"Are you investigating the murder?" Emilia said.

"Yes," said one of the men. "Is your daughter, Karina, here. We'd like to speak with her as well."

"I'm sorry, but my daughter is very tired and is not available," Emilia said.

But Karina, who had been hiding in the hallway around the corner, appeared suddenly.

"It's okay, mama, I'm fine. So you are investigating my father's murder?"

The two soldiers stood up as a sign of courtesy when Karina entered. She had exchanged her heels for slippers.

"Yes," said one of the men. "I am Capitan Hernan Dominguez and this is Coronel Freddy Damas. We need as much information as possible."

"Have you interviewed the witnesses yet?" Karina said. "They have all the information you need."

"We have not yet spoken to any witnesses," the soldier said.

"Well, if you'd like I can send for them and they can come here in a few minutes, then you can ask them whatever you like," Karina said.

"That's not necessary," one of the soldiers said. "We will go to them in due time. But for now, we need to know what your father was involved in. Was he organizing politically?"

"Of course he was organizing politically," Karina said. "He was the mayor of the town."

One of the soldiers nodded. "Of course," he said. "What I meant was political dissidence, socialism. Was he promoting those things?"

"My father's main concern was to help the poor people of this village, the people that the government has forgotten," Karina said.

"Do you have a membership list for us? A list of the people in your father's organization? We suspect one of them is the killer, and without that list we can't help you."

Karina's suspicions about the government's and military's involvement in her father's murder were now confirmed. Karina denied knowing of any list.

"But I will make sure to check his things," she said. "Maybe something will turn up."

The two soldiers exchanged glances.

"Surely your father kept a list of people who were members or followers of his organization. We'd like to have a look for ourselves," the soldiers insisted.

"My daughter told you she does not know of any list," Emilia said.

Karina continued, "As far as I know, my father only held town meetings on Sundays, and kept no lists. This socialism or whatever you say, that is something that exists in Cuba, or Russia, but not here. We are a Democratic village. My father was Democratically elected."

Emilia spoke up.

"I am shocked and insulted that you have come here the day after my husband's death with no sensitivity to what my family is going through. You two should be ashamed of yourselves. Come back when you find the coward who murdered my husband."

"We hope you are right, *señorita*, for your sake," Dominguez said, standing up. "Thank you for your time. Expect us to return soon."

That night, Karina snuck into her father's office in the village auditorium, retrieved his political files and burned them.

One afternoon about a week after the funeral, as Karina walked away from her house, with her dog, Seco, two men approached her from behind on foot and grabbed her by either arm. Karina squirmed but they tightened their grip and continued marching. Neither of the men looked familiar to her.

"We know everything that's going on around here," one of the men said. "If you try to organize again, we will kill you and all your family: your little sisters, your mother, your brother, even your little dog here."

Seco barked and growled angrily at the men.

"*Sueltenme!*" Karina yelled. "Let me go. I am not afraid of you. You are cowards."

An old farmer with a machete dangling from his belt was walking toward them. One of the men handed Karina a small shoebox.

"Here is a little memento from your father," the men said. They released her and walked away in the opposite direction.

Karina peeled open the box. Her father's bloodied fingernails were scattered around the bottom. Karina dropped the box, her face melting into a trembling panic.

The attackers quickly disappeared down an alley. Several people came to Karina's aid, but she brushed them off. She composed herself and told them she was fine, retrieved the box and walked away until no one was watching. With her hands, she dug a hole in the earth and buried the box.

Two days later, someone set fire to the auditorium late at night. By the time the villagers scrambled to the scene with buckets of water, the flames had gobbled the building from the inside, leaving behind only a collapsed tin shell. The arson gutted any remaining morale in the village, and the local CEB went into deep hibernation. The Fuentes school and the mayor's office were also gone. Karina talked to the local priests about promoting a special election for a new mayor, but no one was interested in running for the post. Thus, in one swoop, the growing sapling of Socialism in Tonacatepeque was yanked from the ground, a casualty of an early skirmish that would eventually suck the nation into civil war.

One night a few weeks later, Karina, unable to sleep, heard her mother sobbing. She entered her mother's room and saw Emilia sitting on a chair next to a candle with a pile of papers on her lap.

"Mama, are you ok?" Karina said.

Her mother nodded, but continued crying.

"We're broke," she said. "Your father's pension stopped after he died. We have no money."

Karina sat down on her mother's bed.

"I thought papa had some money tucked away, something in

a bank in the capital, something hidden somewhere," Karina said.

"Mija, your father never saved any money. He spent everything on the school, the books, this house, our clothes, his political dealings. He left us nothing but debt. Karina, I don't even know how we are going to eat. I hate to tell you so much, but you are an intelligent, sensible girl. And I don't know what to do."

Karina walked to her mother and hugged her.

"Don't worry, mama," Karina said. "I'll think of something."

CHAPTER 11

Karina reluctantly accepted Carlos Conejo's marriage proposal. The Fuentes family was in a desperate situation financially and Karina knew that marrying Carlos would ensure that her family would be taken care of by him. She had stifled her adolescent sentiments of romance for the good of the family, and in turn her sacrifice boosted her resolve to try to love Carlos.

But the marriage was doomed from the beginning. Karina didn't bleed like a good virgin on her wedding night, and therefore Carlos Conejo never trusted her. He was an ogre of a man, who drank heavily, had an appetite for Torito and rum, and womanized openly. His suspicions of her quickly disintegrated into animosity.

Sometimes in the middle of the day, he would appear at home just to check on her. He worked only a few hundred yards away in a clearing he had carved out of the jungle for a rustic brick-making factory. If she wasn't home, he'd grill her later. His intimidating temper led her to act submissively, which only bred his suspicion. Adjusting to life with a man like Carlos Conejo was not easy, and Karina never fully adapted.

Carlos seemed to search for reasons to get angry with Karina. When the pupusas were too hard, or the beans too cold, Carlos would yell at her. Sometimes he threw the plate at her, or tossed it on the floor for the dogs to eat the meal. He wanted his house and his clothes clean, and didn't like it when Karina had visitors, even if it was just her mother or sisters. He forced her to wear her hair in a bun behind her, so that men would stop looking at her. But it didn't work.

Mass at 9 a.m. was Karina's daily escape, and she often made trips to the village bodega or her mother's house in the late morning. The more she attended mass, the more she began to lean on her Catholic traditions and beliefs. She prayed vigorously for God to help her family and keep them safe. She prayed for justice for her father's death. And she prayed for God to shed light on El Salvador. She never prayed to God for herself, except when giving Him an occasional chide for her sour marriage to Carlos Conejo.

Karina never complained to her mother about her marriage. Sometimes she felt her mother wouldn't understand, because she only seemed to care about when Karina might have children. And her mother never suspected anything was wrong. Carlos Conejo had kept his promise of helping the Fuentes family financially, and every month, he'd bring Emilia Fuentes an envelope with money, and a healthy smile.

CHAPTER 12

One day after mass, as Karina walked to the market, she saw several wooden statues of religious figures in front of a shack that she had passed many times before. A young, shirtless man with a lit cigar dangling from his mouth, backed out of the shack at that moment, dragging a four foot statue of Jesus, and bumped into Karina.

The man tripped and the statue toppled over, but he caught it before it hit the ground. After apologizing profusely, Karina, who usually avoided strangers, found herself striking up a conversation. The man's name was Hector Elias. He was a sculptor who had moved to Tonacatepeque because he had heard cedar was abundant in this part of the country. The shack was his studio, and he had spent the last two years carving mostly religious figures out of the scented wood. He was thin, had green eyes and kept his long black hair in a pony tail.

They spent the next few minutes getting acquainted. Eventually, Karina told him she had to leave. Carlos was due home for lunch. Hector offered her a statue of the Virgin of Guadalupe, but she refused it. She told him that she couldn't accept it because she was married. She knew her husband would be suspicious and it was better not to instigate the wrath of Carlos Conejo.

From then on, Karina made it a point of passing the shack of Hector Elias. Some days, she'd just walk right past it, afraid to knock on the studio door because she did not want to interrupt his work. But Hector quickly figured out her routine, and he'd make it a point to be outside at that time of the day.

He carved a bench out of cedar and kept it outside for Karina to sit on when she visited. But she rarely sat down, feeling that taking a seat would make her comfortable enough to stay longer and lose track of time. Many times, Karina would just stand quietly off to the side of the alley while Hector Elias chipped and chopped away at wood chunks, more interested in his craft than the man, for she had never met a sculptor, or any sort of artist. And watching him create statues out of wood blocks for a few minutes a day became her favorite pastime. His prized piece was a 3-foot tall, cloaked Jesus figure holding an arm up with two fingers pointing upward.

"I carved the Virgin that they used for your father's funeral procession," Hector once told her. "It wasn't my best work because I didn't have time to finish the details."

"I remember that statue. It was lovely," Karina said.

Karina hid her friendship with the sculptor from everyone else she knew, including her aunt, Maite, and her mother. She never visited for more than 10 minutes, and she never set foot in the shack. She carried herself with the strictest sense of virtue, keeping a marked distance between Hector and herself.

They talked about nonsense such as recipes, the advantages of dogs over cats, the lack of entertainment in the village, favorite colors, the unique smells of churches due to incense. Neither of them talked much about themselves. In the first few weeks after they met, Karina gleaned that Hector was very poor. His only income consisted of the pittances tourists and wealthy Salvadorans would pay for his statues at the market in the capital. Once a month, he'd deliver a few sculptures to a friend in San Salvador who had a kiosk set up in the *mercado* near the cathedral. His friend would skim a percentage of the proceeds and give Hector the rest.

The little money he made by selling art, he used to buy tortillas, beans, coffee and surplus chicken scraps from the butcher in Tonacatepeque. Fresh fruit plucked from neighborhood trees adorned a wooden table that he placed outside the front door. No matter how little he had, he always offered Karina something: a glass of water, a fruit, a carved figurine. Sometimes Karina would bring him a fresh plate of tortillas, or some pastry. His shirts were torn and Karina noticed he wore the same pants every day. Sometimes he wore sandals, but he was usually barefoot.

Hector had peculiar habits. Many times when Karina visited, he would be smoking a cigar-like stick that smelled like incense. He drank coffee all day, but avoided booze. Even though he was poor and had little clothes, he never smelled bad. His teeth were very white, and his hair was well tended and shiny in its ponytail. He never came on to Karina. Unlike most men in the village, he never even mentioned her looks, and from what Karina could tell, he had no woman in his life.

This was a huge point of relief for Karina. She never felt cornered by come-ons and compliments, or pressured to decide how she felt about him. His hospitality made it clear that she was welcome, and her daily presence made it clear she felt that way. She told him that her marriage was somewhat of a disillusionment, and that she hoped to soon have children because that may improve things.

During a particularly rainy week in late June, Karina missed several visits to Hector's shack. She had never gone even two straight weekdays without passing by. But Karina was bunkered up at home, caring for her sick husband, who apparently had contracted the flu with fever and a sore throat. She didn't make it out of the house for several days, until Carlos Conejo felt good enough to return to work. She thought about sending a clandestine message to Hector Elias, but decided against it.

A bedridden Carlos Conejo was even more obnoxious than usual. He criticized everything Karina did, and said his ex-girlfriend (who he still maintained a relationship with) was a much better cook. One night, Carlos Conejo scorched his lips with chicken soup that Karina made for him. He hurled the plate of boiling liquid at her, missing her with the bowl, but splashing her across the belly. Fortunately, Karina was still wearing a sweater and the scolding liquid did not scar her.

The morning Carlos returned to work, Karina got dressed up, went to church, and later walked to Hector Elias's shack. But when she got there, it was locked up. She knocked, but no one answered. There was no noise coming from inside. The cedar bench Hector carved for her visits was missing. Karina smiled at another woman walking by and continued pounding on the door, to no avail. The next day, on Friday, the shack remained locked and Hector was nowhere to be seen.

She never visited Hector on the weekends, because her husband and her family took up most of her time on Saturdays and Sundays. During a visit to her mother's house Saturday evening, Karina barely spoke. And when her mother or sisters talked to her, she was daydreaming and distracted. She retreated into the kitchen, helping her mother cook. Her husband had gone to a nearby *cantina*.

On Monday, Karina skipped mass and went straight to Hector Elias' shack. The door was ajar, and Karina knocked on the frame. A strange man, several years older than Hector, walked out of the shack without saying a word to Karina.

"Un Segundo," Hector yelled from inside. "I'll be right out."

Hector opened the door with a surprised look.

"Karina?" he said. "What are you doing here so early?"

"I came by to say hello," she said. "Where have you been the past few days? It's been all locked up around here."

"I'll show you," Hector said.

He stepped into his shack and dragged out a 4-foot cedar stump. Karina placed her hand on the aromatic wood.

"It's all one block," Hector said. "A client told me where I could get it for free, so I went away for a couple of days to cut it down and bring it back here. The thing is, I noticed you didn't come by here for a few days. I thought you might never come back. So I wanted to sculpt you before I forgot what you looked like. Doesn't that ever happen to you, that you forget what someone looks like, even though you really like the person?"

Karina nodded.

"I couldn't come by because my husband was sick, and I had to take care of him," Karina said.

"I'm sorry to hear that," Hector said.

Karina paused. "Well, so now that I'm here, you won't forget what I look like."

"Good," Hector said. "But now that you're here, I don't need to work from my memory. You can be my model."

"I can't be your model." She said. "What if my husband finds out?"

"He won't. I'll only carve for a few minutes a day. It will be a long term project."

Karina liked the idea of being a model for an artist.

"Fine," she said. "I'll do it. When do I start?"

"How about right now? It's early so we'll get a good head start."

Hector gave Karina what looked like a clean bed sheet.

"I can't carve you in a black dress," he said. "Put this on, it will look more traditional, like a Greek statue."

"Do you want me to wear it over the dress?" she said.

"Sure, that's fine."

She changed into the robe in Hector's house and stepped out into the harsh daylight, squinting her eyes. Hector was sitting on a stool next to the 4-foot cedar stump, smoking a sweet-smelling cigar.

"You know," he said. "Sex is what makes us animals. Art is what makes us human."

"Is this how you want me to wear this robe?" Karina asked.

"Perfect. Stand there in the shade under the tree."

Hector stared Karina up and down and thought for a moment. He then walked up to her and gently pulled her toga down slightly, exposing a shoulder. After adjusting the robe the way he wanted it, he walked back to his stump, glanced at Karina one more time, then applied hammer to chisel. After about 15 minutes, Karina got nervous and said she had to get going. But she returned the next day.

After a few days of Karina posing, gossip about it spread throughout the town.

One night, about an hour after sunset, as Karina swept the floor in her kitchen, she heard the front door open and recognized her husband's footsteps. She listened closely. They were drunk footsteps, staggered and uneven. Karina walked to the living room, still holding the broom.

"*Hola*, Carlos," Karina said. "Where have you been? You never came home for lunch."

"Where have I been? Where have *I* been?" Carlos said. "Where the hell have you been, you sneaky *puta?*"

Now he was close enough that Karina could smell the alcohol

in his breath. She knew a beating was coming. If she walked away from it alive, she knew it would provide the emotional catalyst necessary for her to leave him. Carlos undid his buckle and slid his leather belt out of its loops. He grabbed her by the hair with his left hand.

"Coward," was all she said.

Karina dropped the broom and closed her eyes. The first strike caught her square across the face, knocking her to the ground. She went numb for the rest of it.

Blood had crusted between Karina's cheek and the wood floor. As she opened her eyes and lifted her head, the red paste made a suction sound. It was daytime, probably early in the morning she figured. A splitting headache shattered her grogginess. For a while she stayed quiet, listening for any sign of her husband. When it was clear she was alone, her arm drifted to hear head, where she made out a bulging bruise at the edge of her forehead and hairline.

With great effort, she got up and walked to her bathroom. The person staring back at her in the mirror was unrecognizable. Her hair, spread wild, was pasted to her forehead and face with sweat and blood. The entire left side of her face was covered in dried blood from the chin up to the cheekbone. Her left eye was so swollen and bruised that she couldn't see well out of it. Her bottom lip was cut on the inside and puffy. Her dress was torn between the sleeves and the waist.

She grabbed some clothes and shoes from her closet, stuck them in a suitcase and walked over to her aunt's house.

Karina cleaned herself up in her aunt's bathroom, changed her clothes and walked out the front door against her aunt's advice. After the shower, her cuts and bruises were more defined. She wanted to look that way when Hector saw her.

Hector was outside working on his sculpture when Karina approached him from behind. He stood up with a frightened look on his face.

"Oh no," he said. "This is my fault."

Karina shushed him, grabbed him by the head and pressed her lips against his. Hector squirmed free and gently pushed Karina back.

"I love you," she said. "This proves it. I want to be with you."

The words seemed to knock the air out of Hector, who sat down on the bench with a wasted look on his face. He dropped his head into his hands and sighed. Karina dropped down next to him and grabbed his hands.

"What is it?" she said. "Don't you love me too?"

"I do love you, like a sister," Hector said. "But not the way you love me. I just can't."

"I don't understand. Don't you think I'm pretty?"

"You're beautiful. It's not that. It's me, not you. I can't believe you don't realize what it is."

"What?" Karina said. "Why can't you love me."

"Because," Hector said with a huge sigh that seemed to take 1,000 pounds off his shoulders. "Because I'm a homosexual."

It had been almost two years since Karina married. She was 22. The remnants of independence within her that survived her father's assassination were scattered and beaten down by a brutal husband. Carlos had long ago burned her novels in a drunken rage. She knew she had to leave him.

But Karina knew that any separation from Carlos would have to include an income replacement for the sake of her family.

Her husband's beating and Hector's rejection awoke the dormant sentiment of pride in Karina, fueled by a lucid recollection of her father's voice dispensing advice. Mingled in were memories of aspirations and fantasies. Like the rush a soldier gets when he's about to attack a well-guarded bunker, boldness gripped Karina. She cooked up a plan. No more relying on men.

It was a call for independence.

She spent the night at her aunt's house. The next day, she woke up early and visited her mother. Emilia stared at her daughter with a sad face.

"Mama, I can't take this anymore," Karina said.

Emilia sighed and hugged her daughter.

"Do what you have to do, Karina," Emilia said.

Karina borrowed money from her mother and took a bus into San Salvador the next day. It took her almost 3 hours to get from her hometown to the entrance of the Universidad Autonoma de San Salvador. Professor Victor Descuento was out to lunch. Victor had been a close friend of Karina's father. He was the only person from the capital who had attended Antonio's funeral, and had told the Fuentes family to contact him if they needed anything. Karina waited for two hours sitting on the floor outside his office.

Around 2:30 p.m., he showed up with two students tagging along.

"Hello," he said. "Aren't you Antonio's daughter. My God, what's happened to you?"

"It's nothing, professor," Karina said, lightly touching her scars. "Yes, I am Karina Fuentes."

"That's right, Karina, I remember now. What a nice surprise to see you around here. How is your family doing?"

"Everyone is fine, but I came here because I need to speak with you."

"Sure," the professor said, turning to the other students. "Please return a bit later, as you can see something has come up."

Professor Descuento was a stocky little man, although he wasn't always. In his office were old photographs of friends and students with him during his younger, trimmer days as a professor. Noticing that Karina liked his pictures, he pointed one out.

"There's one of me with you father," he said, pointing at a black and white photograph of several youths taken in the mountains. "So what can I do for you?"

"You told us to come to you if we needed anything. I need to get to America."

"Why do you want to go to America? What's wrong with El Salvador?"

"There are no jobs here for women and I desperately need to work. I've left my husband, for obvious reasons."

The professor discretely nodded to show he understood.

"But going to America is a bit drastic, don't you think," he said. "You can get a divorce now in El Salvador, and find yourself another man."

The suggestion offended Karina. But she persisted.

"My father told me you once worked for the Ministry of the Exterior. I remember him telling me that you once helped smuggle two political refugees to *El Norte*."

"He told you that, did he? You know, Antonio always spoke very highly of you."

Karina smiled.

"Really? What did he say?"

"He said you were not a regular girl. That you were as smart as you were beautiful. I remember him telling me once that he felt you were ahead of your time for El Salvador. How about that?"

Professor Descuento pushed himself back on his chair and opened a desk drawer.

"How does you family feel about you going to America?" he said.

"They don't know anything about it. But I am old enough to make my own decisions."

The professor took an atlas out of the drawer and opened it up to the section on North America.

"Where would you want to go?" he said.

Karina thought of a movie she once saw, Breakfast at Tiffany's.

"I want to go to New York City. Women can do well for themselves there."

"You have this all planned out I guess, then?"

Professor Descuento rubbed his face with his hands.

"Ok," he said. "I will help you. But you will need to do your share. You have a passport, correct?"

Karina nodded. Her father had obtained a passport for her several years ago for an excursion into Nicaragua.

"Ok, good. I will need your passport, a letter of

recommendation which I will write for you, and $400."

"That's a lot of money," Karina said.

"You're asking for a big favor. I need $100 to bribe the visa officer, and $300 to buy you airfare to New York. Are you sure your family will be ok with this?"

"Without this, there is little hope for my family," she said.

"Ok, come back when you have the money and we'll get started."

The next day, while Carlos was at work, Karina snuck into his house, rifled through his stash of cash, which he kept in a glass jar under a floorboard in the kitchen, and stole $500. She counted his savings: $2,436, a fortune in El Salvador.

The following day, she returned to the capital and gave Professor Descuento the money. He took her to the Department of State to fill out paperwork and have her picture taken. A week later, she returned as he had asked, and he handed her an envelope with her passport, plane tickets, and a work visa. The plane was scheduled to depart in two weeks.

"I was able to get your visa hosted by a family in New York," Professor Descuento said. "You will be taking care of their children, and they in turn will provide you with room and board and a monthly stipend. I don't know how much. It's part of a program our country has with theirs. Don't worry, if you want to try other options, your visa allows you to seek employment elsewhere."

Karina hopped up and down with joy.

"Look, just…be careful," he said. "*El Norte* is another world."

Realizing she could not talk her daughter out of her trip, Emilia hosted a going away party in her honor. Karina danced with her sisters, cried with her mother, laughed with her aunt, Maite, who snuck her an envelope with $200 in it. Word must have gotten around that Karina was short on clothes, because friends, family and even strangers showed up with enough dresses, shawls and shoes for her to fill up two suitcases. Her mother gave her the red dress she liked, her aunt gave her a pair of shoes, even her little sister donated her favorite belt.

Emilia pulled Karina aside during the party and told her she was very worried for her. She gave her two Catholic scapulars to wear around her neck for protection. "Remember, if you ever need anything, turn to God. Every church in the world will open its doors to you."

The day before the flight, Karina took a last walk around Tonacatepeque with her little sister, Camila. As though to prepare herself emotionally for the departure, Karina catalogued all the things that annoyed her about her village: the muddy streets in the rainy season, the look of poor, bare-chested children, the smell of burning garbage, the damp, raw look of the foliage. She couldn't stand the way men smiled at her, the ignorance of the populace, or the power outages that left her without a light to read. Men carrying machetes, women gossiping on their porches and bone-thin dogs fighting over chicken bones were all images ingrained in her mind. She put a negative spin on them, and even tried to convince herself that the Salvadoran cuisine nauseated her. If she never saw another pupusa, papaya or plantain again, she'd be perfectly happy, she told herself.

"I can't stand this place," Karina said.

"The plaza?" said Camila.

"No, the whole town, I'm sick of it."

"Why, Karina?"

"Because it's too small," Karina said. "And everyone here is ignorant."

"I'm not ignorant, Karina. And mama isn't either."

"Of course, not you, Camilita."

"I'm sure there's ignorant people in El Norte, too," Camila said.

"You're probably right."

"Do you love us, Karina?" Camila said.

"Yes, Camila, very much. I'm going there because I love you."

"When are you coming back?" Camila said.

"Soon," Karina said. "I'm coming back very soon."

CHAPTER 13

Michael Cervantes had spent hours listening to stories of Karina from the many family members and friends who remembered her. Cervantes jotted down his notes as fast as he could to keep up with Camila. In between, Camila offered him a slice of cake. It had been a while since Cervantes had eaten, and he accepted, hungrily wolfing it down in four bites.

"What happened after she left?"

"For a while she sent money," Camila continued. "At the beginning, it was a little bit. It was not enough to meet all of the family's debt. So my mother had to pull us out of the private school we attended. She also had to fire the woman who helped her around the house. It got really bad. My mom wrote letters to Karina telling her that everything was fine. But I was really worried."

Camila paused, wringing her hands guiltily.

"My mother never wanted to tell Karina about the trouble we were going through. But this next part I remember well because I've always regretted it. I overheard my mother talking once. She was telling my aunt that we were going to lose the house and have to move in with her. The government had no sympathy for our family, as you can imagine. So I wrote Karina a letter behind my mother's back telling her how bad things were. I told her everything. Maybe I shouldn't have done it. Now I think about it and realize how selfish I was. But I was only a girl back then, maybe 15. It must have put tremendous pressure on her. My mother never found out about the letter. But about a month later, Karina started sending these large sums of money, more than what we ever got from her ex-husband.

My family was relieved and very grateful but my mother grew suspicious about where the money came from. But my mother didn't want to create a rift between them, so instead of asking where the money came from, she made Karina promise that she would go to church every Sunday, and come home one day.

"We survived because of Karina's money. I remember she moved a few times, because a couple of times they sent my letters back to me. She always wrote to us when she moved into a new address. I still have some of her letters and pictures. I'll show them to you later."

"That would be a great help, thanks," Cervantes said.

Camila paused again. Michael took advantage of the moment to observe and describe her. She was in her early 50s, but a lifetime of squeezing mops and getting on her knees to clean toilets had taken its toil. Her hair was cropped short like a man's, and her indian-hued skin was wrinkled on the forehead and around the eyes, the places that crease the most when you worry and smile.

"I remember that before she disappeared she said she had met a man who was very nice. That's all she ever said. She never said she was pregnant or anything like that. I wonder if it was a boy or a girl. I bet it was a girl. She would have been as pretty as her mother, I bet."

"And what happened after she stopped communicating?"

"We were all very worried. We went to Interpol. They said they would look into it, but nothing ever turned up. The newspapers in San Salvador wrote about it. We wrote letters to all the friends she mentioned. We called the police department in New York City. We even wanted to hire a private investigator because Interpol told us that was a good idea, but we didn't have the money. My mother started sewing quilts and dresses and selling them at the market after the money ran out. My brother sold fruit on the street. Gladys and I had to drop out of school and help our mother with the sewing. As we grew older, our situation got a little better with money. But then the fighting with the guerrillas started getting really bad. They recruited my brother when he was just 14. He died in a grenade attack in Tonacatepeque in 1981. At one point, the guerrillas took over our house and we had to flee here to San Martin. I moved to

Los Angeles to work when I was 24 and Gladys went a couple of years later. We clean houses there. It's not a bad job. We have enough money to send our mother. I visit my mother a couple of times a year, usually for her Birthday and Christmas. I want her to move to Los Angeles with me, but she says she wants to die in El Salvador."

Camila paused again. She looked Cervantes in the eye.

"I don't know if I should feel happy or sad all over again. But I feel a huge relief."

Cervantes finished his interview and had some pupusas with ground pork and white cheese. Before she left, Camila scoured several boxes in her mother's closet and found letters written by Karina and several pictures of her in New York. She gave them to Michael and asked her to send them back after she made copies.

Isaac drove Cervantes to the San Salvador Sheraton. He typed up his story and transmitted the pictures on a laptop. The editors loved it. But they were hesitant to include Emilia's account of her nightmare. Michael fought to keep it in, and it stayed. He had scooped the cops twice in one week. He knew there would be hell to pay with his sources when he got back home. He lay down in his hotel room bed to watch CNN Latin America, and fell asleep in seconds.

CHAPTER 14

The same day that Newstime ran the story about Reyna's family in El Salvador, the New York Post ran a story saying Connery "would not deny" that the case was getting put on the backburner because the victim was Hispanic.

Headline: *Cops Neglect Case of Latina Mummy.*

The commissioner berated Connery the morning the story ran.

"What in the hell is this I'm reading in the New York Post," Commissioner Cooper said. "Is there any truth to this?"

Sgt. Connery shook his head slowly.

"Sir, I can assure you that this case is receiving maximum attention from this department. We have pulled out all the stops. I think every man in Homicide is involved in one way or another."

Cooper wasn't satisfied. He leaned over his big desk.

"Tell me something, Connery. Are you a racist?"

"No sir," Connery said. "I would take it as an insult if anyone called me one."

"You shouldn't be so insulted," Commissioner Cooper said. "Racism is rampant."

"Maybe sir, but I don't believe it is in this department."

"Connery, I want to tell you something. I will demote you to a smog-snorting traffic director if I ever find out you neglected this case because of the victim's ethnicity."

"Sir, that was an absolute fabrication. Look at the source. It's the New York Post for God's sake."

"Then I don't want to see any more damn fabrications. You

understand?"

If Connery had a tail, it would have been so far between his legs when he walked out of the commissioner's office that it would have tickled his belly. Somebody had obviously planted the asinine idea of racism in the New York Post reporter's head. Connery eyed his detectives in the Homicide Unit. "I better never hear it was one of you nitwits," Connery said.

Then he calmed down and surveyed the situation.

He had noticed that the immigration papers had the name and address of Karina's host family, Edgar and Wilma Stancanato, of Great Neck. Connery had their names run through the New York state license system. He got a hit. The driver's license database said they were living in White Plains north of the Bronx.

With little to do in the office, Sgt. Connery and Poppel endured the traffic on the Throg's Neck bridge and paid a visit to the Stancanatos.

Connery rang the doorbell and an old, overweight man with balding salt and pepper hair and wearing a faded gray jogging suit greeted the officers.

"Let me guess, you are collecting donations again for the Police Benevolent Association. Let me see if I have some cash around here. One second," the man said, turning around to go back inside.

"No, are you Edgar Stancanato?" Connery said, trying to stop the man.

"Yeah," he said, surprised they knew his name.

"Hi, I'm Sgt. Connery, this is Det. Poppel from the Nassau County Homicide Squad. This is my badge and my identification. We're investigating the murder of Karina Fuentes. Mind if we ask you some questions?"

Mr. Stancanato seemed surprised, but invited the detectives in and offered them something to drink.

Spotless Mexican tiles shined under Connery's shoes. Elegant lamps and ornaments decorated every table. It smelled like fresh summer fruit with a clean undertone of ammonia. The house was well lit, but dim enough to seem charming. The décor was modern but cozy, except for an eyesore parked in the middle of the living room – a worn, faded and stained reclining chair where Mr. Stancanato had just plopped himself down.

"Have a seat guys," he said.

Connery was glad to see his seat was an armchair made of polished wood and spotless cushions.

"Is your wife here?" Connery said. "It might help to save time if we speak with you both."

"I think so," Edgar said.

Connery waited for Stancanatto to look for her, but he just sat in his filthy chair.

"Can you call her in?" Sgt. Connery said.

Edgar gave them a long eye, as though he were drunk and couldn't see them well.

"If you wanna talk to my wife, then you call her."

Connery looked stunned.

"What do you mean?" Connery said.

"If you have a cell phone, you can call my house phone and tell her to come to the living room. It's 555-0917. Sorry Charlie, but my wife and I aren't on speaking terms right now."

Connery, obviously annoyed, pulled his cell phone out of his pocket and called Edgar's house. The detectives heard the phone ringing in the kitchen.

"Hello, is this Wilma Stancanato?" Connery said.

"Yes. Who's this?"

"Mrs. Stancanato, this is Sgt. Connery. I'm a homicide investigator from Nassau County. I am sitting in your living room talking with your husband, and I'd like you to join us. It's concerning an investigation we're conducting."

A flawlessly dressed woman with her straight, salt-and-pepper hair neatly tied back, walked out of the kitchen wearing a white, ironed apron, her phone in her hand. She seemed distressed.

"Homicide investigator? What's going on?" she said.

"We are investigating the death of a woman named Karina Angelica Fuentes," Connery said. "She came to the United States about 30 years ago from El Salvador and stayed with you in Great Neck, according to her visa."

"Sure. I remember Reena," the woman said. "What happened

to her?"

"She was murdered, ma'am," Poppel said. "We need you to tell us what you remember about her."

"Poor thing," Wilma said, sitting down.

Mrs. Stancanato rested her head on her hand and concentrated.

"Well, that was a long time ago, remember her, Edgar? Nice girl, though a bit of a mystery if you ask me. I never could figure her out."

Edgar didn't respond.

"How long did she live with you?" Connery said.

Edgar scoffed at Wilma, as though she didn't know what she was talking about.

"If you don't mind my asking, mam, what's going on here between you two?"

Wilma sighed.

"He hasn't spoken to me in two years," Wilma said as she wiped her hands on her apron. "He's upset because I kicked our son, Timmy, out of the house. I had no choice. He was doing drugs and stealing from us. Edgar ignores me. All he does is sit on that filthy chair and watch television. I do my share, though. My house is spic and span inside."

Edgar shook his head. "That's the Ice Queen's account," he said.

"So what can you tell us about Ms. Fuentes?" Poppel continued.

"Here's what I can tell you," Edgar said. "She was the best-looking nanny the kids ever had. But my wife asked her to leave because she was jealous."

"Edgar!" Wilma yelled. "That's a lie. I never got rid of her. She left on her own account."

"Sure," Edgar said, addressing the cops. "Next thing you'll hear her say is that our son Timmy left on his own account too."

Connery stood up, embarrassed to be part of a marital spat.

"Please folks," Connery said. "We're working on a very important homicide case here. Lets try to stay focused."

"So what happened to her?" Wilma said. "We never heard

from her again after she left here. But I think Griselle did. Griselle is the maid at the house across the street, although now she's more like a grandma than anything else. She even lived with Karina in the city for a while, I think. But Griselle went back to work for our neighbors after she got divorced. I can go see if she's there, if you like?"

"Thanks, that would be great," Poppel said.

"Reena couldn't stand it in this house because my wife here treated her like shit. She ran her out," Edgar said, gesturing toward his wife.

"You wouldn't stop groveling over her!," yelled Mrs. Stancanato, apparently picking up the argument where they left it three decades ago. "What did you expect me to do?"

Connery stepped in.

"I think the best thing to do is interview each of you separately," he said. "Mrs. Stancanato, can you wait for us in a separate room for a few minutes? I'll come get you when we're done talking to your husband."

"Sure, officer."

"Thank you, mam."

Wilma Stancanato shot a nasty look at her estranged husband and walked out the front door to go get Griselle at her neighbor's house. She returned a few minutes later with a compact 50-something woman whose block shaped-frame was punctuated by a gray-white puff atop her head. She removed her rimmed spectacles and extended her hands to the detectives. She smelled of cookie dough.

"We understand you knew Karina Fuentes?" Poppel said.

Griselle nodded slowly. The detective asked her to please wait with Wilma in another room until they were done interviewing Edgar.

"Ok, now in your own words, what happened with the girl?" Connery said.

"I don't really remember a lot," started Edgar. "It was a long time ago. We're talking what, three decades here? She was closer friends with Griselle. What I do remember is her looks. The girl was beautiful. I saw her walking across the concourse at the airport when we went to pick her up the first time and I just couldn't believe it.

She didn't have any winter clothes, so I gave her my jacket. From then on, my wife hated her..."

CHAPTER 15

Pan Am's Flight 522 touched down at John F. Kennedy International Airport on March 17, 1965. Following other passengers, Karina collected her bags, cleared customs and started walking to the exit, when someone yelled her name as she walked across an open space. A man with a coat and a felt hat was holding a sign with her name written on it and waving at her. Karina walked over.

"Hi there, Karina?" said the man. "I recognized you from the picture. Nice to meet you. I'm Edgar, and this is my wife, Wilma."

Edgar grabbed Karina's hand and shook it. Wilma did the same. Karina had never seen people so pale. They looked like they had rolled around in flour. Wilma had dark, curly hair packed into a beehive hairdo. Edgar was short and thin, with a heavy beard shadow. Edgar grabbed Karina's bags, and they walked out of the airport on their way to the parking garage. Although the snow had begun to thaw, temperatures still hovered near 40. Karina shivered as the cold slapped her.

"My God, you must be freezing," Edgar said. "Take my coat."

Edgar removed his trench coat and threw it over Karina's shoulders.

"You have winter clothes, don't ya?" Wilma said. But Karina didn't understand.

Wilma turned around to face her. "Winter clothes?" she said slowly. Karina shrugged and shook her head.

"You do speak English, don't ya?" Wilma said. "English?"

"Yes," Karina said. "A little."

"Thank God," Wilma said. "I was worried there for a second."

Karina didn't hear her. She was distracted by the volume of cars clogging the airport roads. They all looked so fancy.

Edgar drove a wood colored Plymouth station wagon. To Karina, it looked ultra modern with sharp edges, like a rocket that might take off in flight. She was a bit disappointed when it merely slugged along the icy streets like the other cars. Edgar cranked the heat and played music. Wilma went on and on about her kids and their hobbies. But Karina was glued to the window, scanning the horizon for the city skyline. It never appeared. Edgar took the Long Island Expressway east toward Great Neck on Long Island. Karina saw lines of red brick tenements crowded up against the highway in Queens. Plenty of sidewalks, dead trees, snow and people in coats. And as far as the eye could see, miles and miles of paved roads stretched in all directions, all of them smooth and new, with bright colored lanes to direct traffic, and an endless stream of cars and colors. But no skyline. After a 20 minute ride, Edgar pulled into the driveway of a sprawling ranch house.

"Here we are, home sweet home," Wilma said.

Karina, who understood the word "home," got out of the car and frantically looked around. She could barely even see a neighbor's house. Skeletal trees framed the driveway. The lawn was covered in white snow. Where were the buildings, the shops, the people? Karina felt the snow crunch under her shoes. She bent down and grabbed a fistful. It felt like sand -- frigid, watery, moldable sand. She dropped it and jammed her hand into the coat pocket for warmth.

As she stood there pondering her utter disappointment, two kids bolted out of the house, climbed on Karina's luggage, and jumped on her, nearly tackling her. The boy grabbed a clump of snow and hurled it at Karina, nailing her on the shoulder.

"Come on Timmy, Tricia, be nice," Wilma said. "This is Karina."

"Hello," Karina said.

"We wanna tie Reena up mom. Like cowboys and Indians. She's the Indian, mom."

"Alright, Timmy, just give her time to settle in," Wilma said. "Then she's all yours."

Wilma flashed a brilliant smile at Karina. It said: behold my wonderful children. Karina wanted to scream.

The Stancanatos had set aside a bedroom for Karina across the hallway from the kids' room. It was plainly decorated, with a twin bed, mismatched sheets, a small clock radio, a reading lamp, curtains and a dresser.

Wilma asked Edgar to retrieve a box of old winter clothes from the attic and gave Karina one of her old coats. Wilma was taller than Karina, so the coat sleeves were a bit too long, and the shoulders were too wide, but it kept her warm. Wilma told Karina she was surprised at how little clothes she had brought. Likewise, the size of Wilma's closet and how much clothes she owned awed Karina. Endless rows of shoes were stacked in little shelves along the closet's back wall. Dresses and blouses formed a layer of garments four feet long.

After a few hours in the house, Karina's throat dried out. She was accustomed to open windows, natural light, humidity. With the heater cranking and the windows sealed shut, the house felt more like a chimney. But she didn't want to complain to her hosts.

Wilma liked to cook. Her specialty was spaghetti with meat sauce, loaded with onions, garlic, oregano and tomato sauce: all weird flavors in Karina's opinion. That first night, Wilma served her famous spaghetti. She set a place for Karina on a little guest table about five feet from the main dining table, clearly separating her from the family. Karina had never eaten spaghetti. She watched how the kids and adults rolled it up in their forks then shoved it into their mouths and sucked in the rest of it. She did the same, but almost vomited. She had never tasted anything so vile, so bitter, so horrible. With all her willpower, Karina gulped down the first mouthful with some water, then she smiled awkwardly.

"You don't like it?" Wilma said. "It's spaghetti. Haven't you ever eaten spaghetti?"

Karina shook her head. The kids cracked up. Edgar hushed them. Wilma served ice cream for desert and Karina gobbled it up.

After dinner, Wilma took Karina on a tour of the house and explained to her what she expected from her new employee. She talked so fast that Karina could barely understand her. But she talked with her hands and mimed her instructions, so Karina somewhat followed. First stop was the kitchen.

"The kids wake up early. You have to make sure they brush their teeth, dress them and serve them breakfast. Timmy likes corn flakes with a little sugar sprinkled on top. That's this white box with the rooster on it. Tricia likes oatmeal. It's in the cupboard right here. Get some hot water from the faucet and pour it into the bowl then mix in the powder. Pour a little honey over it. She loves the stuff. Don't worry about Edgar. He doesn't eat breakfast. He just has coffee. I wake up earlier than he does, so I'll make him the coffee. Don't worry about that, capisci?"

Karina gave her a blank look and nodded. Wilma opened the cabinet doors under the sink.

"Use the Pine Sol there to clean my floors. I like 'em cleaned at least every other day. The mop is right here in the pantry. If the kids make a mess with the snow and all, then clean the floor again."

Wilma led Karina into the garage.

"Pay attention, this is where you do the laundry," Wilma said.

She picked up a pile of dirty white clothes, stuffed it into the washer, then poured in detergent, a dash of bleach and started it.

"You do like that, then when it's finished you put it in the dryer, and hit start. You know how to fold clothes right? Well don't ya?"

Wilma took a shirt and folded it to show Karina what she meant. Karina nodded.

"Fold the clothes and put it back in the basket. Later, I'll show you where to put everything away."

Out of nowhere, Timmy sprinted at Karina, lept in the air and landed on her right foot. Karina winced in pain, lifting her foot to rub it. Wilma grabbed Timmy by the arm and shook him.

"No horsing around with Reena!" Wilma yelled at the boy, then turned to Karina, "You're gonna have to get strict with them."

Exhaustion kicked in after the grand tour. Karina went to her bedroom and lied down in her bed. She was too embarrassed to ask for a towel to shower. Karina assessed her long day when her head hit the pillow. She took stock of all that had happened: the family that had taken her in, her new home, the daily chores that lay ahead, and the spoiled children she would have to care for. What she still didn't know was how much money she could expect to get paid every month, a worry that weighed on her because her family's future in El Salvador depended on it. But for now, Karina concentrated on resting her head on this strange bed in this strange place. Tomorrow, she knew, was the beginning of her new life.

Adjusting to her slew of chores during the first few days drove Karina nearly crazy. Fortunately, Timmy and Tricia knew where their cereal and oatmeal were, and showed Karina how to prepare it. Soon she was running on a schedule: making beds and preparing breakfast in the morning, and tidying the house and doing the laundry in the afternoons.

For the most part, Karina kept quiet. The new language and the strange surroundings made her feel isolated and homesick. Mrs. Stancanato seemed happy with her, helping her along with her chores and trying to make her feel comfortable and part of the family. Visitors to the Stancanato house always showed intrigue in Karina, asking her how she liked New York, what her name was, and where she was from. When she'd say El Salvador, most of them would just nod and smile. Karina suspected they had no idea where her homeland was located.

Karina smiled enough so that her silence did not draw suspicion. Everything she had to say, she put in the letters she sent home. Wilma, who would mail her letters for her, joked that Karina must have been writing a book because she never saw anyone write so many letters.

One afternoon several weeks later, a friend of Wilma's named Sylvia came over with her Panamanian housekeeper, Griselle, to meet Karina. Griselle was a tubby little mulatta with a curly afro. The first words out of Griselle's mouth almost gave Karina a heart attack.

"*Hola*," Griselle said to Karina with a sweet smile that made it seem as though she were just extending a casual welcome. "*Mi jefa es tremenda cabrona y la suya no sabe cocinar.* (my boss is a bitch and yours doesn't know how to cook.)"

Wilma and Sylvia both smiled and asked Karina what Griselle had said. Karina stammered and in broken English told them that Griselle had just extended her welcome.

Griselle, still smiling sweetly, took it a bit further. "*Digale la verdad, que son dos putas tacañas.* (tell them the truth, they are both stingy bitches)" Karina chuckled.

"Griselle's English isn't very good yet," Sylvia said to Wilma. "But she's learning, right Griselle?"

Griselle nodded. "Yes," she said with a heavy accent. "Very good. *Tu marido es pajaro.* (your husband is gay)."

After weeks of not speaking a word of Spanish to anyone, Griselle's company was a godsend. Karina led Griselle to her bedroom under the auspice of showing off her quarters and cracked up as soon as they were out of earshot.

"How do you know they don't understand you?" Karina said.

"If my boss understood Spanish, I would have been fired the first day," Griselle said. "It's the only thing I can do to keep from going crazy. They are so spoiled. They think they are the center of the universe."

Griselle complemented Karina's room. She noticed the closet was empty. She went to get a closer look, then without permission opened the drawers.

"Where is all your clothes?" she said.

"I didn't bring much clothes. At least not the right clothes."

"And your boss hasn't taken you shopping for some?" Griselle said.

"She did take me shopping the day after I arrived, but everything was so expensive, and I don't have much money."

"I bet she took you to one of those ridiculous department stores, right?" Griselle said. "That's the worst place to go. I'll take you to a few places where you can get a whole new wardrobe for the price of a department store blouse. Do you have any days off?"

Karina sat on her bed.

"On Sundays, they take the children to their grandmother's house. They told me I can either come with them or stay here. I guess that's like my day off. But let me check."

Griselle sat next to Karina.

"Ok then, Sunday, we'll take the train to the city and I'll take you shopping. *Esta bien?*" Griselle said.

"*Muy Bien,*" Karina said.

On Thursday night, Karina finished her chores later than usual and took a late shower after the children had gone to sleep. She usually dressed herself in the shower, but she had forgotten to bring her change of clothes. She wrapped her towel around herself and scurried across the hallway into her bedroom. Shivering, she grabbed a clean pajama and a pair of socks from her drawer, and sat on her bed, unraveling her hair from her tight bun.

Her hands were dry and chafed from her housework. She dabbed some cocoa butter lotion Wilma had given her to help moisturize her skin and began massaging her tired hands. Her towel slipped off but in the privacy of her room, she didn't bother covering herself up again. The tropical scent of the lotion soothed her and she went on spreading more of it over her thighs, her stomach, her breasts. She closed her eyes and layed back on her bed, still naked, thinking about El Salvador, the warm nights, her family.

Then suddenly a noise outside her bedroom door startled her. The hallway light flicked on and she heard Wilma yelling "Edgar!" Karina quickly slipped on her pajamas and cracked open her door.

"How could you, Edgar?" Wilma yelled. Almost crying.

The kids darted out of their rooms. Wilma slapped Edgar on the arm and pushed him to the living room.

"Sleep on the couch! You disgust me."

As Wilma stomped back to her bedroom, she gave Karina a dirty look and told her something she didn't understand. Karina herded the children back into their rooms and tucked them in. Timmy was laughing, but little Tricia was crying. The little girl didn't let Karina go back to her room until she fell asleep.

The next day, Karina was awoken to the sounds of Wilma pounding on her door at the crack of dawn.

"Come on," Wilma said. "We're moving you into the garage."

Wilma grabbed Karina's clothes from her drawers and tossed

it on the bed. "Come on," she said. "What are you waiting for?"

While Karina was still trying to make sense of everything, Wilma bearhugged her pile of clothes and left the bedroom with it. Karina followed her into the garage, where Wilma dropped her clothes into a hamper.

"What happened, Ms. Wilma?" Karina said.

"Nothing happened," Wilma said. "I just want you as far away from our bedroom as possible, *capisci?*"

A full explanation never came. From then on, Karina simply lived in the garage, sleeping under layers of blankets to stay warm, locked out of the rest of the house at night. Edgar gave her a space heater but it barely phased the frigid temperature in the garage, which reeked of gasoline. Karina no longer ate dinner with the family. Instead, Wilma brought a plate of food to her quarters every night. If Karina didn't like it, there was no alternative. The ice cream desserts became a thing of the past.

On Sunday, Griselle came early in the morning, and her boss, Sylvia, gave her and Karina a ride to the Long Island Railroad station. A few minutes later, a train showed up and they boarded. Karina told Griselle about her exile into the garage. Griselle was perplexed.

"Maybe her husband is attracted to you and she can't handle it," Griselle concluded. "You're much prettier than his wife. She looks like a witch."

Karina shook her head.

"But Edgar is such a caballero (gentleman)," Karina said. "He keeps to himself. All he does is watch television and play with the kids."

"Don't try to make sense of all these gringos," Griselle said. "A lot of the things they do don't make any sense. For example, my *jefa* is always complaining that they don't have any money, but then her and her husband go out to restaurants a few times a week. It's ridiculous. You can't worry too much. Just keep doing your work. If anything, get even in your own way. You can clean the bathtubs with their toothbrushes, or spit in their water, or clog their toilets with a wad of toilet paper. Those kinds of things always make me feel better when I'm really pissed."

Karina caught a glimpse of something outside the window

and tuned out Griselle's babbling. It looked like a chiseled mountain range on the horizon, black against the gray winter sky. It was New York City, looming in the distance. The sight of the city's skyline made Karina's worries temporarily disappear. After weeks at the Stancanato house in the distant suburbs, the city seemed like an elusive fantasy. She had chosen to block out unrealistic thoughts about a place that she wasn't even sure existed as she had pictured it. She had convinced herself that New York was just a spread of cookie-cutter houses with brown lawns and big cars, and that the movie she had seen and books she had read built it up in fiction. Without access to a map of the area, she didn't even know if the city was close to where she was living. Now it seemed so much bigger than anything she was worrying about.

She grabbed Griselle's arm, both to quiet her and alert her to the view. Griselle turned to look out the window.

"So this is your first time going to the city?" Griselle said.

Karina nodded.

"Then I'll shut up and let you enjoy the view."

As they neared the city, the train slipped into a tunnel. At the end was Penn Station. Karina and Griselle climbed the stairs and surfaced at the corner of 34th street and Seventh Avenue, across the street from Macy's. Karina grabbed Griselle's arm as she looked around.

"The world's biggest department store," Griselle said, pointing to Macy's. "Unfortunately, it's out of our price range."

Everywhere were people, cars, buildings. The Empire State building was off to the left behind Karina.

"I want to stay here. Forget the Stancanatos," Karina said.

The wind was blowing and a chill hit them. They hurried across Seventh Avenue and headed south. After walking for about a block, Griselle led Karina back underground.

"I thought we could walk, but it's too cold," Griselle said. "Let's take a subway."

"Where?" said Karina, whose hands were buried in the pockets of her boss's oversized jacket. "Aren't we here?"

"The city's really big, you have to take subways to get around. We have to get to Greenwich Village. That's where all the good shops are."

Three stops later, they arrived. The neighborhood was eclectic: students, hookers, pimps, immigrants, hipsters, artists, gangsters, poets, professors, thugs and queers. But wrapped up in thick coats and scarves, they all looked the same to Karina, with only their faces visible to transmit any vestige of individuality. Everything looked brown. Brown buildings, brown trees, brown coats, brown snow. It looked like a serious city to Karina. No one smiled or even made eye contact. Everyone walked in a hurry.

Griselle introduced Karina to a cluster of thrift shops and consignment stores in the area. After glancing at a few price tags in the Salvation Army store on 8th Street, Karina knew she had found the solution to her problems. Most of the clothes was fashionable, looked brand new, and cost less than her train ride into the city. Griselle and Karina spent the day stocking up on winter clothes, coats, sweaters, boots, pants.

"For the first time since I got here, I'm having a great time," Karina told Griselle over a cup of coffee at a local diner.

"I'm planning on moving back into the city soon" Griselle said. "I'm waiting to hear about a job. You wanna come with me?"

Karina shook her head.

"I didn't know you lived in the city," she said. "What was it like?"

"When I migrated here from Panama three years ago," she said, "I lived in the city the first two years. I had a good job cleaning a restaurant. But I got mixed up with the owner, and we eventually had a fight, so he fired me and kicked me out of his apartment. I've only been with Sylvia for about 8 months. I got that job through the church. But I hate it. I'm coming back here first chance I get."

A waiter refilled their coffee cups.

"I would love to live in the city. But I just got here. I barely have any money. I don't know anybody," Karina said, sipping her coffee.

"Well, you'll know me when I move here. Call me up when you're ready."

Karina went home with two bags full of new clothes. She couldn't wait to wear them. That night, she tried it all on again in the garage, staging a fashion show for herself. She fell asleep wearing her new coat, made of leopard faux fur and cut short.

Griselle had agreed to accompany her to the city again the following Sunday. Karina went to sleep wishing it was next Saturday night.

Karina's relationship with Wilma Stancanato soured more every day. Wilma treated Karina progressively coldly, correcting her constantly for things like using too much laundry detergent, or putting clothes away in the wrong drawers. Every once in a while, Wilma would rub a windowsill or a shelf with her finger and show the dust to Karina, clearly criticizing her work. One morning, as Karina was sweeping the kitchen, Wilma yanked the broom out of her hands without saying a word and charged into Timmy's bedroom, yelling along the way "is sweeping a room so godamn complicated?" Apparenty, Karina had missed a spot.

A couple of times a week, Wilma would cook up a garlic-heavy Italian meal: spaghetti, garlic chicken, garlic bread, lasagna. Karina made the mistake of telling Wilma that she didn't like garlic.

"Oh, really?" Wilma said, as she diced and crushed a few cloves and tossed them into the frying pan. "That's too bad because we really like it around here."

Needless to say, Wilma increased the number of meals she cooked with the bitter root, and Karina did not eat dinner the nights Wilma spruced it up with *ajo*. In order to compensate for the foregone meals, Karina made it a habit to forage for non-perishable foods in the kitchen during the day, such as butter sandwiches, crackers, cereal, cookies, and an occasional slice of cake. Taking only a few pieces and slices at a time to make sure Wilma did not notice anything was missing, Karina created a stash of emergency snacks in a shoebox at the back of her bottom drawer. She lined the shoebox with aluminum foil and plastic wrap to preserve the food as long as possible and keep bugs out.

The sweet reserves got Karina through the nights when

Wilma would otherwise have seen her go hungry. Karina would savor the bites of cookies and graham crackers, many times making taunting faces at the door that led to the kitchen, as though Wilma could see her savoring the pilfered snacks.

Under siege from Wilma, Karina took refuge in Tricia and Timmy. The children were spoiled, unaccustomed to lacking or even waiting for things they wanted. Timmy was a sneaky operator, sometimes rummaging through his father's drawers in search of knives and other weapons. And Tricia was a tattle tale, keeping check on all her older brother's mischief. Karina, who had helped raise her own young siblings and spent much time with younger cousins in El Salvador, had a keen understanding of child psychology. She earned Timmy's trust by taking the blame for a broken vase that turned up in the dining room, and she won Tricia's love by playing with her and her dolls every day after school. Sometimes the two would sit in the family room and watch I Love Lucy together as Tricia twirled her fingers in Karina's hair. Tricia was the only person in the house who ever asked Karina about her life and family in El Salvador.

"Do they have tea in your country?" The little girl asked once, as she pretended to serve tea to her dolls.

"No," Karina said.

"Do you have brothers or sisters?"

"Yes," Karina said, "I have two sisters, Camila and Gladys, and a brother, Javier."

And so the little girl extracted from Karina the intricacies of her past: whether she was married, had children, went to school, had a best friend and a favorite color. Karina's childhood, annexed by the militancy of her father's socialism, had never been typical. There had been clandestine meetings, recruitment drives, Marxist teachings and study sessions. Toys were not a routine part of her young life. Karina fit her father's mold so well that he didn't bother with the rest of his kids, who grew up on a healthy diet of playing instead of plotting.

As Karina played with Tricia some days, she would drift off into a trance, staring at the dolls and wondering about her life.

"Why don't dolls have fingernails so that I can paint them pink?" Tricia asked Karina one afternoon.

The question sent a chill down Karina's spine, triggering

memories of her father's severed fingernails, delivered to her by the men who killed him. She went pale and walked out of the room. She continued out the front door and stood on the lawn, absorbing the cool May air. The sunlight tickled her cheeks. Leaves were beginning to appear on some of the trees. Tricia followed her into the front yard and grabbed Karina by the hand. A few minutes later Timmy got home from school and the three of them went back inside.

A letter from El Salvador arrived for Karina in mid May. From the unusual handwriting, Karina immediately noticed it was not from her mother, the person who usually wrote to her. It was from little Camila, who always injected a P.S. note at the bottom of her mother's letters. But why would Karina get a letter from Camila? She tore open the letter on the way to her garage bedroom and started reading it as she walked.

4/26/66

Dearest Karina:

Mama just took me and Julio and Gladys out of the *Colegio* (school) and she wants Julio to start selling fruit and water on the street and she says we have run out of money and are going to have to move in with our *tia* (aunt) Luz. Luz only has one bedroom for all of us. We haven't eaten any meat in more than a week, not even chicken because we killed our last chicken last week. I overheard mama talking to Luz today and she told her that she has no money because the money you send is not enough, and that the family *se esta undiendo* "is going under." I don't know what that means Karina, but it doesn't sound good and I am very worried. Mama doesn't want to tell you because she doesn't want you to worry more than you already do. But I know that you always have a good solution to problems. You are our only hope. Please help us. Love,

Camila

Karina had been sending her family about $50 of the $100 monthly stipend she received from the Stancanattos. She couldn't come up with the $200 monthly sum Carlos Conejo gave Emilia

Fuentes every month. Karina knew that was a big difference, but she urged the family to clamp down and curtail their spending for a few months. Still, with the expenses of the children, education, food, and electric and telephone services, and paying the small debts Antonio had accrued to fund his socialist revolution, $200 barely helped them make ends meet. Karina knew she had not been sending enough money to the family. But she had no idea of what was awaiting her in New York. She always figured that living in a big city, opportunities for employment would abound and that she'd get a higher paying job at some point. But instead of the big city, she was trapped in the suburbs. On Sundays, the day she traveled to the city, many of the shops and factories were closed, and finding another job seemed almost impossible.

After Karina's first trip to the city, she made it a habit to go every week. At first, she went only with Griselle. But one Sunday, Griselle cancelled on her at the last minute, and Karina decided to go alone. She had memorized the bus route to the Long Island Railroad station, and figured out the train times.

The city offered Karina a weekly escape. There was no way she would spend her only day off watching Ozzy and Harriet on black and white television. Not with the city so close. Many Sundays Karina didn't spend a penny beyond her train and bus fair. The constant festival of people and faces on the streets were entertainment enough. After a week of caring for spoiled children, the hippies of Greenwich Village, the Asians from Chinatown and even the social elite in Gramercy were a welcome sight.

While exploring on her own, Karina stumbled upon a church in Little Italy called St. Genaro, where they performed Mass several times on Sundays. Even though the Stancanattos had a cross hung over their bedroom door and were raised Catholic, they never went to mass. They told Karina they didn't have time for it with so much going on in their lives. But she figured they just weren't religious.

Karina made it a point to make it weekly to the noon service at St. Genaro. Sometimes she dragged Griselle along, but most of the time Griselle wandered around the neighborhood shops while Karina heard mass. Although most of the people at the noon mass were Italians, Karina always felt welcome. The priest was a tall, red-haired

Irishman named Father O'Leary who liked to sing psalms and chants despite his unmelodic voice. He said the mass in heavily accented English, so it took Karina some time to be able to follow it.

Karina tried a few times to strike up conversations with Father O'Leary after mass, but the language barrier always turned it into a comic affair.

Griselle introduced Karina to several of her friends, most of them housekeepers or dishwashers. When they got together as a group, Griselle took center stage, blaring insults in Spanish at gringos who walked by, flirting aggressively with handsome men in the streets. Griselle was the kind of person that attractive friends clung to, one with few scruples, difficult to embarrass, and a mouth that never stopped charging. She was a woman whose only true attraction was her shamelessness. Karina marvelled at how brazen she could be. Walking through the East Village one afternoon with Griselle and another friend named Tania, Karina nudged Griselle on the arm to call her attention to a good-looking man in pin-stripe suit with a white T-shirt underneath standing on the corner. Griselle grabbed the chance.

"*Oye, Rico,*" Griselle said motioning toward the man with her hand. "My friend Karina, you see her there, the real good looking one. She thinks you're cute."

The man studied Karina for a moment.

"She ain't too bad looking herself," he said.

"So you got a name?" Griselle said.

"Zorro," said the man.

Griselle cracked up. But the man was not amused.

"Yeah, right. Zorro? *Esta loco.*"

The man seemed annoyed.

Zorro said he was from Puerto Rico, and he said he liked pretty girls. His Spanish sounded eerily familiar to Karina, who identified his accent as similar to that of Tomas, the man who deflowered her. Zorro had a thin black mustache over his lip, which he stroked as he stared Karina up and down.

"Are you waiting for your *mami* to come bring you your mask and your sword?" Griselle said.

Karina chuckled.

"You think that's funny?" Zorro said. He couldn't help himself from smiling too. "I guess I do too. So what are you girls doing around the *loisada*? I've never seen you before."

"Shopping," Griselle said, "For handsome super heroes like you."

"You're a sassy little *mamasita*," Zorro said. "How would you like a job? Do any of you need a job?"

Griselle laughed. Her friend Tania laughed louder.

"*Si, seguro*, (yeah, sure)" she said. "Zorro, the superman. What kind of benefits do you offer? Free fencing lessons?"

"If any of you need a job, I'm always looking for some pretty helpers, assistants. I'm usually right around here."

"What kind of job?" Karina said.

"A service industry job," Zorro said, staring at Karina. "It pays really well. You'd be really good at it. A beautiful woman like you I'm sure has many skills (skeels)."

"Sure, *jefe*, we'll mail you our applications," Griselle said, and turned to leave.

As the girls walked away, Karina turned to wave goodbye to Zorro, who was gnawing on a toothpick and staring at her ass. He winked at her and blew her a kiss.

"Griselle, I've been thinking about finding a job in the city and moving there," Karina said in Spanish on the train ride home. "What do you think?"

"Go for it," Griselle said. "That's what I'm going to do."

The gringos on the train stared at them, which usually happened when Karina and Griselle spoke Spanish in public. But for the first time, the disparaging gazes triggered a feeling of power in Karina instead of vulnerability.

The next Sunday, Karina left her clothes in the washer by accident. When she got back from the city, she went straight to the garage. Her clothes was in a soggy pile on the floor next to the dryer, covered in pink and white blotches. It had been heavily bleached.

Karina grabbed some of her garments, which she had carefully selected at Manhattan thrift shops over the past two months, and walked to the family room, where Edgar and Wilma were watching the nightly news with the children.

"Those damn gooks'll pay for going commie," Edgar said as he watched footage of Vietnam on the television. He hadn't even noticed Karina.

"Excuse me, Weelma!" Karina said, holding up a shirt. "What happened to all my clothes?"

"Oh, I didn't realize it was your colored clothes in the washer. I'm sorry," Wilma said, and went right on watching television. Timmy laughed at the bleached patterns on Karina's shirt.

"It looks like a clown costume," Timmy said.

"No it doesn't," Tricia said. "Reena is not a clown."

Karina's nostrils flared. Wilma looked at her and shrugged. Karina turned around and stormed back toward the garage.

"There's spaghetti for dinner if you're hungry," Wilma said. "It's got lots of fresh garlic."

The guerilla tactics Wilma employed to oppress Karina had obviously escalated. That night, Karina hung up all the bleached clothes on wire hangers around the garage and stared at them. It had taken her two months worth of Sundays and a large chunk of the money she made to accumulate the beginnings of a Manhattan-worthy wardrobe. Now Karina stared at her ruined, tye-dyed collection and clenched her teeth, crushing a rhinoceros animal cracker. What angered Karina most was that Wilma had a grievance against her through no fault of her own.

On Thursday morning, Karina served the children their cereal and oatmeal, kissed Tricia goodbye and waited for Edgar and Wilma to leave the house. She wrote a note telling them she had decided to move to New York, not to worry, and that she would drop them a line to forward any mail when she settled down.

CHAPTER 16

Poppel jotted down some notes, nodding.

"How long was she with you? Is that the last you saw of her?" he asked Edgar.

"I think it was only a few months. She was outta here by the time the weather warmed up."

"So your wife was jealous?" Poppel said.

"Extremely. You know how women are."

"Jealousy can be a motive for murder."

Edgar shook his head.

"My wife is jealous, but not crazy, and certainly no killer."

"Did you have sexual relations with her?" Connery said.

Edgar frowned.

"What kind of a question is that? Of course not. I'm married. Like I said, I'm Catholic."

"But you did find her attractive," Connery said.

"Any man would. But there's a big difference between finding a woman attractive and actually getting sexual with her."

A whooshing noise came from the kitchen, followed by a whistling sound. Wilma walked out a minute later with two cappuccinos. Connery and Poppel each reached for one.

"Thank you mam, but we're going to need a few more minutes with your husband."

"Look, we had a bunch of different nannies and babysitters over the years. Karina stuck out in my head because she was by far the youngest and most attractive one. After that, my wife would only hire hags."

"Did you ever sponsor another Visa?" Poppel asked.

"No," Edgar said. "We decided it was more trouble than it was worth."

"Why did your wife move her into the garage?" Connery said.

"Beats me."

Poppel stood up and took a plastic bag out of his pocket. Inside, there was a round, plastic container.

"Can we take a sample of your saliva for DNA testing?" Poppel said.

Edgar hesitated for a few seconds.

"DNA testing? That sounds pretty serious. Do I need to call a lawyer."

Connery shrugged.

"That's usually a question guilty people ask," Connery said. "You're not guilty are you?"

"Of course not. Look, just take any sample you need from me."

"Good," Poppel said.

He handed Edgar a cotton swab and told him to smear it on the wall of his cheek inside his mouth. Poppel then rubbed the wet swab on the Petri dish-type plastic container, closed it and labeled it. Connery fetched Wilma Stancanato from the kitchen and asked her and Edgar for some time alone with Griselle. They agreed and left the detectives alone with Griselle in the living room.

"What we're doing is trying to piece together the pieces of the puzzle at this point," Connery said. "We're trying to chronicle Reena's life before she was killed. She died a long time ago, more than 30 yearss. So what happened with Karina after she left here?"

Griselle shook her head slowly, as though the memories didn't want to return.

"I don't think she was happy here," Griselle said. "A young woman like that stuck in a house with someone else's kids all day. I don't think she really liked it. Sometimes she just went quiet and stared out a window, even when she was with me. I mean, we all came here from somewhere else. We all left families behind. But she worried a lot about them. I mean, too much you know what I mean? It wasn't healthy. The only thing that seemed to make her happy was shopping for clothes. She knew every thrift shop from the Lower East Side to Harlem. For her, buying a new outfit, putting it on, and walking around Manhattan all dressed up was her therapy. She used to tell me that dressing up was her disguise, her way of becoming another person, and seeing the world through a different set of eyes. She said it made her feel powerful."

"Do you know where she went?" Poppel said. "Can you help us piece that together."

"Karina and I were close friends. We lived together in the city. At least, until I got married...."

CHAPTER 17

It was no Sunday stroll. The train was so packed, Karina could barely fit her suitcase inside. Penn Station was a dense concentration of business suits and briefcases. People bumped into her, strode past her, cut her off, even insulted her. They breathed down her neck, pushed her on the escalator, hawked watches and jewelry to her. A couple of shady-looking men with sunglasses asked her if she needed help with her suitcase, but she politely declined. During one of her Sunday escapades into the city with Griselle, Karina remembered seeing lockers. So almost as soon as she arrived today, she ditched her suitcase in one of them.

As she walked across a mobbed Penn Station, some long-haired freaks wearing Indian garb and shirts that looked like a rainbow had exploded on their chests tried to cram a pamphlet into her hand, but she shrugged them off. A group of black men had set up a table, adorned with a posterboard of a fist. Several of them had afros and wore leather jackets. Griselle had warned Karina several times to steer clear of blacks, but she never understood why and was not fearful of them. A nice-looking black man smiled at her and held out a pamphlet harmlessly.

"Don't take it if you don't want it," he said.
In order not to be rude, she accepted it and continued walking. When she looked back, the man nodded to her and held up his fist, and Karina made a fist too and thrust it forward, crumbling the paper by mistake. She tossed the paper in a garbage can around a corner and headed for the stairs to ascend from the city's underground lairs.

A New York workday greeted her. Rivers of suits and hats and trenchcoats and taxi cabs filled the streets and sidewalks. Unsure about her next move, Karina wandered the Penn Station area and ended up at Larry's Diner on 32nd Street and 6th Avenue, where she took an empty seat at the counter and ordered Vanilla ice cream and apple pie. The place bustled with business types and working types with jackets, all hunched over coffee, most of them with a newspaper spread out in front of them, smoking cigarettes. A few people glanced up at her when she walked in but immediately went back to their headlines. The meal cost $1. The Vanilla was so creamy and the pie so warm that Karina figured she could survive on that alone if worst came to worst. With the $43 in her pocket, that came out to, let's see, at three meals a day…a full two weeks that she could live on Vanilla ice cream and apple pie.

With that comforting thought in her mind, aided by an injection of sugar pumping through her in the morning, Karina headed to the East Village. The exact cross street where she had seen Zorro was still imprinted in her memory: Avenue B and 6th Street. Yes, Zorro, who had seemed so nice and offered her a job the moment he met her. There had to be some positive quality about a man like that, so spontaneous, so generous with his offers.

It was a hell of a walk, Penn Station to the lower east side. She had walked the route once before with Griselle on a beautiful day in April. There was always a safe route from one point to another in Manhattan, but it wasn't always a straight line, Griselle had explained. So Karina loosely followed their previous path, heading east to Lexington, then south to 20th Street where she turned east again to avoid Union Square Park -- that was one of Griselle's stalwart warnings: avoid the parks day or night. Third Avenue south took her straight to 6th Street, where she turned left and headed into Alphabet City.

On her way there, she must have passed a half dozen thrift shops and consignments stores, but she resisted the urge to enter, fearing that she would be tempted into buying a masterpiece of modern fashion with the small buffer, $43, she had between herself and complete destitution. One stop she did make was at a phone booth in the Village to phone her friend Griselle. But no one answered at Griselle's boss's house. Sometimes Griselle took the kids to the park or was working in the garage or the yard and couldn't hear the phone. Karina and Griselle never spoke much on the phone anyway, always nervous about drawing the ire of their ever-observant *jefas*.

Zorro was nowhere to be found on Avenue B and 6th Street. It was already almost 10 a.m. by the time she got there. A couple of winos were already gathered outside the bodega on Avenue B, sipping from bottles wrapped in paper bags, and a laundromat nearby had it's front door wedged open to let in the cool Spring air. It's funny how New York neighborhoods contrasted, thought Karina. In some places you couldn't spot a person wearing a suit and tie. In others, you wondered whether anyone ever practiced their fabled American individuality – even their ties all looked the same. She sat on a stoop just down the street from where she had first seen Zorro, hoping he'd show up. Unlike in other parts of Manhattan, where people shunned eye contact, in the lower east side, dubbed *Loisada* by its heavily-accented Puerto Rican residents, everyone stared at Karina, especially after she took a seat on a neighborhood stoop. And they didn't smile either. They looked at her like she was out of place, intruding in a forbidden ghetto. Karina did her best to avert their inquisitive glaring. And sure enough, just before noon, Zorro stepped out of the building where he'd been standing the week before, dressed in a shiny black leather jacket, blue jeans, a white t-shirt underneath, and glossy black shoes. Upon exiting his building, Zorro sparked up a cigarette. Karina liked the way he bent his head forward and cupped the flame, as though he were kissing someone.

Relieved, she stood up to walk over, but for some inexplicable reason, her feet wouldn't budge. For a while her heart thumped faster and faster as she pondered the reasons for approaching a total stranger about a job offer that may have been a joke. Maybe it was the hawkish look Zorro had on his face 50 yards away, scrutinizing the people who passed him on the street, blowing smoke rings at them in defiance. What kind of job could this man really have to offer? He said it was a "service sector" job. But the service sector in New York – as Karina had come to find out, painted everything non-tangible with the same brush. She had never seen so many services available in her life. Real estate and insurance agents, criminal/civil/immigration lawyers, deliverymen, high-rise window washers, chimney sweeps. She remembered seeing an add in Chinatown for a duck plucker, a *duck plucker*. Service industry indeed. But then the alternative washed away her doubts, namely that she was alone in a humongous, hostile city nearly broke and in dire need of money to save her family. Okay, Karina, if you put it that way, then what do you have to lose?

Not until Zorro began to walk away did Karina's feet kick into gear. She got within shouting distance about half a block away. But she hated the thought of shouting out the name Zorro, which seemed so strange to her.

"*Senor* Zorro!" she yelled, immediately regretting the senor part.

Zorro turned around. She could tell immediately that he had no idea who she was. He didn't even stop walking.

"Zorro!" Karina yelled again as she neared him. This time he stopped walking and turned around.

"Who are you?" Zorro said, obviously annoyed, devoid of the charm that he so blithely had projected in their first meeting. Then he took a closer look, and jabbing his index finger, said "Oh, wait. I know you."

Karina caught up to him and nodded her head with a big smile. "Yes, it's me, Karina, I met you last week with some friends, remember? You were standing over there and you offered us all jobs."

Zorro laughed to himself, then without lifting his eyes from Karina, he went for another cigarette – Lucky Strikes, Karina noticed.

"Of course, how could I be so rude? My favorite street friend, so what's shaking, baby?" Zorro said.

Karina didn't understand the expression "what's shaking", so she just smiled and shrugged her shoulders.

"I was wondering about your job offer," she said. "Does it still stand? I'm curious."

Zorro smirked and exhaled away from Karina.

"Like I said, I always have jobs," he said. "I'm always looking for new talent. How about you meet me back in front of my building in an hour? I have to take care of some business right now."

"Oh, thank you, Zorro, thank you very much," Karina said.

"I will meet you there in one hour."

As Karina walked away, she turned around to glance at Zorro, and there he was, puffing away at his cigarette, and staring at her ass. Her first reaction was to smile and blush, but then another feeling, a more eerie and intimidating feeling washed over her. She knew it wasn't going to be that easy, this new attempt at an American lifestyle.

Zorro returned sooner than expected, and immediately put his arm around Karina's waist and led her inside the building. Karina's first instinct was to squirm, but she knew she didn't have the upper hand at the moment. They went up a flight of stairs and Zorro unlocked a door in the hallway.

"Please step into my office," he said.

Karina walked into a neatly kept apartment with wood floors, throw rugs, a big stereo and television, and a fish tank the size of car's windshield. A large leather couch faced the tank, which was positioned next to the television, as though the two competed for an audience. But the piece de resistance was a lifesize lamp of a nude black woman squatting and holding the lampshade in her arms high over her head. On the wall above it all was painted a giant red Z in elegant cursive.

"Isn't that beautiful," Zorro said. "I think it's beautiful art, the body of a woman."

"I've never seen anything like that," she said. "So what about that job you offered us?"

"Now you have..." Zorro said. He quickly changed the subject. "I don't know who you are, or what your represent. Are you a cop?"

"A cop? Me?" Karina said and laughed.

"Well, are you?" Zorro insisted.

"No," Karina said. What did that have to do with anything? Why would he ask her if she was a cop? Karina just needed a decent paying job to send money to her family.

"Okay, good," Zorro said. "Not that there's anything wrong

with cops. But I like to know when I'm talking to one."

In a way Karina felt flattered that Zorro could have mistaken her for an authority figure like a police officer. So she let it slide.

From the way Zorro's slicked back hair reflected sunlight like a tinted window, to the way he dragged on his Lucky Strikes, to the way he dressed like a street gladiator primping on a fashion runway, his image projected smoothness. His little mustache was perfectly trimmed over his upper lip, and always looked clean and shiny. And his style, while in touch with the Puerto Rican street hip of the 1960s, never forfeited itself to shock value.

He was well versed in street talk. Sometimes words would slip out of his mouth in a torrent of cut-off syllables for 20-second stretches, and Karina wouldn't hear a word because she was distracted by the effort he was making to sound seductive. Like Karina, he also spoke rudimentary English, but he evidently picked it up off the streets because he usually limited his English to slang terms like "cool" and "wasted" and "heavy".

"So you want a job?" he said. "That's cool. What are your skills." The pronunciation came out like "skeels".

"Well, what jobs do you have available?" she said.

Zorro raised his index finger, as though to silence her.

"I asked you first."

"Well, I speak English. I can type okay. I can clean, sew, cook. I work very hard."

Zorro walked over to the stereo as Karina ran through her list of domestic skills and flipped on a switch. A loud, rowdy band came on, with a man shrieking and whining, and right then as Karina spoke, Zorro burst into spasmic dance across his living room floor, shuffling his feet right over his rug and twirling his arms like human machinery.

"Yo, baby, you like James Brown?"

Karina shrugged her shoulders and nodded.

"This is 'Out of Sight,' the whole things cool top to bottom," Zorro said.

The music was so loud, Karina didn't feel like trying to talk over it, so she sat back, entertained by Zorro and waited for him to finish. In any other scenario, she might have gotten up. But she had no place else to go. As it turned out, Zorro's "office" was it. So she settled into the couch, which was actually quite comfortable, and tried to appreciate the wild music and the dancer. In El Salvador, the only American music that ever reached local radio were candy-apple numbers from the 1950s that carried mixed messages like "Big Girls Don't Cry," and "It's my party and I cry if I want to." Zorro paused the dancing for a moment to sprinkle some food into his fishtank.

Someone knocked on the door halfway through the album, and Zorro peeked into the peephole before opening. A mulatta wearing a chic, waist-length jacket and fake eyelashes popped into the room and dropped down next to Karina. The girl's heavy perfume blindsided Karina instantly. Zorro disappeared into another part of the apartment.

"Hey honey, are you new?" the woman said.

"New?"

"Yeah, are you new. Are you working for the man or what?"

"No," Karina said. "But I need a job."

The woman leaned toward Karina, as though feigning intimacy.

"Zorro's a good man to work for, but I've known better," she said, then winked at Karina. "He takes a small cut, but he can be a real asshole."

Zorro returned with a yellow letter-size envelope and handed it to the woman. She kissed him on the cheek, whispered something, and left. Every time Karina's thoughts about Zorro drifted toward the cryptic, she checked herself and reanalyzed her personal situation. And this time was no different. She knew by now that Zorro's jobs, if they existed, were at the least unconventional, probably immoral. But she had come this far. And now her curiosity, above all else, kept her glued to that leather couch. Zorro turned down the music and sat next to Karina – close enough that she could smell the gel in his hair.

"So what kind of job is it that you're looking for?" Zorro said.

"I don't know. What kind do you have? You said you had service sector jobs."

"O yeah, yeah. I do have some service sector jobs. Some great ones. They pay a lot of money."

"Well, how do I apply? I need a job."

This question seemed to confuse Zorro. He narrowed his eyes, as though concentrating on Karina's eyes for an answer.

"I'll tell you what," he said. "Today's your lucky day. I need an assistant. Mine just left me and I'm looking for a replacement. I'll give you a one-week try-out. If I like you, then you can stay on the job. How does that sound?"

"Your assistant?" she said. "What exactly do you do? I'm very confused."

"Look, you assist me. That's what you do. The job pays $100 a week and you can stay right here in this place. There's an extra bedroom. The only benefit you get is that I bail you out if you get arrested. Take it or leave it."

The words "$100 a week" wiped any doubts from Karina's minds. Every other word Zorro uttered might as well have been spoken in Chinese.

"Ok," Karina said. "When do I start?"

"Right now," Zorro said, reaching into his pocket for money. "Run to the corner and get me a case, that's 24 bottles, of Budweiser, a couple of packs of smokes and a pack of rubbers. Sheepskin."

Zorro lived in a prewar building, a five-story, light brick walk-up. The fire escape on the front side of the building doubled as a clothes line for many of its residents. As Karina hauled the case of beer and condoms up the two flights of stairs, she could hear televisions playing soap operas behind many of the doors.

Zorro thanked Karina and showed her her room. It was a small space that until now was apparently used by Zorro and his house guests as a dumping ground. That afternoon, she fetched her suitcase from Penn Station and tried her best to clean the room. Old panties, beer bottles, discarded packs of potato chips, old newspapers, cigarette butts, clothes, a dead plant in the corner, which probably suffocated from all the second hand smoke, littered the floor and the few pieces of furniture. It took a few hours to tame the mess.

Zorro took Karina on a general tour of his operation. He led her out into the hallway, which had five doors that opened to it, one to Zorro's pad, which faced the street, three to separate but small one bedroom units and a trash room. A single key opened the doors to three of the other apartments one by one. The three one-bedrooms were sparsely decorated with a bed, a lamp, a ceiling to floor mirror on the wall facing the bed, and a couch in the living room. Zorro explained that his mother and cousins lived in apartments upstairs.

"Here's how it works around here," Zorro said. "The customers come around at all times. I try to greet them out front, but sometimes they gotta knock on my door. But they NEVER go straight to a girl's room. *Entiendes?* That ain't gonna happen, cause my girls are well trained. But just in case I want you to know. I'm the gatekeeper around here."

Karina's suspicions were now confirmed. Zorro was operating a whorehouse, a harem, a brothel, *una puteria*. Karina wasn't thrilled at the prospect of her new job. But it was clear, at least up to this point, that she was not one of his "girls."

Zorro took Karina into one of the rooms and led her into the bedroom. He flipped on the light switch and opened the bedroom closet door.

"Come here, I wanna show you something," Zorro said, stepping into the small walk-in closet.

Karina hesitated, fearing rape or a beating, or worse, being killed. But Zorro walked out, calmly put his arm around her waist and led her into the closet. Adrenaline made her legs shake and her throat dry. She was sure he would try to rape her. Zorro closed the closet door and flipped on a light switch. He and Karina were standing shoulder to shoulder. Zorro stuck his finger into a hole in the wall about 5 feet up from the ground. He pulled back, quietly opening a two-foot by two foot secret door. It looked like a mirror.

"This is my favorite trick right here," Zorro said. "I call it my National Geographic room. It's where we see the animals in action."

He turned off the light in the closet, and the mirror became a window into one of the bedrooms they had just visited. They were positioned at the foot of the bed, probably behind one of the large mirrors Zorro had set up for added kinkiness in the rooms.

"To watch?" Karina said.

"Don't act so surprised. This is how I evaluate my new employees," he said. "It's a useful tool. You'll see."

Karina stirred in the closet. "I'd rather not see anything, if you don't mind. I'm sure you've got it under control. I'll stick to my grocery shopping."

"Your loss," Zorro said. "You'll just miss out on the fun, because this is a fun house, baby, a pitstop for all those hardworking, lonely immigrant men who come here alone to send money back home to their wives and kids, that's all. Did you know that men migrate from Latin America to this country at more than twice the rate as Latin women?"

Karina shook her head, rather surprised to hear Zorro the pimp quote statistics on demographics. She wondered if he really knew what he was talking about.

"Well, it's true. There just aren't enough women for all those guys. So that's where I come in. For fifty bucks, I provide the girl."

Zorro turned to face Karina and put both his hands on her hips, pulling her toward him in the cramped closet. Karina smiled, but gently grabbed his wrists.

"Zorro, let's keep this professional, *por favor*," she said.

Zorro frowned comically, but couldn't resist slapping her ass as she walked out of the closet.

"The world is yours if you give yourself to Zorro," he said.

After a couple of days on the job, Karina was surprised not only by the amount of clients Zorro had on his weekly roster but by their diversity as well. The clientele did include a large number of laborers. But there were many men in suits who spoke no Spanish, and at least one who looked like a doctor, Karina guessed from his scrubs.

Another aspect of the job that surprised Karina was the amount of marijuana that was always around at Zorro's house. He often lit up a joint in the afternoon, then spent the rest of the day lying lazily lying on the couch.

Zorro explained to Karina that his marijuana business was growing, and he needed her more than anything else to be his secretary and delivery woman. He set her up with old cigar boxes that he'd get from the corner bodega every Friday. Karina kept a notepad, a phone and a rolodex, where he kept the phone numbers and addresses of all his clients. Karina was to take orders and make deliveries. But Zorro never let Karina near the pot. He cut it, weighed it and packaged it himself.

About a week after Karina had started, Zorro handed her a small cigar box wrapped in foil and newspaper.

"Take this to this address," Zorro said, handing Karina a small paper. "Make sure you carry it in your purse, and bring me back the packet they give you."

Karina did as she was told. It was the first time she ventured through the streets of Loisada so late at night. The errand took her north along Avenue B, where the streets were filled with threatening looking toughs, many of them in leather jackets similar to Zorro's.

She walked quickly and avoided eye contact with anyone. Finally she arrived at her destination, an apartment in the East Village near University Drive.

When she knocked on the door, a white guy with long dreadlocks opened the door, letting out a fog of smoke that by now Karina recognized without fail. The man let her into the apartment, and asked her to wait for him. Karina noticed another smell in the room, not too different from the scent in a church. On a couch were a couple of other men, both with short hair and round, intellectual type glasses, and a woman with long brown hair parted in the center.

"Hey are you from Vietnam?" one of the men asked Karina.

Karina shook her head. Vietnam? *Estan locos*, she thought to herself.

"No. My name is Karina," she answered them. "I am from El Salvador."

The three hippies looked surprised to hear her speak English so well. Karina figured they had been smoking lots of weed, judging by their bloodshot eyes.

"Is that incense?" Karina said.

"Yeah, it's patchouli. You like it?" said the woman in the room.

"It smells like a church?" Karina said.

"Sorry, man," said one of the hippies, "no saints in here."

The stereo was cranking rock and roll, and conversation seemed to be sporadic. So Karina just sat there until the guy who opened the door came back with a thin envelope for her. She thanked him and went back to Zorro.

The girls who worked for Zorro were nice enough to Karina, but she found it hard to befriend them. They spoke about sex so liberally, often comparing the size of their John's penises and fetishes and boasting about orgasms. Zorro had a total of 7 girls working for him. The turnover was high because of the nature of the business. Girls sometimes ran off with a John, or stole cash, or got tired of Zorro and moved on to the next pimp. They were mostly poor girls from Puerto Rico, Cuba, Dominican Republic, all of them young and dark-skinned with dark brown or black hair, except for a bleached-blond Cuban woman named "Pepa" who had a foul mouth. She loudly used "*coño*," "*pinga*," "*mierda*," "*cojon*" or "*maricon*," curse words which used effectively could deliver a stunning verbal sting. And her barrages usually increased tenfold when the topic of Fidel Castro came up.

One day, one of the Puerto Rican girls questioned whether the Cuban Revolution was bad.

"Socialism is supposed to be good," she said. "It's supposed to help everyone."

Karina made the rare move of jumping into the conversation.

"The only reason socialism hasn't worked well yet is because it has been imposed on people by force," Karina said. "In El Salvador, we were experimenting with Democractic Socialism. It's a system that can work if adopted correctly, especially in poor societies where the wealth is so concentrated among the rich."

Pepa was shaking her head angrily.

"That's a bunch of shit. If you like socialism so much, then go live in Cuba. You think that's paradise? You think that's what the world should be like. *No jodas*," Pepa said to Karina.

"I think Fidel Castro has good intentions," Karina said. "If anything, he has shown courage, standing up to the United States that way. He believes he is doing what's best for his people."

Big mistage. Pepa got in her face, yelling with her index finger pointing this way and that.

"*Ese maricon barbudo que le falta la pinga y no tiene cojones no sabe ni mierda, que coño?*" Pepa roared, using all her favorite words in a single sentence.

Karina would never have associated herself with people like this. But her job forced her to. And no matter the strength of her will, Karina's moral defenses slowly began to deteriorate under the influence of her new band of colleagues.

"Why shouldn't sex for money be legal," they argued. "Sex is the most natural thing in the world. We're just performing a service for these lonely men. Inhibitions about sex in this country are a relic from the days of the puritans and quakers."

What the hell were quakers and puritans? Karina didn't know. But she did know they sounded stern and outdated. It's amazing how a paycheck will justify moral degradation, Karina thought. Soon after starting her job, in order to preserve her position and her income, she stopped viewing the girls and the jobs they performed as pathetic. She prayed to God to protect her, to guide her through this valley of darkness into the light. But she felt that the more she prayed, the less God heard her. Her situation was purely her own doing. As conflicted as she felt, she stopped looking for another job, which would surely pay her less.

No matter how much partying Zorro did, he always remained in control. Even as he staggered around after a night of devastating substance abuse, he'd remember who to collect payments from, how many tricks each girl had turned, who his next customer was, what room was vacant, and what girls were working. His operational hours would effectively end around morning, sometime after his girls passed out on his couch, or the johns stopped coming, whichever came first. It was at those off hours, when the only sounds outside came from street sweepers, car horns and ambulances, when Zorro lived up to his reputation as an asshole. After the johns were gone, and the girls were exhausted, he'd come out to complain – and to scold.

But for some reason, maybe because she was not one of his hookers, Zorro didn't scold Karina. But he made it a point to have sex openly with his girls while Karina was around. She couldn't help but see it. And in a bizarre way, it made her jealous.

Zorro hit on Karina constantly, and eventually, she gave into him. Karina regretted it immediately after it was over, but for a few days afterward, Zorro feigned loyalty to her. He rebuffed the other girls in front of Karina, he bought Karina flowers, he invited her to dinner at a restaurant. But the honeymoon didn't last. A few nights later, Karina walked in on Zorro having sex with another one of his girls and stormed out of the room.

Later that night, Zorro told Karina that he wasn't interested in an exclusive relationship with her. Then he said something that made her blood boil.

"I think you could have a good future," Zorro said. "If you become one of my girls."

"One of your girls?" Karina said. "One of your *putas*?"

"You're really incredible in the sack, baby," he said. "You could make a lot of money. I'm talking $500 a week or maybe more."

"I'm not a *puta*," she said, the $500 weekly figure bouncing around in her head. "I will never be one of your girls."

Still, the temptation lingered. Making that much money, Karina could work for a year or two, send most of the cash back to El Salvador, where it would stretch much further, then go back to her family.

When she had first started working for Zorro, the thought of selling her body for money had not crossed her mind for moral reasons. Later, she considered hooking out of the question for other reasons, namely fear and disgust. Although many of the johns were not ugly, she couldn't imagine having sex with a man she didn't love, much less one she had never met before.

But with every visit to the little spy room, and with every account from a hooker of how great this john and that john were, Karina's own excuses for not hooking seemed to resonate less and less in her conscience.

One Friday evening, as the girls had been trying to convince Karina to try hooking just once just to see if she could handle it, Zorro walked in with the first John of the night.

The first customer to arrive on any given night was the luckiest because he got to choose between the two or three girls who were available. The man had a bald spot on the crown of his head, and although he wasn't fat, his body looked thick from too much heavy labor and rice and beans.

"Can I get you anything, a beer, a cigarette," Zorro said to the man.

"No," the man said. "I want to get straight to business."

"Alright," Zorro said. "You know the price. $50 per girl. The tip is up to you. Take your pick."

The man took a wad of wrinkled cash out of his pocket, fished out $50 in tens and fives and handed the money to Zorro. At this moment, the girls would routinely quiet down and strike seductive poses. Suddenly the John turned to Karina and gestured toward her with his chin.

"You," he said to Karina.

It wasn't the first time a John had wanted her over the other girls. Usually Zorro stepped in at this point and explained to the John that Karina wasn't available. But Zorro stayed quiet, counting the bills in his hand without looking up. Karina's head swam as she searched for her own excuse. The John took a step toward her. He didn't offer so much as a smile.

"Come on," he said to Karina.

Possessed by a power beyond her comprehension, Karina took the man's hand and walked out of the room with him. She shot a hot glance at Zorro on her way out. But Zorro just stood there, watching Karina with his relaxed eyes and rubbing his mustache. Just before she looked away, Zorro winked at her. She couldn't believe it. She was furious. The other girls in the apartment erupted in yelps and whoops.

Karina led the man into the room with the two way mirror in front of the bed. Somehow, she knew Zorro would be watching.

The wedding ring on the man's left hand made Karina feel a sudden pang of guilt. She went through such hasty motions with the John, stripping off her own shirt and quickly going for his belt, that he told her to slow down.

"Hey, what's the rush, baby," he said, putting his hand on her shoulder. "Take your time."

Karina tried her hardest not to look pissed. She smiled and

slowed down. She kept glancing at the mirror, knowing that she was being watched. She imagined that this is what it must feel like to act in a movie. The last thing she wanted to do was give off the impression that she didn't know what she was doing. So she tried to take charge by taking off the man's clothes. But it turned out that this John was very particular about what he wanted and how he wanted it.

"Take off my pants," the man said. Karina noticed for the first time that the man had horrible coffee breath.

She began to undo his zipper and take off his pants. But his shoes were still on. So she removed the man's shoes, and then pulled off his pants. Once he was in boxers, Karina got nervous. She noticed the lump in his underwear and the look on his face. A wave of nausea shot through her. Second thoughts sprouted up in her mind. But she quickly suppressed them by glancing at the mirror. It looked so real. Was there anyone really behind the reflection, watching her every move?

She found herself in a sexual situation configured out of duty, like the myriad times she had sex with her husband in El Salvador *out of duty*. So Karina resigned herself to do what she had been paid to do, suppressing any doubt or inhibition that still lingered in her head. So mechanical were her motions that the man kept giving her instructions on how to move and act. Everything disgusted her: his smell, his sweaty belly, his anonymity. The man finished his deed, and tossed a $10 bill at her for a tip. He left without a word.

Instead of getting dressed and seeing the man out, Karina stayed in bed, trying to justify to herself what she had done. Then Zorro strolled into the room with his imperious gait, and his relaxed eyes and a slight smile.

"Not bad," he said.

Not bad? Karina's head dropped into her hands.

"I knew you had it in you," he said. "Now fix yourself up before the next John gets here."

Karina began to whimper. She thought about her family, about God, about her father. What if her father saw her right now? What would he think of her. Or what if her mother, or sisters or brother knew. This, she could never explain. She felt like she was on a collision course with hell. If she died now, her soul would not be saved. She had done something bad, something very bad. Karina sifted through the tidbits of religious philosophy embedded in her mind to come up with some sort of justification for having sex for money.

Karina dressed herself, and with her chin held high, she walked back to Zorro's apartment, where one of the girls was hanging out. The other two girls were busy working. Karina's makeup had been smeared all across her face by the tears. But she hadn't bothered to clean it.

Zorro walked in. He was about to say something to Karina, but she gave him such a look of hatred that he turned away instead. A John walked in behind Zorro and immediately chose the other girl after giving Karina a ghastly look. When Karina and Zorro were alone, she told him she wanted to quit.

"I can't do this," she said. "It's not me."

"Of course it is," he said. "You were great."

"I can't," she said. "I'm leaving tomorrow."

"O yeah, where are you going to go?" Zorro said.

"I'll find somewhere. Anywhere is better that this," she said.

"You're not leaving, baby. You and me are going to make a lot of money together. A lot of money."

"I want to leave. This was never part of the agreement," Karina said.

"I won't let you leave. How about that?"

"Then I'll call the police, how about that?" Karina retorted.

Zorro suddenly grabbed her by her hair.

"You're not going anywhere, bitch," he said, reaching into his pocket and pulling out switchblade. "You're in too deep here. If you leave, I'll track you down and cut your fucking throat."

Later that night, all the girls congratulated Karina and welcomed her into the operation. Karina just smiled and thanked them. By 5 a.m., the Johns stopped coming and all the girls congregated in Zorro's apartment. Some left. Two passed out on the couch. By dawn, everyone in the apartment was asleep, including Zorro. Karina, who had gone to her room to wait out the end of the party, had packed her bags in the meantime.

Before she left, she had some unfinished business. She took

the rolodex of names and addresses of Zorro's clients and stuck it in her suitcase.

Then quietly, she opened the door to Zorro's room. Through the dim light now coming in from the window, she could see that he was lying on his bed, with his pants still on, but without his shoes or a shirt. Hanging on a chair by the bathroom door, Karina could see Zorro's black leather jacket. She crept over to it, ever so quietly. Zorro stirred, but didn't wake up. With her hands, she probed both pockets of his jacket.

She sat gently next to Zorro on the bed. He was facing down, his head buried in a pillow. She put both hands on the small of his bare back, the way a masseuse would do to let the temperature of her hands adjust to someone's skin. Zorro didn't move. Slowly, she slid her hands down, past his belt, to the seat of his jeans. Each of her hands wriggled into his back pockets and pulled a wad of cash out from one and a wallet from the other. Zorro suddenly turned around and grabbed Karina by the waist with one arm, half asleep.

"Later, Gigi, later," Zorro said, obviously mistaking Karina for someone else.

Karina waited until he nodded off again, then gently pried his arm away from her and laid it on the bed. She put the cash and the wallet in her own pocket and walked out of his room. An uncontrollable urge to giggle sprang up from the pit of her stomach as she hurried away from the building. She strained the muscles on her face to keep from contorting them into a gleeful smile.

From a payphone, she called the police and reported Zorro's operation. She tossed Zorro's rolodex into a trash can and continued dragging her suitcases, until she flagged down a cab.

Not until the taxi dropped her off at the doorstep of St. Gennaro Church, where Karina sought refuge, did Karina take stock of the money she was carrying: $483 taken from Zorro's pockets, plus another $162 from her paychecks.

She figured she had been the most expensive woman Zorro ever recruited.

CHAPTER 18

Using the serial number and company name taken off the barrel, Det. Poppel traced it back to a company in New Jersey, Carey Steel & Containers. Company records showed it had been manufactured in 1963, giving the murder a broad time frame. Records showed the barrel had been sold by Carey Steel & Containers to a Manhattan plastics company called Melrose that same year. He reported his findings to Sgt. Connery.

"Great, it's only a 25-year span, no problem," Connery said. "So much for putting the case to bed in 72 hours. What else have you got? Any word on the Zorro character? Talk about a motive for murder."

"Zip. No record of the 'Zorro' alias going back to the 60s. But I got property records for the house," Poppel said. "The house was built in 1957. It's had 7 owners since then, if you include the new guy."

"Fuck, that reminds me," Connery said. "That fucking asshole from Newstime broke the news to him about the body. So what do the property records say? Who are we looking at here?"

Poppel served himself his morning cup of coffee, sat on the long conference table in the Homicide department's "brainstorm room" and opened a file. One by one, he briefed Connery on the house ownership history.

"First owner, George Talbot, lived in the house from the time it was built in 1957 until 1971. Second owner, Salvador Salmaggi, lived in the house from 1971 until 1976. Third owner Thomas Jenkins, lived in the house from 1976 to 1980. Fourth owner…"

"Hang on a second," Connery interrupted. "That crawl space looked like it was under an addition. What do the permits say?"

Poppel leafed through the pile.

"Here we go. A back extension was added to the house in 1969. It looks like the basement wasn't extended. That's probably when the crawl space was created."

Connery nodded and took note.

"Back to the owners. Where was I, let's see the third owner, Thomas Jenkins. The Fourth owner, Frank Rothfeld, lived there from 1980 to 1983. The Fifth owner, Lydia Frankel, lived there from 1983 to 1991. The sixth owner Cohen. And now we have Bazi."

"How are we doing on contact numbers?" Connery said.

"We're working on it," Poppel said. "A couple of the owners still live on Long Island. The rest are elsewhere. But we've got social security numbers, drivers license numbers. We'll find them."

"Anything else?"

"We also got the test results in from that grain we found in the barrel. Forensics says it's industrial-grade plastic. That's it. All those little pellets are melted and used to make stuff. I still can't figure out why anyone would have stuffed plastic pellets in the drum. They don't absorb moisture or smell. They just made the barrel heavier."

Connery stood up in a frenzy of thought. He called in three more detectives who had been assigned to help Connery on the case.

"Ok, Poppel, you make it your priority to get addresses and phone numbers for all these previous owners. When you're done, report back to me. I want them all interviewed in person. I don't give a shit if they live on Mt. Kilimanjaro in Africa. We'll go talk to them. Mazur, get the name of the contractor or company that added the back extension to the house, see if they are still alive, and try to get the names of all the workers who worked on it. I know we're working with a time deficit, but that's what we have to go with right now. McGuire, go to Albany, get with the division of corporations and pull as much information as possible on this Melrose company that the barrel was sold to. When you're all done, report back to me."

CHAPTER 19

Newstime, ever avaricious for new copy, craved a fresh angle as the "Body in the Barrel" story began to get stale. Editors pressured Michael Cervantes to scoop the competition. The basics were old: a mummified woman from El Salvador buried about 30 years ago in their quiet suburbs. Her family in El Salvador missed her. But they wanted more now.

Cervantes called Poppel to press him for the rest of the immigration file.

"No way," he said. "You're not getting them from me. That's part of our investigation."

"Come on, I won't tell anyone where I got it. I'll just say it's a public record. Those lazy asses at Immigration will take their time to get it to me. By the time they mail it, the case will be over. You guys are kicking butt. You'll get someone soon."

"I don't know. I better clear it with Connery."

"Just make me a copy. I'll swing by to pick it up. Look, I treat you guys well. I make you out to be heroes in my stories. And I'll do that again with this case. Come on, I need your help."

Poppel sighed.

"Ok, come by later. But I still don't know if by the time you get here I'll have made you that copy. I'm still deciding."

Fifteen minutes later, Poppel leaked the papers to Michael Cervantes. He pointed out that Karina's immigration papers had been red-flagged by the FBI when she arrived in the United States. But he didn't know why because the FBI was taking their sweet time getting back to them. A Fed contact on Long Island had promised an answer two days ago, but was "still dicking us around."

There was a big hole, a vacuum of plot vandalizing Cervantes' thoughts. Why had this young, attractive immigrant's file been flagged by the Feds?

Cervantes picked up the phone. He tapped his source at the Feds, FBI Special Agent Holly Jacobs, an old college friend who worked for the bureau in Washington.

"Holly, hey, this is Michael Cervantes, how've you been?"

"Michael Cervantes? I used to have a friend called Michael Cervantes, but he dropped off the face of the earth about three years ago," Special Agent Jacobs said.

"I know, I know, I've been terrible. I'm sorry. So how've you been? Really."

"I'm great. I tried to call you a few times, but never heard back from you. So I figured you'd call me when you were ready."

Cervantes laughed nervously.

"If you weren't an FBI agent, I would lie to you and tell you that I never got your messages. But they probably teach you guys how to detect lies in someone's tone of voice over the phone. So I won't bullshit you. I'm a bad friend. I got the messages and never called. I've just had tons of work and never have time to call you for a good chat. Also, being married is a big job. All that extra time I used to spend talking to friends or going out I now spend with the wife."

"Ok, ok, forget about it. I'm just giving you a hard time. It's great to hear from you. All's well here. I'm doing counterintelligence analyses. Still single. Having fun. You know. Doing Fed stuff. So what's up? What can I do for you?"

"I need some help. I have this case…"

Jacobs listened as Cervantes relayed all the pertinent information in Karina's file: her immigration number, the year she emigrated, her date of birth, point of entry, etc.

Cervantes killed the whole day waiting for Special Agent Jacobs to get back to him. He took a long lunch, swung by the police department, chatted it up with beat cops. It was another day of nagging from editors. But Cervantes didn't want to write a story with holes in it. He wanted to wait and see what Jacobs turned up. But Holly took her time and after a while Cervantes thought she might be taking revenge on her for not returning all those calls. He started badmouthing Holly. He wrote a few times on his computer screen: "she never liked me anyway," only to erase it right away.

By the time Special Agent Jacobs got back to Cervantes, it was already 6 p.m. and the editors had stopped expecting a story.

Special Agent Jacobs sounded excited on the other end of the line.

"You're gonna love this," Jacobs said. "All off the record of course."

"Of course."

Cervantes typed away on his computer excitedly.

"You're girl Karina here was apparently a potential communist instigator, at least that's what her file shows. The CIA branded her in El Salvador so we wanted to make sure we kept tabs on her stateside."

Cervantes was shocked and eased off the keys.

"Communist instigator?" he said in disbelief. "What the hell is that supposed to mean?"

"I have a few pages I can fax you," Special Agent Jacobs said. "It was in her file. It took me a while to get to it because it's an old file and it was buried in the warehouse."

"What do you have?"

"Mostly internal CIA and FBI memos. The Bureau included them as part of the file here. It's on the list of files to declassify, but they just haven't gotten around to censoring it for sensitive materials yet. Back in the height of the cold war they flagged immigration files every once in a while. If these memos weren't in her file here, you'd probably never see them. Getting anything out of the CIA is next to impossible. Sounds like she was in deep trouble in El Salvador when she emigrated over here. Listen, unless your cop buddies have a friend like me, they'll probably never see all these reports. So you didn't get this from me, got it?"

Cervantes cracked away on his keyboard, taking frantic notes, not pausing to respond.

"Got it. Thanks. I owe you big Holly."

Cervantes stood by the fax machine, scanning the newsroom nervously, making sure no editors snuck up behind him. A few seconds later the machine whirled, spitting out 11 pages in the life of Karina Fuentes. The first thing Cervantes did was fax a copy to Poppel, with a simple note: "just got this from a source."

DOCUMENT INSERT   5/16/64 Teletype report, Latin American Intelligence Division, Central Intelligence Agency, San Salvador, El Salvador; Tomas Robaina to Richard Stempleton. CONFIDENTIAL/HAND POUCH DELIVER

Richard:
The more time I spend in El Salvador, the more I think the socialist movement here is growing roots similar to the ones that took hold in Guatemala a decade ago.

Through a contact, a vetted informant named Amado Soypaz, I've arranged to attend a rally sponsored by one of the country's leading rural organizers, Antonio Fuentes. He was one of the university students whose civil disruptions triggered the formation of the CEB here.

Mr. Fuentes is the mayor of the small town of Tonacatepeque located about 10 miles from the capital. He is apparently organizing peasants to demand land reform and socialist policies from the government. His movement has grown in recent months and apparently is spreading to neighboring villages.

I saw this happening in the Cuban countryside while Fidel Castro was in the Sierra Maestra. Batista's government largely ignored these organizers because he thought attention should be focused on the armed rebels instead of the masses. It was a mistake.

Speaking from experience, I believe that if we want to stop the reds from running across El Salvador, we have to begin by weeding out the cause of the problems. I need to find out a bit more about Mr. Fuentes before making a final recommendation.

After my meeting I will brief you in detail.

Tomas Robaina

DOCUMENT INSERT   5/20/64
Teletype report, Latin American Intelligence Division, Central Intelligence Agency, San Salvador, El Salvador; Tomas Robaina to Richard

Stempleton. CONFIDENTIAL/HAND POUCH
DELIVER

Richard:
I attended a meeting Sunday of the
CEB group being organized by Mr.
Fuentes in Tonacatepeque. I saw for
myself how this man is clearly making
headway in promulgating socialism to
the people in the rural countryside.
The meeting was attended by more than
200 farmers and laborers. Mr. Fuentes
has great speaking abilities and made
several references to the admiration
he has for Fidel Castro and the Cuban
Revolution. His ideals are clearly
communistic in nature. He promotes
nationalization of property, strongly
criticizes the rich and middle class,
and on various occassions clearly
stated that violence is not out of the
question in attaining his goals.
I met him after the meeting and
quickly gained his trust by doubling
as an agent of the Castro regime. His
daughter, Karina Fuentes, apparently
is his right hand and is leading the
charge to spread the group's message
across the countryside. I invited them
both to a dinner at a hotel in the
capital next week. I wanted to give
you enough time to respond and suggest

a solution.

It is clear to me that Mr. Fuentes stands alone as the leader of the movement. His daughter is intelligent and educated, but she seemed to lack the charisma and stage presence of the father. I believe that we can resolve the situation through Mr. Fuentes alone. According to my informant, Mr. Fuentes's organization would not likely survive for long without him. I await your instruction.

Tomas Robaina

DOCUMENT INSERT   5/24/64
Teletype report, Latin American Intelligence Division, Central Intelligence Agency, San Salvador, El Salvador; Richard Stempleton to Tomas Robaina.   CONFIDENTIAL/HAND   POUCH DELIVER

Tomas:
Good work in El Salvador. I couldn't agree with you more about the need to confront this red menace wherever it rears its ugly head. Mr. Fuentes sounds like a serious threat

to the stability of the Salvadoran government, which the United States considers a close ally.

Proceed with caution with your plan to resolve the situation with Mr. Fuentes. As for the daughter, I leave her situation up to your discretion.

Richard Stempleton

DOCUMENT INSERT 5/27/64 Teletype report, Latin American Intelligence Division, Central Intelligence Agency, San Salvador, El Salvador; Tomas Robaina to Richard Stempleton. CONFIDENTIAL/HAND POUCH DELIVER

Richard:
The situation with Mr. Fuentes has been resolved. However, after spending some time with his daughter, Karina Fuentes, I believe she can lead us to more of the organizers who are bound to rear their heads in the area. She may also be able to produce the names of the organization's members, which would be very useful down the road. My informant tells me that Karina Fuentes has vowed to continue in her father's footsteps and maintain the meetings. I

will deal with this situation appropriately.

I have moved to a safe house in Santa Anna while the dust settles in Tonacatepeque, but will continue to monitor the events there from a distance.
Tomas Robaina

DOCUMENT INSERT 2/06/66
Teletype report, Latin American Intelligence Division, Central Intelligence Agency, San Salvador, El Salvador; Richard Stempleton to Tomas Robaina. CONFIDENTIAL/HAND POUCH DELIVER

Tomas:
For the new year, President Johnson has requested an update of all Soviet/communist activity in Latin America. I have good information from the updates you send me regularly from El Salvador. But I noticed one loose end. It concerns Karina Fuentes, the daughter of Antonio Fuentes. Your last communique to me hinted at the possibility of obtaining the names of members from Mr. Fuentes's

organization. You also mentioned that you would continue to monitor his daughter.

President Johnson specifically wants intelligence on communist and socialist groups in Central America, their numbers, their weapons capacity, and their level of militancy. It seems as though Mr. Fuentes's group was organized at the time. Is there an update here? What of Karina Fuentes?

Richard

DOCUMENT INSERT 2/06/66 Teletype report, Latin American Intelligence Division, Central Intelligence Agency, San Salvador, El Salvador; Tomas Robaina to Richard Stempleton. CONFIDENTIAL/HAND POUCH DELIVER

Richard:
A coincidence you should ask about Karina Fuentes. After her father's movement lost its leader, Karina tried to replace him, but could not muster the support of the people. We braced her for the files, but she apparently

destroyed them. After expressing our concern about Karina's organizing efforts to her in a crystal clear manner, she subsequently married and settled down, abandoning the socialist cause.

She remained dormant until about a week ago. As I was scanning the foreign visa applications at the American embassy, I came across her file. She has been granted a visa to enter the United States through New York next month and live with a family there.

I think it is important that we monitor her during her stay in the states. A reliable informant tells me that a left-leaning university professor of a high position helped Karina obtain her visa. That indicates to me that she may still be harboring some communist tendencies. I recommend the Bureau keep an eye on her.

Tomas

DOCUMENT INSERT 3/08/66
Teletype report, Latin American Intelligence Division, Central

Intelligence Agency, San Salvador, El Salvador; Richard Stempleton to Tomas Robaina. CONFIDENTIAL/HAND   POUCH DELIVER

   Tomas:
   I have passed along your warning about Karina Fuentes to the FBI. I have also copied them with pertaining background information in order to facilitate their understanding of the case. It's one thing to have these reds in neighboring countries. It's a quite more serious matter to have them infiltrating ours. Good job on the follow up.

   Richard

   DOCUMENT INSERT   8/17/67   Field Report, New York Office, Federal Bureau of Investigations, SA Don Greer to SAC Vincent Dover.

   Sir:
   The subject, Karina Fuentes, has been dormant since her arrival in the United States about a year ago. Several spot checks have revealed no suspicious activity. She is living in

Brooklyn with two friends and has a job as a waitress/dishwasher in a Red Hook diner.

I think we may be wasting our time with the subject, who appears to have more interest in economic progress than political ideology. I recommend scaling back surveillance from every other month to once a year in order to focus on more pressing matters.

Greer

DOCUMENT INSERT 8/17/67 Internal Memorandum, New York Office, Federal Bureau of Investigations, SAC Vincent Dover to SA Don Greer.

Greer:
Point well taken regarding the Karina Fuentes case. Scale back operations as you see fit, but I'd like you to update the file at least once a year for procedural reasons.

Dover

DOCUMENT INSERT 8/22/68 Field

Report, New York Office, Federal
Bureau of Investigations, SA Don Greer
to SAC Vincent Dover.

Sir:
Interesting development in the
Fuentes case. In the last year, she
has taken a job at a plastics factory,
Melrose Plastics, by the east River.
According to interviews with a
disgruntled former factory official,
she has made headway in organizing a
small labor movement that has the
potential to threaten the stability
and profits of the company.

My contacts say Fuentes has met
clandestinely with co-workers at off-
site locations to promote the labor
cause. Fuentes spawned the idea
several months ago.

While she has not expressly
declared her intentions communistic in
nature, and she has no clear links to
socialist or communist groups in New
York, she is clearly establishing
left-leaning practices in a private
industry. I recommend doubling the
surveillance of the subject to twice
yearly.

DOCUMENT INSERT 3/26/69 Field Report, New York Office, Federal Bureau of Investigations, SA Don Greer to SAC Vincent Dover.

Sir:
Ms. Fuentes has stopped attending her job and is in an unknown location. My contacts tell me she may have moved to another city or left the country altogether, although they have no real indication of her whereabouts. Apparently the subject was pregnant when she departed. She gave no notice at work, and did not share leads with co-workers.

I recommend putting out an alert in the New York office to keep her in mind. She may turn up again in a different scenario such as a radical student organization, the labor party or the communist party.

Either way, it seems the situation has been resolved at her place of work. Labor practices have returned to normal and the situation has stabilized. Let's hope this one decided to take a one-way ticket home and doesn't turn up again.

Greer

DOCUMENT INSERT 5/05/70 Closeout Memorandum, New York Office, Federal Bureau of Investigations,

Ms. Karina Fuentes has not been located in the United States in more than a year, and a Central Intelligence Agency report states that she has not surfaced again in El Salvador.

CHAPTER 20

The phone lines lit up at the Nassau County Public Information office and the Homicide Unit. Reporters, dozens of them, were seeking answers.

Was it true? Had the case of the body in the barrel taken on an aura of international intrigue? Did this information bring the cops any closer to the killer?

Karina Fuentes's name was on headlines in major newspapers across the country.

Sgt. Connery didn't bother showing up at the office. He turned off his cell phone and his pager, knowing the story would raise the Commissioner's ire to a new level and lead him to call Connery to scold and complain.

Newstime's report opened up a whole new range of potential motives and suspects for the murder. The report complicated the case because it diluted the theory that Karina's killing had been an act of passion, a murder about love gone bad. Could it be possible that the FBI or CIA were involved? If so, to what degree? Do they know anything else about her disappearance?

Connery called the FBI's office in Long Island on his cell phone and scolded the public information agent, knowing in his heart of hearts that chastising the FBI would only further entrench them. Connery and Poppel entered police headquarters through a back door. In the hallway before entering the Homicide Office, a Lieutenant from the Narcotics division made a strange face at Connery, by clenching his teeth, pushing back the corner of his mouth and motioning with his eyes toward the Homicide office. The look told Connery: there's trouble on the other side of the door.

Commissioner Gilford Cooper was sitting in the middle of the Homicide Office when Connery walked in. He was holding a copy of Newstime. Three Homicide detectives were scattered about the office, trying their best to look busy in front of the top dog.

"I want you off the case," he said to Connery.

"Sir, I can explain. This reporter has a contact in the FBI. I assure you we put in for this information last week," Connery said. "The Feds take their time getting back to us."

"You know what people are saying out there," Commissioner Cooper said, nodding out the window. "They're saying Newstime is going to solve this case. Do you know what that makes us look like?"

"Sir, that is not going to happen," Connery said, turning both palms toward the floor and raising and lowering his hands, as though calming a rabid dog.

"No, it isn't," The commissioner said. "Because I'm giving this case to Nugent. He should have had this case from the beginning. I don't know why this case was assigned to you."

"Sir," said Connery, as he pulled up a chair and sat next to Cooper. "Give me one more day, 24 hours. I know we're close. I can feel it. Give me until tomorrow, and if there's no progress, I'll hand the case over."

The Commissioner stood up.

"This case has been a nightmare," he said. "You have 24 hours left on this case. After that I'm calling a press conference and announcing that a new "task force" is being put together to investigate. You won't be a part of it."

The last time the police commissioner had pulled a Homicide Sgt. off a case was 13 years ago, when Sgt. Sal Smitty bungled a drug case by arresting the wrong suspect. Smitty retired a month later. Everyone knew Smitty had been forced out. Now Connery, who boasted an illustrious career, faced a similar fate. But he'd be damned to go down like Smitty.

After the commissioner left, Connery went straight for the Homicide unit's well-stocked cache of over- the-counter pharmaceuticals. Off to the corner was a little yellow box of Vivarin, an over-the-counter stimulant college students often took to pull all-nighters to study for tests. Connery popped one, and served himself a cup of coffee.

Connery's detectives had fanned out across the area, even flying to Florida, to interview people tied to the house and other evidence. Their reports and updates trickled in through phone calls throughout the day.

Connery flipped through the files on the Karina Fuentes case. The coffee and Vivarin turned his eyes into two spotlights prying every sentence apart for potential clues. The files were a mess because several detectives were constantly looking at different aspects of the case. Connery reviewed all the notes from the interviews conducted with property owners, with contacts that had surfaced from Karina's address book. He also reviewed the documentation on the case: the blueprints for the house and additions, the contractors and builders who had built and remodeled the house, the state file on the company that manufactured the barrel and the limited state files on the company that had purchased the barrel in the 1960s. Connery flipped through hundreds of pages. At this stage of an investigation, combing through documentation was like gambling on a game of memory. The goal was to find a connection between segments of the investigation: between Karina and one of the previous homeowners, or contractors, or neighbors.

The afternoon zipped by on a caffeinated wave of alertness. Connery didn't look up from the paperwork for three hours. And when he finally did, it was to get another cup of coffee. The other detectives in the squad didn't dare address a word to him, knowing that Connery's Irish temper only needed a spark to ignite. The office quieted down when Connery walked into the main office for a coffee refill. All eyes seemed to track his movements, but none made direct contact with him. Not that he noticed. His mind was hooked to the files and seemed to only have given him enough slack to make a quick coffee and bathroom run. His eyes were wide and vacant like a zombie. His brain was crunching data, a human computer running on all its cylinders. Back in the brainstorm room, Connery continued to spread pages out on the table, drew charts in his notebooks to show connections between people and places. He stared at the charts, seeking a clear answer. He could feel he was overlooking something.

Suddenly, an incredible pang of frustration struck him. It was a pang like those students feel during a test, when time is running out, and the answer is just at the tip of their minds but doesn't rear itself. Another hour must have passed. The coffee was now cold, but that didn't stop Connery from sipping away. His hands held up his head as he concentrated. His eyes glanced at the table in front of him. More pages made their way across his fingers: statements, notes with bad handwriting, dates, names. He felt a bit nauseous. It was the caffeine gnawing on an empty stomach.

He looked up again, it was 5 p.m.. He had left strict orders in the office to divert any and all calls from media to the public information office, which had nothing new to work with. Pissed off reporters camped out in front of police headquarters, hoping to intercept Connery at the end of his shift.

But Connery didn't end his shift that night. By 7 p.m., the day shift was out, the night shift was in. The day guys had told them not to mess with Connery because he was on a tear. So Connery hadn't even noticed the shift change. By the time he emerged from his cave, it was 9:30 p.m. Two of the night guys were out on a case, and only a black detective named Engels and a night clerk were in the office. The clerk handed Connery a note. It was from Poppel.

"I'm gonna check out another contact from the address book first thing in the morning. Her name is Catalina Fernandez. She still has the same phone number and address today as in 1967, when she met Karina. The address is 298 West 32nd St. Apartment 364. We'll be there at 7."

The note depressed Connery. While he had been willowing away helplessly on the paper trail, Poppel and the others were making *real* progress on the case. Suddenly, Connery felt as if the whole day was wasted, as though his last stand to solve the case had been a charade to quell the rising tide of doubt sweeping his self-confidence.

The only place he could turn to now was Danny's, an Irish pub two blocks from police headquarters where Connery used to knock back Jack Daniels and water after work. A swollen liver had caused him to cut back on his drinking eight years ago. So it had been years since he went to Dannys on the night shift. He only knew the day staff who served lunch. When he walked inside, it was like the twilight zone: same bar, but different faces all around: different bartender, and waitresses and manager, and barflies bent over drinks.

He ordered a Jack and coke, figuring he wanted to ease his body from the caffeine to the booze. A Yankees game was playing on a television at the corner of the bar. The Yankees were up 10-2, a typical spanking. It didn't interest Connery. During lunch hour, that same TV always had MSNBC on so the bartender could watch the stock ticker at the bottom of the screen throughout the day to monitor his investments. Christ, everybody had some cash tied up in the markets these days. Everyone was getting rich. That Nasdick index or whatever you called it seemed to be doubling every month. Connery had never invested, outside his police pension, in stocks. But every time he bothered to look at one of those tickers, they had spiked again, making a lot of people a lot of money, including the bartender. This thought depressed Connery. He looked at the TV again. Yankees, no news. The night-shift bartender preferred sports to equities. One set of faces in the day, one for the night. Connery massaged his hands and felt his wedding ring embedded in his thick finger. His wife would be calling him any second. But she wouldn't get through because he had never bothered to turn his cell phone and pager back on all day. He checked them to make sure they were off. The bartender came up to him after a few minutes.

"I thought I recognized you from somewhere," he told Connery.

The bartender pointed to a framed cutout of Newstime's front page dated 1992 hanging over the bar. It was a photo of Connery escorting Amy Fisker out of police headquarters. Connery was 15 pounds lighter in those days.

Connery stared at the Newstime picture, drifting off to some point in his past. The sound of the bar door opening next to him distracted his attention. A middle-aged white man wearing a suit walked in with a black woman dressed in a white blouse and knee-length khaki skirt. Connery never understood interracial relationships. They just didn't make sense to him. Stick with your own kind, that's what he figured. In fact, he couldn't remember the last time he had seen a black face in Danny's Irish Pub in Mineola, New York. But he looked again. The woman was very pretty, with a light, smooth complexion, curly hair held behind her head in a pony tail, showing off the wrinkle-free skin of her face. The makeup on her face had lightened the sockets around her eyes. And her eyelashes seemed to go on a mile. It was strange. The curve of her large hips, the apparent firmness of her breasts, her feminine grace as she placed her hand on the man's. Connery found her...attractive.

The bartender placed the Jack and coke in front of him and said something. But Connery didn't hear the man's voice. His mind had sprung out of the cobwebs of innebriation and had seized on something. The old detective's facial muscles went slack. His eyes glazed over, as though they were fixed on a distant point. All sound was cut off from his skull. He jumped up from the bar, now with a determined expression on his face, took some cash out of his pocket and tossed it on the counter, and hurried back to headquarters.

The two Homicide detectives on duty nodded hellos, but he ignored them and went straight to the brainstorm room. The papers he had been sifting through all day were still exactly where he had left them, scattered around the table, on chairs, in apparent disarray. But he knew exactly what he was looking for. It was, after all, a game of memory. On the far side of the table, in a pile of folders, was the file on the former owners of 97 Forest Dr. Thomas Jenkins, third owner, 1976 to 1980. Nope. Salvador Salmaggi, second owner, 1971 to 1976. Nope. There, the first owner, George Talbot. He lived in the house from the time it was built in 1957 until 1971. He set Talbot' file aside.

Then Connery walked to a chair on the other side of the table, where he had set aside some detective notes on interviews with the former homeowners. He found the interview with Talbot, conducted earlier that day at Talbot' current home in Palm Beach, Florida. Det. Spinner had conducted the interview.

He flipped through Skinner's notes.

"Do you remember ever seeing a barrel under the house?" Skinner had asked Talbot.

"No," he had answered.

"Why would this barrel be under your house?"

"I don't know."

"Where did you used to work 30 years ago, when you lived at 97 Forest Drive?"

"At an industrial factory in Manhattan, Stern Industrials, it was owned by my father-in-law," Talbot said.

Connery placed that notebook with Talbot's property file. Then he walked to the far end of the table, to a file Poppel had pulled from state corporate files on the Jersey company that manufactured the barrel in 1963, Carey Steel & Containers. He separated that file and placed it with with the other papers. Connery wiped his forehead. He hadn't even bothered to remove his suit jacket, and after all those Jack and Cokes, he had begun to sweat up a storm. He was frantic, sifting through piles for a specific file, unable to locate it, checking the chairs, slamming his hand on the table. He pushed aside a pile with an angry "fuck," and looked down. There, on the table, the file he was looking for. It was thin, only a few pages in the cream colored folder. Connery snatched it and opened it. It was the file Poppel had pulled on Melrose Plastics, the company that had bought the barrel from Carey Steel & Containers in 1966, about 6 pages long. In the mayhem of identifying the victim, dealing with the media onslaught, and interviewing former homeowners and contacts from Karina's address book, Connery had only given the file a passing glance the first day Poppel turned it over to him. He studied the file. Names jumped out, accounting figures blurred his scanning, corporate mumbo jumbo diluted his concentration. His heart raced. There, on page 3.

"Melrose Plastics, a subsidiary of Stern Industrials. Registered for dissolution in 1971; Registered Agent, Jeff Katz; Treasurer Gary Schneider; Vice President, Gunther Briggs; President, George Talbot."

Connery let out a loud "ha!"

He sat on the nearest chair and took a deep breath. The Jack and Cokes and high caffeine levels clashed in his skull. His head swirled. The sweat had seeped through his shirt. His neck was sticky. He fanned himself with the Melrose file he was clutching in his hand.

"So, Mr. Talbot," Connery said aloud to himself, "you had a weakness for Latinas?"

Raging thunder – along with caffeine-induced excitement -- kept Connery up most of the night. By the time he drove across a fog-enshrouded Triboro Bridge, Connery's head was heavy with sleeplessness. It was a horrible day. Rain seemed to be slashing at his Ford Crown Victoria from the sides. Traffic was heavier than usual because of the weather, and it took him more than an hour to get to Catalina Fernandez' apartment on West 25 Street.

Det. Poppel – wrapped in a soaking trench coat -- was waiting for him in the lobby of Catalina's building.

"We're booked on an 11 a.m. Flight to Palm Beach," Connery said to Poppel. "I don't think this guy Talbot told us everything he knows."

"Ok boss," Poppel said.

They buzzed the super's apartment, and a tall Romanian man dressed in a robe emerged a minute later to open the door.

They took the elevator to the sixth floor and knocked on the door at apartment 6-H. They could hear someone approach the door from the other side.

"Who is it?" a woman said.

"Mam, are you Catalina Fernandez?" Connery said.

"Yes, I am."

"We're police officers mam," Connery said, holding his badge up to the peephole. "Roger Connery and Daniel Poppel from the Nassau County Homicide Unit."

"Oh, please, one moment. I wasn't expecting any visitors."

"Take your time, mam," Connery said.

A couple of minutes later, the woman opened the door and let them into her apartment. She was short and stocky, and had not bothered dying her graying curly hair, which was cut short. Dressed in a pair of polyester brown slacks and a black blouse with flowers on it, the woman seemed like a relic of the 1970s. At her request, Connery and Poppel removed their coats and Catalina hung them up on a rack by the front door. She led Connery and Poppel to a couch and sat on a chair next to them.

"I think I know why you're here," she said, her voice sanded down by decades of Marlboros.

Connery and Poppel looked at each other quizically.

"Why is that?" Connery said.

"Because of Karina." Catalina said it in such a way that her deep affection for Karina was not betrayed.

"That's right," Connery said. "We're trying to piece things together."

Catalina lit a cigarrette, holding it gently between her fingers. She held out the box to offer smokes to the cops, but they politely shook their heads. She offered them coffee or juice, but they declined those as well.

"I've been wondering what happened to Karina for 30 years," she said, letting out a cloud of smoke.

"So you knew her?" Connery said. "What can you tell us about her?"

"I didn't just know her. Karina and I were practically best friends. We met at St. Jean D'Arc residence for women in 1967. That girl was really something. Talk about a woman that turned heads. She loved to dress up. She loved style and fashion. But it wasn't like the Sex and the City set, you know, they felt great about themselves and had great confidence and wanted to dress up. For Karina, dressing up was almost an addiction. If she couldn't wear the clothes she loved, it would depress her. Jobs with uniforms? Oh my God, forget it. She hated them. But going anywhere with her was fun, to get a coffee, to a movie, to a store. People always stared, especially the men. We'd go out for subway ride and people would turn to look when she passed. When we met, she was looking for a job, so I set her up at a factory, a place called Melrose Plastics."

Connery glanced at Poppel.

"Go on," Connery said, taking a notebook from his pocket and clicking on his old silver Parker pen to jot notes.

CHAPTER 21

Griselle told Karina she was moving to Brooklyn with a friend and invited Karina to room with them. The first time Karina set foot in Griselle's Park Slop apartment, she was shocked at how nice it was. Yami, Griselle's roommate, explained to Karina that it was an excellent neighborhood.

"I used to work for an old couple nearby when I first got here from Puerto Rico," Yami said as they entered the apartment through a tiny foyer. "Every since I left this neighborhood, I've wanted to move back because it's so nice and so close to everything. I looked at the real estate listings every week for a year to see the apartment prices. Finally I found this one. It's only $175 a month."

Karina noticed the polished wood floors, the crown moldings over the doorway, and engraved moldings around the ceiling, the floor boards. Two large windows in the living room opened to the street, where the view included treetops, the building across the street, and off to the side, a view of the Statue of Liberty in the distance. Griselle grabbed Karina's hand.

"You have to see the bedrooms," she said. "This one's Yami's. It's a little smaller, and the bathroom is in the hallway. Ours is here."

"Ours?" Karina said, a bit surprised. "There are only two bedrooms?"

"Yeah, that's all we could afford," Griselle said. "I don't mind sharing a room if you don't. We all have to share the bathroom. You can sleep on the couch if you prefer."

"I don't mind sharing a room," Karina said. For some reason, the thought of splitting a room with Griselle put a damper on her enthusiasm. "So how much rent do I have to pay?"

"Well, since Yami has her own room, she's going to pay $75 a month. We each pay $50."

It didn't sound too bad to Karina.

"You don't have a bed, do you?" Griselle said.

Karina shook her head.

"Well, we're going to have to go buy you one at a thrift store or something."

The apartment was located on 8th Street just off Sixth Avenue, about three blocks from the Seventh Avenue stop on the F-subway line near Prospect Park. The building was a six-story brick apartment built after World War I. Handsome gothic trimmings decorated the edges of the building, and an arch curved over the walkway that led to the courtyard in the front. The street itself was lined with mature sycamore and oak trees, which had just begun to sprout leaves.

Griselle showed Karina where to get the subway and told her where that train took her: up Manhattan as far as Central Park. Most of the people who lived there were white Anglos or Europeans. Like everywhere else in the city, they mostly whizzed by Karina and Griselle without so much as a glance.

It didn't take long for the women to find a slew of Thrift shops and other stores on Fifth Avenue, Park Slope's main business artery. The thrift shops and second hand stores here were even cheaper than the ones in the Village, and soon Karina built up her wardrobe to the level where it was before Wilma Stancanatto had sabotaged a load of her clothes with bleach. Her closet filled up with tight blouses that buttoned up to the neck, v-neck sweaters, slim straight-leg trousers and mini-skirts, bringing 1960s supermodel Twiggy to mind.

Karina landed a job as a cashier at a 24-hour laundromat just up the F-line. For a few weeks, she worked a 7 p.m. to 3 a.m. shift, which she hated, but eventually a daytime shift opened up and the manager let her work days. But the daytime shift was much busier and stressed her out, so she quit.

After a couple of unemployed weeks, Karina landed another

job as a waitress at a Red Hook diner named Pappy's. The pay wasn't bad: minimum wage of $1.25 an hour plus tips, which usually came out to about $50 a week. The job required her to wear a white uniform with an apron, and a crown-like cap that made her look like a World War II nurse. All the dockhands and laborers who worked at the Red Hook ports – Germans, Irish, Polish, Russians – were stingy with the tips but generous with the flattery. It sometimes bordered on harassment, but since Karina didn't understand much of what they said because of heavy accents, she usually didn't complain unless someone felt her up or grabbed her ass. Otherwise, she'd smile away at any comment they threw at her.

But that wasn't the worst part of the job for Karina. More than anything, she hated the damn uniform. She felt that it stymied her individuality, and lumped her together with a team of other women who she had nothing in common with. But most of all, she didn't like the way it made her look. It was boxy on her curves and fell too low below the knees. Her favorite part of the day was getting home and changing into her own clothes.

In El Salvador, fashion and style rung hollow in the ears of poor women. In New York, Karina discovered that being poor didn't mean having to dismiss a sense of personal style. In fact, she began to feel that her clothes was the only way to convey who she was at a glance, and she dressed accordingly. Cosmopolitan and Vanity Fair became standard guides for the kind of clothes she would target at thrift stores. Hemlines inched up on Karina's legs, which were a great asset, with strong, rounded calves and long thighs that curved gently into her hips. She wore miniskirts with decorative tights and pantyhose. Gaudy accessories, such as perspex rings and earrings and gold chain-belts, helped to get the message across. She found them all for pocket change in Brooklyn.

But one Sunday, after work, she and Griselle headed to a thrift shop they had heard about next to St. Michaels Church on the Upper East Side. Apparently, all the rich Catholic women turned over fashionable dresses to the church after wearing them once, sometimes even before the clothes even went out of style for the season. Betsey Johnson and Barbara Hulanicki dresses lined the racks. Most had been worn once, or not at all. Some still had the price tag on them. The prices were a little higher than at regular Brooklyn thrift shops. But an $80 dress was still retailing for as low as $5 at St. Michaels: White boots and Zombie glasses by Pierre Cardin; trouser suits by Andres Courreges; Christion Dior dresses with dipped armholes and plunged necklines that revealed Karina's generous bosom; Mondrian dresses by Yves St. Laurent; Afghan coats, beads, beatle Jackets, body paint; stark white, pastel or checked fabrics were among Karina's favorites.

And Karina didn't overlook shoes or makeup. Ankle and calf-high boots, mostly black leather, chisel-towed slingbacks, white mid-calf go-go boots all lined her closet. She bought enough makeup to darken her eyes and lighten her lips almost every day. Karina tamed her hair not with hairspray, but with barettes and ribbons, and let it grow so that it passed her shoulders and eventually her shoulder blades.

Karina had noticed that in several pockets of Manhattan, particularly in the East Village, many young women had adopted a peculiar dress style to look like men as much as possible. Hippies, they were called. They didn't take care of their hair. They wore brown jackets that looked like they had been lifted from a battlefield. They rejected makeup. At the thrift stores, these woman would target the ugly brown and military green clothes in the men's section. They almost never went for the brand name women's clothes. This phenomenon was a mystery to Karina, who couldn't explain why so many American women would collectively decide to skirt social standards for attractiveness. Karina, unable to connect with Hippie mentality, decided to avoid the places where they congregated, such as certain thrift shops run by tough-looking women with shaved heads and army-green fatigues.

But these hippies seemed to be everywhere sometimes, often staging protests in Midtown or Downtown, tying up traffic, holding up signs and hanging out in groups. Fortunately, once you entered Brooklyn, the number of hippies hanging around plummeted.

After about six months, Yami got married and moved out of the apartment, leaving Karina and Griselle alone. Griselle took over Yami's old room and Karina kept their old room. With Yami gone, the subtle differences between Karina and Griselle were suddenly amplified. Karina noticed that Yami and Bolo had kept things normal in an apartment with Griselle's impertinence at one extreme, and Karina's pride at the other. It wasn't long after Yami moved out that Karina realized she didn't really like Griselle all that much. Beneath her humorous, extrovert exterior lay an angry girl quick to insult and criticize. It didn't help that she rarely dated and had a complex about being too fat. Although Griselle shared Karina's enthusiasm for fashion and shopping at thrift shops, she never wanted to experiment with her new clothes in public, which is what Karina thought the whole thing was about. Meanwhile, Karina began to look like a knockout to any man that passed her on the street: anglos, Hispanics, blacks, whoever. Like Griselle, Karina seldom dated. But she didn't lack suitors. Every once in a while, a man would call the apartment. A couple of times, men even followed Karina home, and she had to ask the super – an Italian man name Gregorio – to please escort the pursuers out of the building.

As the seasons changed, Karina adopted her dress. She bought a coat that resembled the one Lara wore in Dr. Zhivago, a movie Karina had seen with Griselle in a theater in Chelsea in the fall of 1966. But the two women drifted apart. Griselle eventually started dating a Puerto Rican man named Juan, or "Don Juan" as Griselle liked to call him. Don Juan had his own apartment, and Griselle began to stay at his place more and more often. After a couple of months, Griselle moved out and left Karina alone. Karina felt horribly lonely. Griselle and Yami called her every once in a while, but she had no one to talk to or model her new dresses in front of on a daily basis. She stopped dressing up, and started wearing the same Dr. Zhivago coat, which was relatively non-descript, everywhere she went. Instead of going for walks or to catch movies after work at Pappy's, Karina just went home, and watched more television than she ever had before. Unable to handle the rent by herself, Karina asked Griselle and Yami and a couple of other friends to help her find a place to stay or a roommate. But they never came through. After a month by herself, the rent was due, and Karina didn't have the money to pay it all by herself. She asked Yami and Griselle for money to help her out, but they both declined, saying they were hard up for money themselves.

So Karina turned to Father O'Leary again. She showed up at his church on a Sunday. It had been almost a year since she had seen him because while living in Brooklyn, she had attended another church closer to where she lived. Father O'Leary greeted her warmly and invited her into the rectory for a cup of coffee.

Karina explained her situation to Father O'Leary. He listened intently and without an expression of judgment on his face, much like he did when hearing confessions. When Karina ended, Father O'Leary looked up and took a deep breath.

"Well, I know you need a place to stay right away. I'd let you stay here again, but we both know the church frowns upon having guests for prolonged periods in rectories. I suggest you go to St. Joan D'Arc not far from here in Greenwich Village. Have you heard of it?"

Karina shook her head.

"I don't know father. Is it a safe place? I wouldn't know anyone there."

"Well, it's a wonderful place run by the Sisters of St. Joseph, a good group of the Lord's servants that dedicate themselves to young ladies such as yourself. It's really a wonderful operation."

It wasn't the answer Karina was hoping for, but it did sound intriguing. Father O'Leary phoned the headmistress at St. Joan.

The nuns at St. Joan placed Karina in a room with two other women for $13 a week. One of Karina's roommates was a gigantic Polish girl named Helen that showered once a week and spoke extremely limited English. The other was an African woman from Zaire named Jasa, who scared Karina at first glance, but quickly gained her confidence with her educated conversation and extreme politeness. Jasa's physique resembled Karina's. She was about 5 feet 4 inches, with an athletic figure. She kept her side of the room clean, and had a mix of traditional African garb and modern American clothes she bought in

Harlem thrift shops in her small closet space. Helen seemed to have two outfits: an ankle-length light blue dress made of heavy cotton, and a blue blouse she wore with jeans that she seldom washed. Standing at 6 feet tall, Helen easily weighed more than 200 pounds, and had short, curly brown hair held back by a green bandana. Helen was wearing the blue blouse when Karina met her. Despite her hygienic backwardness, Helen had a sweet personality, and smiled awkwardly at Karina.

"Welcome," Jasa said. "I am Jasa. They told us you were coming, and so I cleared out the bed over here for you."

"Oh, thank you very much," Karina said, still a bit apprehensive about the black woman, who was dressed in an orange, knee-lengh dress.

"My name is Karina. I am from El Salvador."

The third-story room had a sink and a mirror near the door. They shared showers and toilets with nine other girls on their floor, and a common area on the first floor had a television and two telephones that the girls could use to make local phone calls. Helen slept on a bed on one side of the room, and Jasa on the bottom of a bunkbed on the other side. The only divider between the two sides of the room was a large wooden desk that looked like it had been used by women there for two centuries. Jasa had stationary set up on the desk and told Karina she was welcome to it. Karina took the top of the bunk bed, leaving Jasa on the bottom. Jasa's side of the room was meticulously decorated with dark-wood carvings of animals and masks spread out over a shelf and Jasa's nightstand. Beautiful red, green and yellow weavings were hanging on the walls. And she had deodorized her side of the room with a bowl of potpouri of natural spices. Helen's side of the room was a dismal sight in comparison, with a pea-green towel draped in front of the only window in the room as a makeshift curtain, a framed photograph of the Pope and two boxes with her things inside.

Jasa and Helen couldn't believe how much clothes Karina had. From the half empty suitcase Karina had brought from El Salvador, her clothing collection now required three large suitcases to transport. Needless to say, there was limited closet space in the residence room, so Karina had to select a few items to hang in the closet. Helen let Karina keep her suitcases under her bed, since Jasa was already using the space under her bed as storage. The few trinkets she had brought – a lamp, some books and magazines, and a box of letters from her family – fit on a shelf above her bed near the ceiling.

The residence was a microcosm of American immigration in the 1960s. Women from all over the world had taken refuge at this one spot in Greenwich Village, which was specifically for immigrants. Some had been battered by boyfriends. Some were former prostitutes or drug addicts trying to return to the path of righteousness. Some, like Karina, simply had nowhere else to go. Many of the girls spoke no English at all, so the ones who did were always translating for others.

The rent was cheap and the rules were simple: no drugs, alcohol or men were allowed in the rooms at any time. The women had to be in their rooms by midnight, and they had to volunteer to cook, clean, sew, translate, or counsel others at least one day a week at the home. If they were unemployed, they had to be actively seeking a job. If they became pregnant, they had to leave. They had a chapel downstairs where Karina occasionally lit a candle or prayed, but she continued attending mass on Sundays at St. Columbus. St. Jean D'Arc served three meals a day. But the girls with extra money often ate out to avoid the sometimes frightening cooking by the nuns and their cadre of volunteers.

For the first few weeks, Karina commuted to her job at Pappy's Diner in Brooklyn. But Pappy's changed the hours on her when one of the night-shift waitresses quit, forcing her to work from 5 p.m. to 1 a.m. Since this was incompatible with Jean D' Arc's midnight curfew, Karina quit, rejoicing in the fact that she'd never have to wear that depressing uniform again. According to her calculations, Karina had enough money saved up to live at St. Jean for four months without working if she had to, and still send some money to her family. Karina had been giving her mother more than $100 a month – almost half her monthly income -- ever since she started working at Pappy's. Karina's remittances along with the modest income Emilia made from sewing and selling clothes in Tonacatepeque were keeping the Fuentes afloat just fine, Emilia happily reported in her letters.

Karina began her job hunt the next day, consulting one of the residence counselors, a woman named Catalina Fernandez from Mexico. Catalina had once live at St. Jean D'Arc, but had saved enough money to move into her own apartment on West 25th Street. She had grown so attached to the nuns and the women that she still volunteered at the center once a week. Not only did Catalina have a couple of job leads, she also invited Karina to her apartment that night for a home-cooked Mexican meal. Catalina surprised Karina with pupusas and Papaya juice, Salvadoran staples which Karina hadn't eaten in the year and a half she had been in New York. Over dinner, they talked about immigration, food, and U.S. Citizenship. Catalina was planning to take the citizenship test soon and promised Karina to help her become an American *ciudadana*. Karina marveled at Catalina's collection of Mexican and Central American tapestries, some of which were framed and hung on the walls. Catalina's apartments was on the sixth floor of a building with an elevator, which Karina considered a luxury. It had a couple of windows in the living room that looked out to the street, and Catalina had set up a window bench to sit and look outside. Catalina was a heavy smoker, constantly puffing on Marlboros. When she was home, she'd mount her cigarettes on a long, black, slender cigarette holder like the kind Karina saw in flashy magazine ads and television shows. Although Catalina was short and a bit overweight, she carried herself nicely, always dressing well, wearing makeup and keeping her curly black main held back with clips. She was 28, only a bit older than Karina. Catalina explained to Karina that she had moved from Mexico to Los Angeles at 15, but that she hated L.A. because the white people treated Mexicans like if they were subhuman. When she was 21, she followed an older cousin to New York, fell in love with the place, and stayed. She had few kind words for Los Angeles.

"Over there, if you're Mexican, you fall in the Mexican class," Catalina said. "Over here, there are so many different immigrants that no one pays attention anymore. It's about what you can do, not what you are."

Karina told her about her abusive husband in El Salvador and her decision to leave to escape her marriage and help her family financially. That impressed Catalina. Karina also confessed that she fantasized about living in New York ever since she saw the movie Breakfast at Tiffany's, explaining much of her ultra sensitivity to personal style and glamour.

"In El Salvador, my life was about politics and revolution," Karina said. "But here, it takes a whole different kind of skills and qualities to *sobrevivir*. It's true what you said about people not judging you here by your ethnicity. But they do judge you very much based on your exterior, on your looks. At least I think so. Dress like a woman from Park Avenue and see how people look at you differently. Here I am poor, but I don't feel inferior to anyone."

They talked on and on like this for hours, until it was almost midnight and Karina had to leave.

Three days later, Catalina visited Karina at St. Jean D'Arc with good news. A friend of hers who worked at a plastics factory in Chelsea told her the company was hiring women. Catalina arranged for Karina to meet the woman, Marta, outside the factory at 8 a.m. the next morning so that Marta could personally introduce her to her supervisor.

"What kind of a job is it?" Karina said, a bit apprehensive. "I've never worked at a factory before. I don't know how to do any of those things."

"Don't worry, *mija*," Catalina said. "It's not rocket science. All factories are the same. They teach you in ten minutes how to do your job, and in two days it becomes routine. It's a great location for you, right there on the Hudson. You can probably walk there. But there's also a bus.

Suddenly, Karina hugged Catalina.

"*Gracias*," she said. "You have been very good to me."

"Nonsense, *mujer*," Catalina said. "Tell me how it goes tomorrow. Remember, it's right on the river. A place called Melrose Plastics."

CHAPTER 22

Karina landed the job at Melrose Plastics with ease. It didn't hurt that the person interviewing her was a man, Ronald Bauer, and that she showed up at the interview looking like Audrey Hepburn at the premier of one of her movies. Like anyone who lands a needed job, excitement prevails at the beginning. It turned out the factory made plastic flowers, and Karina liked the idea of recreating one of nature's prettiest things, even if it was fake. Karina bought Catalina a basket of flowers and a bottle of wine, and thanked her again. Catalina and Karina went out to dinner at a diner to celebrate.

The job paid minimum wage, which in 1967 was $1.40 an hour, which came out to $56 a week. Her supervisor, Ronald, placed her in a station that arranged the fake violets, roses, orchids, Irises, tulips, etc. in arrangements with fake leaves and branches. The work did not require Karina to handle any heavy machinery, which was good, because Karina had never been very good at manual labor. The room where she worked had a high ceiling with a huge fan ventilating air over the rafters at all times. But the room was designed so that the air never blew down below, so as not to disrupt the papery leaves and petals that were set up at the tables.

Another 13 women shared the 20 by 20 foot cavern with Karina, each of them with a desk, and the supplies necessary to make the arrangements: wires for tying bundles, green peat moss for embedding stems, small pots. Karina's favorite fakes were the red roses with dew drops decorating their petals.

Like her job at Pappy's Diner, the job at Melrose Plastics required wearing a uniform, a medical-green, short-sleeved, button-down tucked into pants of the same color. But since Melrose had a locker room, Karina could wear her own clothes to work and change into her uniform at the factory. Karina decked herself out in miniskirts, dresses, slacks, blouses every morning, fully made up and showed up at work as though ready for the modelling runway. Once there, she changed into her uniform in the women's locker room. She never wanted to be seen in the uniform outside of the factory.

Her co-workers teased her about her precociousness, but it didn't bother Karina. She'd just smile and tell them that she liked to look good. After a while, some of the younger women started coming to her for fashion and beauty tips. They'd congregate in the morning near Karina's locker, trying to speculate what she'd wear that day, a miniskirt, a blouse, a sweater, slacks, a dress?

While Karina got along well with her co-workers, the honeymoon with the job didn't last. As the summer months approached, the temperature rose steadily in the factory, until it seemed that it was hotter inside Melrose Plastics than in the hellish streets of Manhattan. Ronald the Supervisor refused to let the girls turn on the ground level fan because any slight draft would blow away the paper-thin plastic leaves and petals. Some of the women kept clothes and handkerchiefs nearby to pat down their necks and foreheads regularly.

Also, as factory deadlines loomed toward the end of every month, the supervisors would lengthen working hours. By the end of each month, with deadlines near, Karina and the women in her unit were working almost 12 hours a day, weekends included. And the women didn't see a penny of overtime. To make matters worse, bathroom breaks were frowned upon, lunch was strictly 30 minutes, and supervisors were verbally abusive to some of the women.

Working conditions steadily irritated Karina until she finally snapped one afternoon. Karina had made plans to go to Griselle's wedding on a Saturday afternoon. But it was the end of the month, and on Friday as the women were trimming and binding away at the plastic flowers, a tall, well-dressed man stepped into Karina's unit and approached Ronald the supervisor. After a brief exchange of whispers, Ronald the supervisor made an announcement.

"Ok, ladies," Ronald said, with the man still standing next to him. "As you know deadline is approaching and we haven't met our quotas, so we're going to need you to come in all day tomorrow."

The women in the room let out a collective "aaaawe." But no one objected. If they did, it could mean their job. Karina felt rage boiling within. She'd have to cancel on Griselle the night before her wedding, which would be an insult. Ronald the supervisor and the mysterious man were standing right next to Karina. This mysterious man had unwittingly ruined Karina's weekend.

Something about this man's presence made Karina nervous. Karina could sense him checking her out from above. So she stopped what she was doing and slowly turned her head up to look at him. She stretched back a sweaty shoulder, allowing her partially unbuttoned shirt to reveal a strap of her black bra. She gave the man a tired smirk. Who was this guy anyway? The man immediately looked away. He pulled a handkerchief out of his breast pocket and dabbed his forehead.

Suddenly, Karina stuck out her hand and said loudly to the man, "hello, I am Karina Fuentes." One of the women in the room gasped. This so surprised the man that he stumbled briefly on his own words in reply.

"Um, oh, yes, right, nice to meet you," the man said, quickly shaking her hand. Then he looked at the arrangement Karina was working on and said, "Nice job there."

This was quite amusing to Karina and the other workers. One of the women behind Karina giggled. Ronald -- obviously embarrassed that one of his workers had dared address a word to his guest – told the women to "get back to work."

Karina didn't take her eyes off the man the whole time. Before he left, he turned around, gave the room a sweeping glance, and locked eyes with Karina for a split second before exiting.

In the locker room after work that night, Karina was the first to speak up.

"I can't believe we have to work again tomorrow," she said. "How do they get away with this?"

An older Jewish woman from Czechoslovakia named Ingrid sitting on a bench near the back of the locker room laughed.

"Why don't you try to sweet talk Mr. Talbot into giving us better working conditions," Ingrid said.

"Who's Mr. Talbot?" Karina said.

"George Talbot is the man who you met today in the room. He owns this company. He is the one who decides all this. He seemed to like you."

The other women in the room giggled.

"He was checking you out all the way," said a young Puerto Rican woman named Doris. "He is such a fox. I wish he was checking me out, Karina."

Karina pursed her lips, and took off her scrub-colored shirt. She took some paper towels from the bathroom and patted down the sweat on her chest, stomach and back. Then she removed the pants and stood there in the middle of the locker room in bras and panties. There were a couple of other women also changing, but a small crowd formed around Karina.

"Look at this girl," said Doris, the feisty Puerto Rican. She walked up to Karina and walked around her slowly. Karina let her hands hang down by her sides. "If I was a guy, I'd be checking her out too."

There were some giggles, but a couple of the older women nodded their heads in agreement. Karina flipped up her hair and stretched her arms up, flaunting her figure. Then she laughed and got dressed.

"If any of you are serious about getting better working conditions, then let's meet tonight at the Go-Go diner for a milkshake and talk about it," Karina said.

Ingrid and some of the older women scoffed.

"That's the surest way to lose your job around here," Ingrid said. "It's a foolish thing. We are all lucky that we even have jobs."

"Do you all feel that way?" Karina said.

Some of the women nodded, but Doris spoke up.

"I feel lucky to have a job, but I wouldn't mind if the job was a little better. You never know unless you ask."

"So let's go," Karina said.

Of the 14 women who worked on the assembly line, Karina and four others went out for a milkshake at the Go-Go diner in the West Village about 5 blocks away. They were all under 30. Three of them changed into casual clothes at their locker room. The other two came dressed in their uniforms. As the waitress placed the milkshakes down in front of them, Karina glanced around the table.

"I'm tired of this," she said. "I can't stand this job anymore."

The other girls pitched in. "The hours are awful," "the pay is brutal," "the supervisor mistreats us," "we have to work weekends."

"And the heat, *Dios mio*, I feel like we're chickens in the oven," Karina said.

"So what do we do?" one of the women said.

"We get together, we sign a petition, and I'll go talk to that man, Mr. Talbot or whatever," Karina said. "I think I connected with him today. Something tells me he will listen to me."

A couple of the girls giggled.

"What makes you think so?" one of them said.

"Just women's intuition," Karina said.

"What the hell's that?" Doris said.

"This thing I read about in Cosmopolitan," Karina said. "It says that intuition is a woman's ability to make clear decisions with limited information."

"Yeah, alright, whatever," Doris said. "I'll sign."

"Me too," said another one of the women. "What good is a job if it doesn't give you time to live your life. I'll never find a man like this."

They all agreed to sign. Karina wrote up what she thought was a reasonable petition requesting shorter work hours, overtime pay, and a record player to hear music in the room where they worked. On Monday, she clandestinely circulated the petition among the women at work. Only two more women signed, bringing the total to seven, or half the people in the group. The others said they supported the cause, but couldn't risk losing their income even for a week.

On Monday afternoon, during one of her breaks, Karina scouted the cavernous factory. On the second floor toward the back of the building, a string of offices overlooked the main work area. Karina scanned the faces in the offices, but didn't recognize anyone familiar. All around her, machinery was humming, plastic was boiling, workers wearing masks and gloves were handling molten plastic. Making her way closer to the offices, a supervisor in the molding division asked her if she was lost.

"No, I have to deliver something to Mr. Talbot' office tomorrow for my supervisor," she said. "Which is his office?"

The man pointed to the center office on the second floor.

"It's through those doors," the man said. "Talbot comes in around 8 every day, but his secretary doesn't get in until nine."

"Thank you." Karina did an about-face and returned to work. She was already plotting the meeting in her mind.

Karina woke up at 5 a.m. the next morning to get ready, pissing off her roommates. She had methodically planned every inch of her attire: Andres Coureges knee-length white boots, which were exposed beyond the lower frontiers of her white Mary Quant miniskirt. The skirt's hemline, which flirted with the limits of decency, ended a full 6 inches above the knee. Karina had unbuttoned her sleeveless, royal blue, Christian Dior sweater vest down to her mid chest. The sweater was tight and emphasized cleavage. Her face was made up with dark eyeshadow and pale colored-lipstick. Her long, black hair was held back by two berets on either side of her head, and she had crossed a fistful of hair over from the left side of her scalp to her right, and held the flip in place with a blue ribbon.

The Melrose Plastics warehouse was practically abandoned at 8 a.m., with only a couple of mid-level managers unlocking doors and flipping on light switches. Karina entered through the front door, and walked through the main industrial space at the center of the warehouse. The light in Talbot's office was on, as was the light in another office at the end of the second floor, probably another early bird manager. Some of the lights in the warehouse were still off, giving Karina a feeling of sneaking around in the dark.

She climbed the stairs to the second floor, trying not to make too much noise with her heels. She checked herself out in the reflections of glass doors in unlit offices, making sure she still looked perfect. The door to Talbot' office was closed but unlocked. Looking through the glass, Karina could see that a reception area with a desk where the secretary sat was partitioned off from another room in the back. Before she went in, Karina turned around to capture the view of the warehouse from this second story overlook. It was like being the God of Melrose, the all-knowing eyes that took everything in and made judgement calls from above.

The door made a slight creaking sound when Karina opened it. A man's voice from the back room said "Connie, is that you?" On the secretary's desk next to her, Karina saw a name sign that said "Constance Briglio, secretary," ie, Connie.

Karina panicked. She felt her pulse quicken. But instead of beating a retreat, she hurried toward the back room and turned the door knob.

"Connie, what are you doing here so early?" the man said, his voice growing louder as Karina pushed the door open.

Karina stepped into view with nary a smile. Light from the window behind Talbot, which faced West and offered a nice view of the Hudson River and New Jersey beyond, forced Karina's eyes to adjust to the glare. Her shy, yet brazen entrance, with her face slightly downcast yet her eyes looking straight at Talbot obviously caught the man off guard. He sat back in his leather chair and said only, "Oh."

"Mr. Talbot, May I come in?" she said.

"Please do," Talbot said, gesturing toward a chair across from his desk.

It took him a full 10 seconds to soak in the sight before him. And in that time, Karina made her own assessment of him. He was middle aged, his chin was well defined, and he had a full head of hair. Although he had middle-age wrinkles around his eyes, his face retained a youthful look with tight skin and a well-pronounced jawline. Under his jacket, Karina could tell that he was thin and fit, without the slightest hint of a belly hanging over his black leather belt. His black hair was cut short, and had sprouted just enough white strands to make him look elegant. Add to that his stature, his wide shoulders, and a penetrating pair of blue eyes and he was quite a sight.

Talbot stayed quiet for so long that Karina wondered whether she had overdone her appearance. Finally, a smile crept up on Talbot' face. This was the reaction Karina had hoped for.

Karina noticed that Talbot sniffed the air ever so slightly. She knew it was the Chanel perfume, which she had sprayed on sparingly. Talbot stood up to shake Karina's hand. Instead of presenting a limp set of fingers, she squeezed his hand tightly, and felt his big hand squeeze back snuggly around hers.

"I know you," Talbot said.

"You have very good memory," Karina said. "I met you last week in the assembly unit. You had come in to talk to our supervisor."

"O yes, right," Talbot said.

It was then that Karina noticed something different in the air in Talbot's office. He wasn't sweating, neither was she. In fact, she felt a slight chill. It was air conditioning, cranking from a huge wall unit to the left. Then she realized Talbot' office looked ridiculously out of place for the warehouse. Once you entered this threshold, rust colored ceilings and florescent lighting disappeared. Talbot's office was lined with dark wood paneling and wood shelves. A cream colored, wall to wall, rug covered the depressing concrete floor. His desk was three times the size of his secretary's. The lights were soft and the ceiling had been paneled off to conceal the steal beams. A black leather couch, flanked by a matching leather chair and facing a wooden coffee table comprised a seating area near the bookshelves. The coffee table rested on a Persian style rug. Karina noticed another open door led to a bathroom off to the side.

On his desk, Talbot had several photographs of his wife and three children, a large black telephone, some paperwork neatly piled in front of him, and all illuminated by a soft-light lamp that turned on and off with the pull of a string.

"I have come to talk to you because I feel that I can trust you," Karina ventured.

"Oh, I see," he said.

"By the way, you have a beautiful office," she said.

"My wife, Judith, is the one to compliment," he said. "She did all the decorations."

"Well, it's very nice," she said. "I came today because when I met you last week, you seemed like a nice, sensible man, and I wanted to see if you could help us."

Talbot leaned back in his leather throne, interlocked the fingers on his hands and rested them on his stomach.

"Us?" Talbot said. "Who is us?"

"Myself and a few of the women I work with," Karina said. "We are all grateful to have a job here. And we like what we do. We take pride in our work. But we feel that sometimes we are not treated fairly. That we are not appreciated for what we do."

Talbot frowned.

"Not appreciated? What do you mean?" he said.

"For one thing, we work much more than just 40 hours a week, but we don't get paid overtime," she said. "Many of these women have families that need them. And they can't be with them because they are always working. Another thing is we work almost every weekend at the end of the month, and again, we get no extra pay…"

Talbot interrupted her.

"If it's overtime you want, you won't get it," he barked. "Most of the factories in Manhattan treat their employees the same. It's standard practice."

Karina smiled disarmingly.

"I know you have deadlines to meet," she said. "And you meet them because of us. We do a good job for you. But the women tell me they have not seen a raise since the government raised the minimum wage."

Talbot seemed to relax a bit, and he leaned forward on his chair.

"Karina," Talbot said, pronouncing the name correctly, much to Karina's surprise. "I don't force anyone to work here. If somebody doesn't like the job, they can quit and find another one. That's the beauty of this country. I pay minimum wage. That's it."

Karina took a paper out of her purse.

"Some of us have signed a petition to formally request either a pay raise or overtime pay," she said. "We would also like air conditioning, like the one you have here. At the least, we'd like a record player to hear music while we work. If we can't have the fan on, at least we can hear music. In the men's locker room they have a radio that they play all the time. We can hear it all the way in our locker room."

Talbot humored her.

"And what kind of music do you want to hear?" Talbot said.

Karina dug another piece of paper out of her purse and glanced at it. A factory friend had given it to her.

"Aretha Franklin," she said. "The record with the song 'Respect' on it."

Talbot smiled, obviously amused, and rubbed his chin.

"So, you've signed a petition?" he said. "How many people signed it?"

"Seven," she said. "Half the girls in my unit. Some of the girls wanted to go to the government to complain. But I said I preferred to talk to you first. Because, like I said, you seem like a very nice man."

Then, emboldened, she continued, in an attempt at lightheartedness. But her humor veiled a message she wanted dearly to communicate to Talbot.

"Working such long hours presents a certain problem for some of us women, you know," Karina said, smiling shyly, and stirring in her seat.

"What's that?" Talbot said.

"Many of us, me included, are single," Karina said. "And we want to be able to date and find husbands. But working so much here makes it very difficult, because we cannot meet men while we are working here, and we don't have free time to go out and meet them elsewhere."

Now she noticed that Talbot' eyes had drifted from her face to her legs, which were crossed and exposed almost to the hips. This man, this wealthy, American, man was studying her with a deep interest.

"I guess that does present a problem," Talbot said. "A young, beautiful woman such as yourself should have enough time to navigate the social scene and find a partner. I can understand that."

Karina didn't know how to respond. Something insider her —

women's intuition perhaps – told her to end the meeting on that note. So she stood up, walked around the desk, and stuck out her hand. Talbot, rather dumbfounded, reached up and shook it.

"I don't want to take up any more of your time," she said. "I hope you consider our requests. We would be extremely grateful, especially me."

Then she about-faced and slowly walked out of the room. Immediately outside the door, she let out a huge breath and fanned her face with her hand. She couldn't believe what she had just done. A delirious sensation practically blinded her as she walked out to the overlook. It was past 8:30 and the factory had come alive. She walked downstairs, with machines whirring all around. Workers had manned the melting stations. Supervisors were studying their clipboards. It seemed as though every man on the factory floor stopped what they were doing to look at Karina as she walked by: her white boots, her miniskirt, her non-chalant expression. That included Talbot, who had come out of his office to watch Karina walk across the factory from his bird's eye view on the second floor. She noticed him watching just before she entered the locker room to change for work.

"R-E-S-P-E-C-T. Find out what it means to me…"

The song blared from the assembly unit as women entered the room the next morning. The younger ones were so shocked that they broke out into dancing, turning the furnace-like assembly unit into a temporary nightclub. One of the girls grabbed Ronald the supervisor's hand and twirled herself in front of him. Ronald lowered the volume on the music.

"Mr. Talbot has decided to install a radio at the assembly unit to," Ronald the Supervisor cleared his throat. "To raise morale."

All the women gave Karina elated glances. Karina was so happy she could hardly imagine having to sit through an entire workday. She wanted to go out with her friends that moment and celebrate, and dance all day. The women didn't openly congratulate her that morning, for fear of branding her as the origin of the idea. But at their lunch break, they all gathered around Karina' table in the cafeteria.

"So you convinced him," Doris said. "I knew you would. How did you do it?"

One of the older women chimed in, "tit for tat."

They all laughed. Karina smiled, but shook her head.

"No, I just told him in a nice way that if we were happier, we would be better employees."

"Do you think he will give us everything we asked for?" another asked.

"I don't know," Karina said. "But this is a good sign. Even if we just get a radio, it was worth it."

The older worker weighed in again.

"No man gives something for nothing," the woman said. "Sooner or later, he will ask for something in return."

Friday morning, as the women were settling down to work and the radio was cranking a Buddy Holly album brought in by one of the younger women, Ronald asked Karina to have a word with him outside.

"Mr. Talbot says he'd like you to join him in a meeting in his office after work," he said. "So what's this all about? There's something different about you lately."

"I don't know," Karina said.

Ronald narrowed his eyes behind his eyeglasses, and lifted his head, looking at Karina down the length of his nose.

"Be careful, honey," he said. "This isn't a game you're playing."

"I don't understand," she said. "If Mr. Talbot wants to see me, then I will go see him."

"I know exactly what's going on," he said. "Don't think I

don't know about your little petition. I've had troublemakers like you before. And it never ends well for them."

Karina went back to work, wondering what Talbot wanted to see her about. It wasn't clear whether he wanted her to come dressed in uniform or her own clothes. Luckily, she had dressed nicely for work that day. So she decided that she would change into her own casual clothes for the meeting. Karina changed into the clothes, which she had hung neatly in her locker, and doused some perfume on her neck and wrists. She retouched her lipstick, and made sure her hair was neatly held back with berets. A couple of the other women invited her to join them for a milkshake, but she declined, saying she had other plans.

Karina crossed the factory floor and walked upstairs, drawing looks from some of the men who were working late. Connie, Talbot' secretary, had already gone home for the day, so Karina walked straight to Talbot's personal office and knocked on the door.

"Come in," he said.

Talbot was standing by the bookshelves, looking for something.

"Oh, Karina, it's you," he said. "Thanks for coming. I know you probably want to get out of here as early as possible on a Friday night."

"Not at all, it's my pleasure," she said. "It's not like I had a hot date or anything."

Talbot smiled and took a moment to appreciate Karina's attire, a pink dress that ended above her knees with a white belt that pressed against her curvy hips, and high-healed white shoes. The dress was sleaveless and cut low to reveal the upper chest and back. Talbot' eyes froze for a moment on the muscular striations of Karina's neck and the shallow indentation where her neck met the center of the clavicle. Hanging there were the two scapulars of the Virgin Mary, which Karina's mother had given her. Her hair was held back by berets and hung over her shoulders. Karina pushed some hair behind her right ear.

"Sir, now that I'm here, I want to thank you for the radio," Karina said. "We are all very happy with it."

"Please, call me George," he said. "Don't even mention the

radio. It's the least I could do to show good faith."

Talbot walked over to a dresser-like piece of furniture and opened the top to reveal a full bar. The top button of his shirt was unbuttoned and his sleeves were rolled up halfway up his forearm. Talbot served himself a scotch.

"Can I get you a drink?" he said.

Karina shook her head. "No thank you, George."

Talbot sat on the leather chair in front of the coffee table and gestured toward the couch with his hand, where Karina took a seat. She wondered where this was all leading.

"Karina, when you came into my office the other day, I must admit, you showed some courage," Talbot said. "And I admire you for that. It takes a certain kind of woman to take the initiative you took to come in here and make requests like that."

Karina did not react.

"I'm looking for a woman in this company to advise me on certain matters," he said. "You know, employee relations and morale, lowering turnover, things like that. So what do you think?"

"Mr. Talbot…" Karina said.

"Please, George."

"Oh, right, George, I don't have any experience on these matters. I don't know if I would be very helpful. There must be someone else who knows more about those things than me."

"Maybe you're right. That's all very true. But none of them would impress me the way you do. There's something about you that I can't put my finger on. It's something I can't identify in a job interview. You opened my eyes to something this week. You helped me become a better boss and gave me advice on how to run a better company. You didn't have to do that."

The air conditioner had cooled the room significantly, and after a day of working in the heat, the brisk air chilled Karina. She shivered and crossed her arms in front of her chest. Talbot must have noticed, because next thing Karina knew, he fetched his hanging suit jacket and draped it over Karina's shoulders. It covered her so completely that it felt like a poncho. The lemon' scent of Talbot' Guerlain cologne emanated around Karina. The jacket was so warm, it felt as though Talbot had just removed it and his body heat was still clinging to it.

Talbot walked to his desk and grabbed a folder. He took a seat right next to Karina on the couch and placed his drink on the coffee table. Karina fidgeted in her seat, as though making sure the distance between them was appropriate. But part of her lost interest in etiquette. Talbot opened the folder and showed her several complaints filed against his company by former employees. They ranged from verbal abuse to sexual harassment.

"Look at these," he said. "I've been trying to figure out how to deal with the conditions that triggered all these complaints. I've tried firing supervisors, hiring more employees to take on some of the workload, hiring consultants and lawyers."

While George was talking, Karina kept her eyes fixed on the paperwork, but occasionally, she glanced over at Talbot. As he spoke, he seemed genuinely concerned about the complaints, his eyes showing sincerity as they pored over the file. Suddenly Karina felt comfortable, even sheltered. Maybe it was the coat draped over her shoulders, or the soft leather couch, or the feeling that she could set the price on whatever Talbot wanted.

"Have you ever tried promoting women, or hiring a woman as a supervisor?" Karina said.

Talbot fixed his eyes on her face.

"No," he said. "I never have."

"Why not?" Karina said. "Women are just as capable as men, and probably have a better understanding of how to treat fellow workers, especially if they are women."

Talbot pushed up his eyebrows, as though struck by sudden enlightenment.

"So, tell me a little bit about yourself, Karina. Where are you from? What's your background? Where is that interesting accent from? I bet you're Spanish."

"I am from El Salvador, a small country in Central America," she said.

"Of course, El Salvador," he said.

"My father was the mayor of my town, Tonacatepeque," she said.

"Tonatepiki?" Talbot repeated. Karina smiled.

"Close enough," she said. "Anyways, my father was assassinated in 1965. He was the only breadwinner. So last year, I came to New York to help my family."

"You know, my grandmother moved here from Russia with her sister when she was 20. They were fleeing Jewish persecution there. I always admired her for coming here without any men."

Karina sighed.

"It isn't easy," she said. "I miss my family very much. My mother still lives there with my two sisters and my brother. But there's more opportunity here than in El Salvador. How about you, George? It must be hard to own such a big company. It seems like so much responsibility."

Talbot liked the question.

"Well, it is. But actually, I don't own the company. My father-in-law does. I just run Melrose Plastics. So people just say I own it. I guess I married into the business. I always wanted to be a great industrialist, but I never thought it would be making flowers."

"You do a fine job," she said, then paused and put on a coy smile. "You are a good man."

Talbot looked Karina in the eyes.

"You really think I am a good man?" Talbot said.

"Yes," she said. "I do."

Then Talbot provided another dramatic pause.

"Do you think I am a handsome man?" he said.

Karina froze. His blue eyes were penetrating so deep into hers that she didn't dare even twitch. She was sitting back on the couch, and George was sitting forward to her right, as though poised for some sort of action. Karina swallowed heavily. She knew that there was a moment of truth here. This seemingly powerful man was asking her a question that was obviously a trap. If she said no...well, if she said no she'd be lying. The truth is she thought Talbot was one of the most handsome men she ever met. The way he carried himself, with confidence, yet attentiveness exuded a sense of security in who he was. His voice was so smooth, he sounded like a radio commentator. His clothes was obviously top notch. Karina had snuck a close look at his suit: it was custom cut in Italy and made of the best fabric.

Karina decided she didn't want to lie.

"I think you are very handsome," she said, without breaking eye contact. Then she knowingly tossed a wrench into George's question. "Your wife is very lucky," she said.

He responded quickly. "She doesn't think so," George said. "All I get from her are complaints."

Hearing Talbot take sides against his wife further eroded any safeguards that Karina had erected to maintain a professional relationship with him. George smiled. He folded the file, placed it on the coffee table and inched ever closer to Karina.

"You know, I didn't just invite you up here to talk about business," he said.

The conversation had gotten Karina's heart racing. She shrugged off George's jacket and place it on the chair next to her.

"Then why did you invite me here?" she said.

Talbot answered by reaching behind her neck and placing his warm right hand underneath her hair. Karina didn't flinch. The feeling of his hand rubbing the tiny fuzz at the back of her neck electrified her. She leaned toward him, and at the same time, George moved in and kissed her. The kiss started off with closed mouths, but progressed into a wetter version. Talbot placed his hand on Karina's knee and she suddenly stopped him. She caught her breath and stood up, straitening out her dress. She wiped a bit of saliva off her lips. Talbot had a lost look in his eyes, as though someone had pulled the plug on his brain.

"George, you are a very handsome man," Karina said. "But you are married. And you are my boss."

Talbot stood up and kissed her again. She kissed him back, but only momentarily. Then she pushed against his chest.

"I can't, George," she whispered. "You are married."

Karina grabbed her purse and hurried out of the office, wiping her lips as she walked out the door. She felt so lightheaded, she thought she would faint as she hurried down the stairs. George walked after her, but stopped chasing her just outside his office. He didn't call out to her for fear of creating a scene among the few workers still at the factory. But he watched from above as she crossed the floor.

Part of Karina felt naughty, part of her felt aroused. But the one feeling that permeated her entire soul was love. She wanted nothing more than to let George have his way with her, but she had stopped herself with a dose of strength she didn't know she had. Deep down inside, she knew that if she gave herself up so easily, he would not respect her. On a cloud of feminine power, Karina practically glided out of the factory.

She spent a giddy weekend shopping with Catalina. At one point, she asked Catalina what she thought about dating married men. Catalina warned her about the perils.

"They promise you the world, but they'll never leave their wives," Catalina said.

On Sunday, Karina went to mass and asked God for guidance and strength. She also thanked God for putting Talbot in her path.

Monday morning, the women showed up to work and were struck by the air temperature. It was actually bearable inside the assembly unit. Ronald the Supervisor explained that company maintenance men had installed an air conditioner over the weekend. The women were ecstatic. They rallied around Karina again, this time more openly in front of Ronald. No one broke a sweat in the assembly unit that morning, or any morning after that. With the record player and the air conditioner, work became more bearable, and the long hours that had tortured the women before went by quicker.

Karina didn't dare visit Talbot. The air conditioner was a clear confirmation to her that he still wanted her. But she didn't know how to follow up. She figured she would let Talbot make the next move. And he did.

That Friday, Ronald the Supervisor again pulled Karina out of the assembly unit and again told her Talbot wanted to meet with her after work. So when the shift was over, she decked herself out in a khaki skirt and a tight, button-down black blouse after work and went to see him.

Talbot was wearing his suit jacket and sitting behind his desk when she knocked on the door and walked in. Immediately, she noticed a sea change in his demeanor toward her. The personable charm he had showed her on their last visit had now morphed into pure professionalism.

"Hello, Karina," he said, gesturing toward the chair across his desk. "Please have a seat."

There was no offer of a drink, or retiring to sit on the couch. So Karina reciprocated by calling him Mr. Talbot again.

"Thank you, Mr. Talbot," she said.

"I just wanted to make sure we understood our mutual positions," Talbot said. "What happened last time was a terrible mistake on my part, and I apologize. It won't happen again."

Karina was devastated. If there was one thing she didn't want to hear was that Talbot didn't want to kiss her again. Talbot continued rambling on about some corporate challenge or other, but Karina was so depressed that she just watched his lips move and wondered why he had changed his mind about her. Maybe she was wearing the wrong clothes. Maybe Talbot hated beige skirts, or black blouses. Or maybe she smelled bad – Karina sniffed the air around her just to make sure she didn't. Maybe she didn't put on enough perfume, or her makeup was too heavy, or her shoes made her look shorter today.

Maybe he had rekindled love and respect for his wife. And to this, Karina could not object. But she hoped that wasn't the case. It occurred to Karina that Talbot might be playing a game. But why would he play such a malicious and cruel game with her? Suddenly her attention turned back to what Talbot was saying.

"...So can I still count on you as an adviser?" he said.

"Of course," she said. "I will help however I can."

"Good," he said. "Then I'd like to start meeting once a week, on Friday after work, like we have been the last two weeks. Does that work for you?"

"Yes, that's fine," she said.

So for the next few weeks, Karina ended her Fridays by changing into her clothes after her shift and visiting George Talbot in his grand office. When she'd arrive, he'd close the shades behind him to block out the descending sun. For the first two weeks, Talbot spent the better part of the hour talking about his business, and the ideas he had that his father-in-law, a man named Jonathan Merl, never considered good enough to implement. Using his father-in-law as a jumping board, Talbot would segue the conversation to his marriage and his wife, Judith. He did his best to cast a dark shadow over the prospects of his matrimony, always giving Karina the impression that it was doomed. Karina, like a good counselor, would simply sit and listen, sometimes feigning to take notes on a yellow notepad.

Talbot painted the portrait of a man oppressed by a marriage that had attached him not just to a woman, but an entire life of servitude to her family. He complained about her adherence to Judaism, and the insistence that they follow rules such as observing the Sabbath and Holy Days. He couldn't stand it. He explained to Karina that many times, he spent the weekend at an apartment that he owned in the city under the pretext that he was working and had to meet deadlines. Karina couldn't really sympathize with his problems. Instead of being grateful for the position he held in society, he seemed resentful of the people who had made it possible. The only story from Talbot she could relate to was his grandmother's tale of immigration from Russia.

It was during those days that Karina, feeling as though she had to size up her competition, got a good glimpse of the photographs of Talbot's wife that he had on his desk. She was about his age, fortyish, with blond hair cut short like a boy's.

The following week, Karina entered Talbot' office after work hiding something behind her back. Talbot was sitting on his couch, having a drink. He stood up when she walked in. The blinds were still open and the hot sun was pouring into the room. Karina was decked out in a black miniskirt and a red satin shirt.

"What do you have there?" Talbot said.

"It's a gift," Karina said, revealing a framed photograph of Russian women disembarking from a boat on Ellis Island next to the Statue of Liberty in 1917. "I found this in a thrift shop. Maybe your grandmother was on this boat."

Talbot put down his drink, his eyes transfixed on the photograph, and he walked to Karina. His face was so serious, she wondered whether she had offended him. He lifted the photograph and glanced back and forth from it to Karina's face.

"I don't know what to say," Talbot said.

"Don't say anything," Karina said, then in a quick move, she pulled down his neck and gave him a welcoming kiss on the cheek. She knew her Chanel perfume had lashed Talbot. As Karina pulled back, he grabbed her by the waist and pulled her toward him. Standing there, chest to chest, it was Karina who made the move to kiss him. She grabbed Talbot' head with her hands and brought it down to her lips. Almost immediately, he slid his hands under her skirt and squeezed her ass. From there, his hands seemed to want to touch her everywhere at once. They stumbled toward the couch, where they collapsed in a tangled bundle. Just as Karina suspected, Talbot had thick chest hair.

Talbot's apartment, on East 66th Street, had a balcony overlooking Central Park. It was sparsely furnished, evidently with a man's touch, because it lacked brightness of color. Like Talbot' office, his apartment was decorated with dark wood and pronounced corners. The queen size bed in the bedroom was nestled in a dark wood frame, and a wood bar in the living room revealed itself with the touch of a button. Both the living room and the bedroom were decorated with original paintings of ships and boats. Talbot explained that he had a yacht and a sailboat and escaped to sea as often as his job permitted. He promised Karina he'd take her out on the water on one of his escapades.

After talking for an hour or so in Talbot's bed, Karina explained to him that she had a midnight curfew at the residence where she lived and had to get home. Talbot drove her to St. Jean D'Arc in his sports car and told her he wanted to see her the following day.

So the next afternoon, on Saturday, he picked her up and took her to the Metropolitan Museum of Art and lunch at a fancy restaurant. And on Sunday, he took her to another museum and another nice lunch. The following week, Karina and Talbot saw each other every day, either after work or during the lunch break. And the following weekend, Talbot gave her a black Anne Taylor dress and took her to *Bouchon Du Provenence,* one of the finest restaurants in Manhattan.

The saddest part of each day for Karina was when Talbot would drop her off at St. Jean D' Arc.

Toward the end of August, a single-person room had vacated at the residence, and Karina had moved from the room she shared with Helen and Jasa into a smaller room by herself. Living alone had its pros and cons. It worked for her because no one could really tell if she did or did not sleep in her room. But it depressed her because on the nights she didn't spend with Talbot, there was no one to talk to when she turned off the lights in her room and waited for sleep to come.

In September, Karina wrote her family a letter telling them about her luck in finding a good man. Without revealing Talbot' identity, she described him as a man of high stature in the community, a handsome movie-star like American who had gained considerable wealth through his hard work. She neglected to mention that he was married, or her boss, but these were details she didn't feel a need to convey.

In response, Emilia Fuentes wrote to her daughter about God and religion. And much to Karina's surprise, Emilia made a vague reference to Karina's sexuality.

"I hope you are still adhering to your religious obligations by attending mass on Sundays and maintaining your womanly virtue," Emilia's letter to her daughter said. "I am not there to guide you. For this, you must rely on your upbringing, and your own judgement. And you must remember that the eyes of God never close. They are all-knowing. The only thing a woman has is her *virtud.* And once she gives it up, it is gone for good. Protect yourself against temptation, *mi hija.* Don't wager yourself for just anyone. Any man worthy of you will respect your wishes and your virtue until you are married by the Church."

Karina felt depressed after reading the letter. Her sense of absolute joy dissolved into horrible guilt. Her mother was right. Her mother knew it all. She had compromised her virtue. She'd probably be damned to hell.

But it wasn't against her wishes. There was genuine love here. God could not possibly frown upon a woman following her heart.

But Karina knew. In that Catholic-tinged conscience with a safeguard heavy on guilt, any justification she gave herself was an excuse to sin, not acceptable reasoning. Talbot was married. She was sleeping with him, committing adultery. She was putting a family at risk.

But maybe the one sinning was Talbot's wife, for keeping Talbot away from the woman he really loved. His wife was such a selfish, ugly wench. The bitch's talons were so tight they were driving him away. And Karina was simply inheriting a man broken by a soured marriage.

Yes, Karina decided, it was Talbot' wife who was sinning by maintaining her grasp on a man who didn't love her, by trying to control him with the help of her father, by oppressing him day to day. Karina was in the right, wasn't she? God would surely understand that. It wasn't Karina who was married anyway. It wasn't so bad. It wasn't really a sin, not one of the serious ones. She'd probably go to purgatory, not hell. She could live with that. She felt that she'd been living in purgatory and hell her whole life and only recently had discovered heaven. Yes, the devil had more evil fish to fry. She was through with living in a worldly purgatory. Talbot made her happy and that was that.

Karina tried to maintain secrecy about the affair. She confided in Catalina, who knew how to keep a secret. Catalina did not try to talk her out of it, but when pushed for advice, Catalina told Karina she should break it off. But Karina didn't want to end it. Nothing, in her opinion, could beat the feeling of having her handsome, rich, boyfriend drive her around the city.

It was much harder to hide the affair at work. Karina's relationship with her co-workers eroded as the perks of Karina's relationship grew more brazen: the long lunch hours, the short work days, the reluctant respect from Ronald the Supervisor. Sometimes Karina would excuse herself in the middle of the morning, visit Talbot, and wouldn't come back until the mid afternoon. And Ronald would just turn a blind eye. This special treatment so irritated her co-workers that any recognition she had gotten from them for getting air conditioning and a radio was soon forgotten. In the locker room, the women joked in Karina's face.

"Hey Karina, you wanna come with us to grab a Vanilla milkshake. O, I forgot, you'll get a hot one from the boss later," one of the women told her.

The situation at work worsened one Friday afternoon in late September when Ronald the supervisor made an announcement to the women in the assembly unit.

"Ok, ladies, it's the end of the month, and you know what that means. All of you have to come in tomorrow for work. Except, of course, Karina. She gets to go sailing."

Karina gave him an icy stare. When Ronald dismissed everyone, Karina stayed behind to talk to him. She waited until the room had emptied out, then walked right up to him.

"Why did you have to say that?" she said. "That's not even true."

"What's not true, that you're Mr. Talbot's girlfriend? I think that's true," he said.

"My personal life is none of your business," she said.

"Sure it is," he said. "I'm still your direct boss. I can still do whatever I want with you."

Ronald grabbed Karina and tried to kiss her. He was holding her so tightly that she couldn't pull herself off, so she bit his lip. He slapped her and pushed her away. Karina yelled and stumbled over a desk.

"You think you're so elegant," Ronald said. "You're Talbot's flavor of the month."

The incident so disturbed Karina that her knees were still shaking nearly an hour later, as she sat in the locker room trying to compose herself for her meeting with George. But even after she washed up and changed, she could not conceal the red mark on her face, nor did she want to. Talbot noticed it the minute she walked in. He stood up, his eyes opened wide with anger.

"Karina, what happened?" he said.

"Ronald hit me," she said.

"He did what? I'll fucking kill him."

Karina had never heard George curse before. He stormed out of the office and ran down the stairs. Karina followed a few steps behind as he charged into the assembly unit. But Ronald wasn't there. He had already gone home for the night.

Needless to say, Ronald the Supervisor was history. And Talbot turned heads in the entire factory when he name Karina as Ronald's replacement. She was the first woman who had ever been promoted to management at Melrose Plastics. And in her first week as supervisor, Talbot raised the pay on all the women in the group from $1.40 an hour to $1.65. He explained to Karina that the government was planning to raise the minimum wage from $1.40 to $1.60 an hour in 1968, which was just three months away. So he might as well do it now. It would help Karina's credibility and win the support of her skeptical colleagues. It was a full $10 a week raise, and the workers in the assembly unit responded with joy. They apologized to Karina for judging her. They brought her gifts of fresh baked sweets, makeup and real flowers. The jokes in the locker room ceased, the women treated Karina with the respect any boss receives, such as suddenly ordaining her as the funniest person in the factory, and Karina got a nice raise.

The new management position made Karina's schedule even more flexible. She trusted the women in her assembly unit to do their jobs well, and often disappeared for half the day. None of them complained when Karina asked them to work late or come in on weekends. The extra money in their pockets and the air conditioning had smoothed them over.

As for Karina, Talbot introduced her to the sort of privileged life that sweeps away a person of humble roots. From the car to the apartment to the restaurants to the gifts, Karina became acquainted with a side of New York that she had only fantasized about. Talbot spent more and more time away from his wife and children, sleeping at his Manhattan apartment under the pretext of working. He let Karina redecorate his apartment.

He bombarded Karina with expensive gifts: purses, jewelry, shoes, clothes. They went shopping often, on Fifth Avenue, at Saks, in the elegant West Village. He never turned down a request from Karina to buy her something. The highlight came when they stumbled upon Tiffany's one day on Fifth Avenue. Karina had lived in New York for years now and had never bothered going inside, knowing she could not afford it. But Talbot gave her his left arm and led her inside, where she was struck by the immense height of the ceiling, the infinite glass cases with jewels, the smell of wealth and luxury that emanated within. She walked out of Tiffany's that day with a new pearl necklace that cost Talbot $400.

A couple of times, Talbot invited Karina on his boats. Once he took her sailing, the other time, he took her for a spin on his yacht. But Karina became so seasick in the first few minutes that he had to turn back around and head for shore.

The only arguments the couple had were over Talbot's wife. Every once in a while, Karina would tell Talbot that she couldn't see him any more because she didn't think that he really loved her. But Talbot assured her repeatedly that he loved her. He promised Karina that he didn't have sex with his wife any more, and that he would soon leave her for Karina. Indeed, Talbot was spending progressively less time at home, and more time with Karina. He would spend almost every weekend in the city, and sometimes a night or two during the week. The only thing he expected from Karina was absolute availability. She had to respond when Talbot called on her, whether she was at work, or at home sleeping.

Since Karina spent all her free time with Talbot, she had little left over for her friends. Catalina stopped calling Karina for Sunday shopping sprees. Griselle never treated her the same after she had missed her wedding because of work. Doris didn't bother inviting her for milkshakes after work anymore. Karina didn't realize how detached she had become from everyone until Talbot took his family skiing for two weeks in the winter of 1968 and left Karina to fend for herself. They were the loneliest two weeks she had spent in New

York. She left messages for Griselle, but never heard back from her. She went out after work with Doris and some of the other workers one night, but felt out of place, as though the group couldn't really let their hair down because the boss was among them.

One afternoon, she ran into Catalina at St. Jean D'Arc, and told her she needed to talk. Catalina invited her for dinner, and Karina broke down crying in Catalina's apartment.

"He's with his family. He still loves his wife. He's been lying to me all this time," Karina said.

"I told you," Catalina said. "That's how married men are, they promise you one thing and deliver another."

"What do I do? I love him."

"You have to give him an ultimatum," Catalina said. "Tell him that if he doesn't leave his wife, you're going to break it off."

"But I don't want to break if off," she said. "What if he says he's not ready to leave her. I don't want him to break up with me."

Catalina, smoking from her long cigarette holder, shook her head and blew out a cloud of smoke. She had opened a bottle of wine and served herself and Karina a second cup.

"Sometimes I don't know what you love more, George, or the lifestyle he provides for you," Catalina said.

"The one thing I really want from him, he can't give me."

"What's that, a new car?" Catalina said sarcastically.

Karina laughed, then shook her head. "No. I want him *exclusivamente para mi*."

Upon his return from the mountains, Talbot immediately called on Karina at St. Jean D'Arc. It was a frigid Sunday night in February, with snow piling high in the streets. He showed up at her residence unannounced at 8 p.m. and asked one of the nuns to please fetch Karina for him. She took her time coming to meet him. Talbot was sitting in his car outside when Karina walked out dressed in a fake-leopard skin coat, a black scarf, and mittens. He immediately got out of his car to open the passenger door for her, but Karina beat him to it and plopped down on the passenger seat of his car.

Her mood matched the weather. She reluctantly pecked him on the cheek inside the car once Talbot got back in. She showed Talbot an icy side of her personality that seemed to intimidate him.

"I've been dying to be with you ever since I left," Talbot told her, as he drived north on 6th Avenue with snow pelting the windshield.

"I don't believe you anymore, George," Karina said.

"Honest, it was torture. I had to sleep in the same bed with her and she wanted to have sex every night. But I refused. She's so repulsive to me."

"Then leave her. Leave her already."

Talbot looked straight forward, took a deep breath and exhaled loudly.

"Karina, I promise, I'm going to leave her. I can't stand the sight of her anymore. She is completely repulsive to me."

"But you still go home to her at night," she said. "You still share your bed with her."

"I've told you before Karina, I only do it for the children. I don't want to hurt them right now. It's really over with my wife. We barely even speak. It's the children Karina, it's them."

Karina sneered. "Ha," she said. "That's baloney."

"I'm here, aren't I? I'm with you because I love you."

"You're with me because you haven't had sex for two weeks and you're horny," Karina said. "It isn't about love with you. It's just about what you need and what you want. You don't care about me. You're never going to leave your wife."

They were stopped at a red light at 6th Avenue and 42 Street. The lights from Times square were glinting off the snowflakes on the windshield. Talbot turned to look at Karina with such a wounded face that she nearly fell for his act. Here was this wealthy man putting on a face like a boy sent to his room for being bad.

"Can't you just be happy to be with me when we're together?" he said.

The light turned green. A car behind them honked. George accelerated, his tires skidding on the ice before catching traction.

"You're a coward," Karina said. "You can't even admit to me that you are lying about leaving your wife."

"I'm not lying, Karina. I am going to leave her eventually."

"Fine," Karina said. "Then maybe I'll call her and tell her about us. Maybe that way it will happen sooner."

George slammed the breaks. Karina had to press her hand against the dashboard to keep from hitting the windshield. A car behind them screeched and skidded to avoid hitting them.

"George!" Karina yelled.

George Talbot looked at Karina with a face so stern, so angry, that she felt afraid for her safety. He held up the pointer finger of his right hand

"You will never call my wife," he said. "Ever. Do you understand me?"

Karina decided to push it. "Why not?" she said.

"Because you'll regret it," he said. "Because nothing good can come of it. When the time comes, I, and only I, will talk to my wife."

Karina crossed her arms in front of her chest and stared straight ahead. They drove on in silence until they arrived at Talbot's apartment. The lovers quickly made up and went to the bedroom. The sex was a fumbling mess. Talbot's urgency to get his pants off and free his stiff penis, the way he bent Karin over and buried his face between her ass cheeks, the way his tongue licked her non-stop, were all evidence of his celibate vacation. The man's pent-up appetite for Karina was overwhelming. He didn't even remove her panties before entering her, he tugged them to the side, ripping them. He stopped only to bend down and rub his face and tongue in her wetness. This was a side of him she didn't know, insatiable, wild. He rubbed her natural lubricants over her ass and tried sliding his penis in. Karina jerked down, but he grabbed her hard and sodomized her as she yelled with pain and pleasure. He pulled his penis out with a "thwack" and stuck right back in her pussy, where he came in a quivering fit of groans, right inside of her.

Karina worried at first, because George had never ejaculated inside of her. But in a way, she saw it as a new sign of commitment. For months, Catalina had been telling her to take birth control pills or force George to use condoms. But Karina had ignored the warnings.

From that night on, Talbot made it a point to ejaculate inside Karina every time they had sex. Although she knew getting pregnant out of wedlock would be devastating, she took no precautions to prevent it. In early June 1968, she missed her period. And by the end of the month, a visit to the doctor confirmed her pregnancy.

Karina was happy about the news, until she told Talbot. He immediately begged her to have an abortion, a procedure she couldn't even believe existed. She wouldn't even consider it. By the end of August, Karina's morning sickness was so bad that the other women at St. Jean D'Arc began to suspect her condition. A month later, she had stopped wearing her tight, sexy miniskirts because they simply didn't fit. One of the nuns confronted her, and she came clean.

The nuns had been good to Karina. They had turned a blind eye to her affair with a married man, tolerated the nights she spent at Talbot's apartment. But the pregnancy was too much. St. Jean D'Arc had a strict policy of not allowing men, babies, or pregnant women. The nuns told Karina she had a month to move out.

Talbot offered full support. He rented a one-bedroom apartment for Karina in a working class neighborhood in Hoboken, which was across the Hudson river in New Jersey. Karina moved there in October. Two weeks later, Talbot asked her to consider quitting her job to avoid the storm of gossip that would hit Melrose Plastics if she turned up pregnant. The uniform at work was baggy, and Karina's slight belly was undetectable. But it wouldn't remain so for long. So Karina, with a heavy heart, quit her job. Talbot promised to pay her rent and give her a monthly stipend of $100, which was less than half of what she was making at the factory.

Karina leaned on her friendship with Catalina and went over to her house often for dinner. She found herself visiting St. Jean D' Arc in the middle of the day for company and attending church services as often as she could. Once Karina quit her job, she didn't see Talbot as much. They had agreed that she wouldn't show up at the factory pregnant, and so she had to rely on Talbot to come to her. Early in the pregnancy, Talbot would pick Karina up on Friday nights and take her to his city apartment for the weekend. But as the months wore on, and her belly grew, Talbot began producing more and more excuses not to spend the weekends with her. At first, she expressed understanding. Then she grew concerned. Then later on Karina realized Talbot was feeding her the same kind of bullshit he would tell his wife: "I have a lot of work to do", "We're behind on deadlines", "My people need me at the factory for the next couple of days."

With her income slashed, Karina's remittances to her family dwindled from a peak of $200 a month when she was a supervisor at Melrose Plastics, to barely $10 a month. She explained in her letters that she was out of a job and the economy was bad. Her mother wrote back that she understood, that their finances were stable for the time being. But Karina knew the family wouldn't stay afloat in Tonacatepeque without a monthly injection of American dollars. So one by one, Karina pawned the jewelry George had given her, the earings, the necklaces, the rings, the broache. She managed to get about $400 for items that must have had a total face value of more than $4,000. Every penny she got, she sent to her mother back home.

Suddenly detached from her entire life and six months pregnant, Karina began to suffer from depression. Her clothes didn't fit her. She gained weight. She felt sick. Her neighbors argued loudly in a strange language. As temperatures plummeted in the winter, Karina went out less and less, until her only weekly outings were to the grocery store and to mass. Instead of venturing to the city with her big belly, Karina asked Catalina to visit her more often. And she did. During the entire pregnancy, it was Catalina who gave her pep talks, who bought her some maternity clothes, who kept bringing her the fashion magazines that Karina used to love to read.

Talbot became a practical no-show. He'd drop by once a week, usually on Saturday, with a bag of groceries, or a batch of flowers, or a new story to tell. He wouldn't stay long, and stopped offering to take her to the city. Although Karina had a phone, Talbot rarely called. In fact, to get in touch with him, Karina often had to leave several messages with Connie, his secretary. Talbot usually didn't return her calls immediately. He stopped promising to leave his wife, and Karina stopped asking him to.

On a freezing morning in late January, an acute pain shot through Karina's belly, followed by another and another. The pain subsided, but started again toward morning. It got so bad that Karina thought she was going to give birth. With her ar m embracing her belly, she phoned Talbot at the factory at 8 a.m. sharp. He didn't pick up the phone. She called back at 9 and told Connie the Secretary that it was an emergency. By 10 a.m., she called an ambulance to her apartment. The paramedics rushed her to the hospital, where doctors told her her pains were a symptom of false labor. Karina was relieved she wasn't giving birth, because she wanted to have Talbot around when she did. The hospital kept her overnight, and released her the next morning. She took a bus straight to Manhattan and showed up at Melrose Plastics at 9 a.m. Karina walked into the factory eight months pregnant and wearing a plain brown winter coat, attracting more stares than she ever did before. There was no music playing.

Connie was at her desk when Karina walked in. Talbot made her wait ten minutes before seeing her. Karina could hear him yapping on the phone in his office. When he finally let her in, he scolded her for coming to see him at the office.

"Do you know what people will say," he said. "This is a scandal."

"This is your scandal," she said. "This is your baby, George. Do you know that I was in the hospital last night? I thought I was going to have the baby. I tried calling you. Where were you, George? I have no one else."

The phone rang on Talbot' desk and he picked it up. In the months that Talbot and Karina had dated, he had never interrupted a meeting with her to take a phone call. Obviously things had changed. George put his hand over the receiver.

"Give me a minute. This is important. I'll be with you in a second."

That was it. Karina stood up and walked out of his office. She heard him calling to her, but kept right on walking without turning around. She knew he wouldn't chase her, for fear of making a scene.

She knew there was nothing more he wanted of her.

CHAPTER 23

With most of Karina's old coats cut to fit a svelt, attractive figure, the stock of clothes in her closet that actually fit had dwindled. Only two loose-fitting wool pullover sweaters could stretch over the watermelon-size lump on Karina's midsection. It became a mission just to find a clean garment and shuffle down the flight of stairs for milk and eggs. Weeks had passed since she took a bus because the wait in subfreezing temperatures was unbearable. The only shops within walking distance were a small market, a laundromat and a bar.

It was early February and Karina was two weeks away from her preidcted delivery date. Poverty kept her from preparing for the baby appropriately. Without cash, Karina couldn't afford a cradle, baby clothes or a stroller. Her own diet suffered, as fresh chicken and beef gave way to red beans and rice, black beans and rice, rice with salt and eggs, and eggs with bread and milk.

To send $30 to El Salvador, Karina had pawned her black and white television a week ago. The only book she had to read was a bible which a group of Jehovas witnesses had given her during a Saturday missionary visit in December.

The pregnancy had been a nightmare: morning sickness, false labor, lower back pain, weight gain, cravings for foods she couldn't afford, like the chocolate eclairs she had for breakfast once with Talbot at La Boheme bakery in Midtown. There was an excellent Italian bakery about three blocks from where Karina lived, a distance she would have walked under normal circumstances, but never as a pregnant woman with labor looming.

Boredom sunk in. The radio she always kept on became background drivel. There weren't enough ingredients in her kitchen to actually cook anything. She read and reread the letters that her family had sent her in New York over the last three years. Two themes kept jumping out at her: her mother's insistence that she go to Church; and her mother's refusal to mention a word about her murdered father. Since Karina moved to Jersey, she wrote less and less to her family. Without good news to deliver, Karina didn't want to write more than once a week. Her mother had no clue she was pregnant, that she was living alone, or that she was destitute. Karina hadn't volunteered the information. In her most recent letters, Karina had painted a rosy picture of the Northeastern winter, all based on her recollections of Fifth Avenue – its glittery storefronts and snow-framed window panes -- when Talbot had taken her there more than a year ago during the holidays. To explain the sudden drop in remittance money, Karina said that she had lost her job and was living with a friend in New Jersey while she found a new one.

By now, Karina's little sister, Camila, had graduated from high school in El Salvador, and was helping her mother sew and sell blankets and dresses at the market. It made Karina feel guilty that her family didn't ask about the drop in remittances, or mention their own economic hardships. Not even Camila, who so boldly had informed Karina of the family's dire straights more than two years ago, hinted at any financial struggles.

After Karina's unscheduled appearance at Melrose Plastics, Talbot hadn't visited her again. Sure, he called her a couple of times, to check how she was doing, and ask her if she needed anything. Karina could think of a million things she could use, starting with a massage on her aching lower back, but she would just say "no thank you."

The last time Talbot called, it was Saturday night, and he was slurring his speech. Karina had a hard time hearing him through all the background noise. He told Karina that he loved her and missed her, that he was at a restaurant with someone, and that he had been drinking. Karina urged him to come visit her, just so she could see him. But he ignored the question and went into a drunken monologue about how things had gotten complicated. He said he wanted to get his life back in order, he said he loved Karina more than his own wife.

"I don't even know why I'm still with her," he said. "I can't stand seeing her when I go home."

But Karina had heard it all before. She sat at her tiny kitchen table and listened quietly, nervously examining her unpainted fingernails as he spoke. Then through all the background noise where Talbot was calling from, Karina heard a woman's voice interrupt Talbot's rant: "Georgie, let's go. Georgie, I'm drunk. Let's go back to your place."

She heard Talbot cover the phone and scream back at the voice, "Hang on a second. I'm talking to someone."

"Who is that, George?" Karina said.

"Who's who?" George said.

"That woman calling you 'Georgie?'"

"She's nobody," George said. "Just some crazy lady who won't leave me alone."

Karina then heard the woman's voice come closer to the receiver.

"Hey, who are you calling a crazy lady? Hang up the phone and come here. I want you, Georgie. Take me back to your place."

Karina was livid: "George? George? Who is that?"

But George didn't register. Jazzy background noise was all Karina got in response. The phone hung up. Karina grabbed her telephone and hurled it across the kitchen. The tears flowed freely from her eyes, aided by the hormonal imbalance of late pregnancy.

Karina awoke with a fever the next morning, shivering under three blankets. She didn't get out of bed all day. A horrible headache accompanied the chill. It occurred to her that Talbot wouldn't be there when she delivered her baby, or any day afterward. Karina wet her bed and lied in the urine for three hours, wanting more than anything to die and be swallowed by the earth and never have to face these devastating feelings. Maybe if she just stayed in bed indefinitely, things would correct themselves. She didn't eat. She used the bedsheet and pillowcases to wipe her eyes and nose.

In El Salvador she could have had any man she wanted, she thought to herself. Things could be so different. She could have had an abortion and continued living her Cinderella life with Talbot, or she could have stayed in El Salvador. Karina's bed-ridden delirium lasted a day and a half. The feverish chill had struck so deep in her bones that she wore two pairs of socks and a sweater, even under her wool blankets.

The memories of El Salvador were so poignant she felt as though she were dreaming with her eyes open. There was her dog, Seco, scampering in her yard; and her father standing on the stage during a rally; and her mother slicing papayas in the kitchen; and Camila rummaging through Karina's "secret box."

Then around noon on the second day, Karina registered a memory that suddenly cheered her up. She thought back to her aunt Maite, the one who had married three different men, and had more money than any other single woman, and never seemed to let a depressing thought seep into her mind. She remembered Maite sitting on her porch, talking about men as though they were interesting pets that had to be kept muzzled and caged. Maite had said: "Much is deduced about a woman from her taste in men." But that never made much sense to Karina because in El Salvador, a woman's taste in men was expected to be expressed only once: when she chose a husband. And Karina couldn't stand to think that people would judge her based on who she had chosen as a husband. Karina tried to identify her taste in men. What could people deduce from her for loving Talbot, other than the fact that she was an imbecile for falling for a married man? Karina had come all the way from El Salvador to connect with Talbot. She hadn't settled for mediocrity. In choosing a man, she thought, she had aimed high.

Maite had said something else: "Sometimes you have to fight for your man." The memory of this thought was what gave Karina the will to finally get out of bed, shower, change her bedsheets. She suddenly felt invigorated. The haze cleared from her mind as the early plotting of a mission sunk in.

Naked, Karina stood next to her closet and picked out her outfit. Black lace thong panties, which still fit, were the first garment she stepped into, followed by thigh-high black stockings. A black, wrap-around skirt was the only matching piece she could fit around her belly. She managed to stretch a button-down pink cardigan over the belly. Although she wanted to perch herself up on high-heeled shoes, her swollen feet made her settle for red, low-heeled pumps.

For the first time in weeks, she felt good about herself when she stood in front of the mirror. That is, until she turned sideways and glimpsed her bulging profile.

After brushing her hair, which was still past her shoulderblades, she combed it and held it away from her face with a pair of black berets. After a session in front of the mirror with an eyelash curler, a compact, lipstick and blush, Karina felt quite satisfied with her appearance. In fact, she felt she looked damned good. But something was missing, something decorative with color.

She opened the top drawer in her dresser and took out a carved wooden box, where she had once kept all her jewelry. By now, anything of value had been pawned: the pearl necklace Talbot gave her from Tiffany's, the diamond earrings he bought her for Christmas 1968; the emerald jaguar he had bought her to remind her of Central America; the gold necklace and matching wrist loops. So she took the few items she couldn't pawn and put them on: a locket inscribed with the words, "Patrice, Love Uncle Phil," which Griselle had given her for her birthday when they were living in Brooklyn; a gold wedding band, with the inscription, M.H.R. XII-59, which she had bought at a thrift shop to help ward off unwanted come-ons; and a jade ring.

Now she looked at herself in the mirror again. She was all made up. Her neck and ears were bedecked. Her face was pretty and her skin looked smooth, if only a little swollen. She puckered her lips and then smacked them, and even sprayed some perfume on.

By the time she got ready, it was about 2 p.m. on Monday. From her pocketbook, where she kept the names, addresses and phone numbers of all her friends, she retrieved George's home phone number. Early in her pregnancy, she had copied it from George's own pocketbook in case of a life or death emergency. The few times she had asked Talbot for his home number, he had refused to give it to her. If he knew she had it, he would have had a fit.

Karina picked up the phone in her kitchen. Her heart began to race. She dialed Talbot's home number. A woman answered the phone.

"Can I please speak to Judith?" Karina said.

"One moment, please," the woman said.

A few second later, another woman took the phone at Talbot's house.

"Hello?"

"Is this Judith Talbot?" Karina said.

"Yes it is. Who's this?"

"You don't know me. My name is Karina Fuentes. I have something very important to talk to you about."

There was a pause on the other end.

"Well, what is it?" Judith Talbot said.

"I am pregnant. And the father of my baby is..." Karina was breathing heavily. "The father of my baby is George."

"Who is this? Is this some kind of joke?"

"This is not a joke. I am living in an apartment in Hoboken that your husband pays for. He loves me. He wants to marry me."

"This is absurd. Look, I don't know what you want. But you're wasting my time. Goodbye."

"Wait!" Karina yelled. "Please don't hang up. I am not lying to you. George used to take me to his apartment next to Central Park. I have been his girlfriend for more than a year. All those times that he told you he was working late, and trying to make deadlines, he was with me. I am about to give birth to his baby any day now. If it's a boy, I plan to name him George, just like his father."

"Who do you think you are, calling me!"

"I love George, and I wanted you to know the truth."

Judith slammed the phone down and the line went dead. Karina sat down on her couch, breathing heavily as though she had just climbed five flights of stairs. Her hands pressed down on either side of her face. The next couple of hours were a blur. She switched the dial on the radio to a music station and danced around her apartment listening to The Beatles, The Rolling Stones, The Mamas and The Papas, The Doors, Led Zepellin. She worked up a sweat.

A few hours later, around 5 p.m., the phone rang. It was George.

George's voice trembled with fury.

"I'm going to fucking kill you," George murmured into the phone.

"George, I'm sorry. I love you. Don't be mad, George.

Please."

George slammed down the phone. Karina panicked. She didn't know what to do. She called Catalina, and told her what had happened. Catalina promised to come to her as soon as possible. What would Karina tell George? How would she explain this? She prayed to God for an answer. As Karina waited nervously, she took a pen from her bag and wrote on a carton grocery bag: "Don't be mad, I told the truth." She clipped the piece of paper and put it in her purse, along with her cosmetics and her pocketbook.

CHAPTER 24

Det. Poppel sat back on the chair in Catalina's humble co-op.

"The little paper in her purse helped us crack the case," he said. "It made us realize this was a crime of passion."

Catalina shook her head.

"She called me here, right here in this apartment. Karina was crying. She's crying and she tells me that she has called her boss's wife to tell her about their affair and the baby. She knew she had made a huge mistake. She immediately regretted it. She tells me that her boss is really angry and has threatened to kill her. She pleads for me to come be with her, so of course, I get dressed up and take a bus over there…"

Catalina paused, staring out the window. She folded her arms in front of her chest, warming herself from a chill that originated within. Connery and Poppel were waiting on the edge of the couch, all ears.

"But when I get there," Catalina continued. "– and this I will never forget as long as I live – the door is unlocked. I walk inside. Karina is not there. There are beans on the stove, still warm. But the gas had been turned off. The slippers she wore around the house were near the couch. Her winter coat was hanging on the rack. I waited there for a couple of hours. But she didn't show up. I went to the police station to get help, or to file a missing person report, but they told me that since I wasn't a family member, that I would have to wait 24 hours to file one. I came back the next day and they told me to wait some more. The cops didn't seem to care at all. Maybe it's because she was just some missing spic or something.

"I've always wondered what happened to Karina. I want to

know. I've been wanting to know for 30 years. I never saw her again."

CHAPTER 25

If New York was hot in September, Palm Beach was a steam bath. Clouds of swarming gnats and mosquitoes, always prolific after a good storm, added to the muggy horror. It was summer here, like it was for most of the year.

Det. Poppel wasn't built for the Florida heat. He sweated right through his suit jacket before they had even put their seatbelts on in the rental car. Connery, who vacationed in Naples every summer, handled it better.

The detectives drove to Boca Raton, where George Talbot lived in a big two-story house on a relatively new development called Brisk Heights. The green lawn was expansive and the yard was nicely landscaped.

"This is what happens when you drain a swamp to build houses," Sgt. Connery said to Poppel as they stepped to the front porch, the only shady spot in the yard.

Connery noted the white Lincoln Town Car parked in the driveway and figured it belonged to an old man.

According to the research they had on Talbot, he was 73, still married to his wife of 42 years, and had three grown children. He was a retired industrialist who hadn't worked a day since he cashed in on his share of Melrose Plastics in 1972 and moved to South Florida.

The doorbell played a vignette of classical music. An older man answered the door.

"Mr. Talbot?" Connery said.

"Yes?"

"I'm Det. Sgt. Roger Connery and this is Det. Daniel Poppel from the Nassau County Homicide squad. Mind if we come in and ask you some questions?"

"I already talked to one of your detectives. I told him everything I know, which is really not that much."

Connery glanced at Poppel.

"Well, consider this a follow up interview. It won't be too long."

Talbot shrugged and said "Alright, come in."

Age had curved the old man's back a bit. But it didn't betray his stature, still more than 6 feet. He was dressed in a royal blue Lacoste shirt, white pants and moccasins. The shirt fit snuggly enough to reveal that Talbot kept in shape and had never submitted to the extra pounds that years can add. His thin gray hair was combed back on his head, as though he had just walked out of a pool.

Through the glass doors at the back of the house, Connery could see a brick courtyard, a shimmering blue pool, and off to the left a fenced-in tennis court.

"You play tennis?" Connery said to Talbot.

"Yes, as often as I can," Talbot said.

An older Hispanic woman came scurrying across the living room.

"Oh. Mr. Talbot, I was in the bathroom when I heard the doorbell. I'm sorry."

"It's okay, Maria, these two gentlemen are here to see me. We'll be in the kitchen."

The woman smiled at the two detectives and walked off to another wing of the house. They walked into a massive kitchen with a steel refrigerator the size of a two-door closet. When Talbot wasn't looking, Connery signaled to Poppel to prepare him.

"Nice maid," Connery said, then waited for Talbot to turn around so he could see his face. "So, I see you haven't lost your affinity for Hispanic women."

Talbot screwed up his eyes.

"Meaning what?" Talbot said.

"Meaning we know about your affair at Melrose Plastics," Connery said.

"What affair?" Talbot said. "What are you talking about?"

"The affair that all the workers knew about, Mr. Talbot.

They all remember."

Talbot sat on a leather chair at the immense mahogany table. Poppel and Connery sat directly across from him. Connery laid a folder on the table.

"Who told you that, a bunch of women? It's all gossip. That Melrose Plastics was a darn sewing circle."

"Well, we have people telling us that you had a pretty long affair with Karina Fuentes," Connery said. "We hear it got pretty serious."

Talbot swallowed hard. He started blinking, as though suddenly angered.

"Look, what is this? I told your detective everything I knew. I don't remember anything about this Karina Fuentes you're talking about."

"Are you denying the affair?" Connery said.

Talbot took a deep, loud breath.

"What do you want from me? I'm a man. I had a couple of flings when I was younger, but I don't even remember the names of the women."

"Does your wife know about your flings?" Connery said. "I'm sure she wouldn't think they were trivial, irrelevant matters, like a fishing trip or, I don't know, a tennis match."

Talbot stood up. "That's it, I'm going to have to ask you to leave," Talbot said. "My wife is coming home any minute, and I don't want her to find you here."

Connery and Poppel didn't budge from their seats.

"We don't think you're telling us everything you know," Connery said. "Did you have an affair with Karina Fuentes? It's a simple question. Maybe her picture will refresh your memory."

Connery slipped a photograph out of the folder, and laid it on the table in front of Talbot. Talbot didn't even glance at it.

"I had an affair with a woman in Melrose Plastics. But I don't remember her name or anything about her. It was just a tryst. It didn't mean anything."

"It must have meant something," Sgt. Connery said. "You got her pregnant and put her up in an apartment in New Jersey, didn't you? Or was that part of your regular routine? Getting women pregnant and putting them up in apartments."

"That's it," Talbot said. "I want you both to leave."

Connery stood up and walked around the table. He took a bag from his pocket, and opened a plastic kit with what looked like a cotton swab inside.

"Sure thing, we'll be gone in a second," Connery said. "Just give us a swab of your saliva so we can compare your DNA with that DNA of the dead fetus we recovered from Karina's womb and we'll be on our way."

Talbot grimaced.

"No," he said, as though insulted. "Certainly not. That's preposterous."

Now Poppel stood up. He got face to face with Talbot.

"We know you killed her, George," Poppel said.

"Get out of here. You're crazy." Talbot said, trying to push Poppel's arm.

"We have the evidence," Poppel continued in a cold, calm tone.

"I don't want to hear it. You two are just here on a fishing expedition because you're desperate."

Poppel let the old man lead him across the living room.

"All we need to bring you in is a sample of your saliva so we can prove you were the father of that dead baby. What happened, George? Your wife found out about the affair? You knew her father would disown you and send you back to the gutter if she divorced you? You couldn't stand to lose that plumb job. Not George Talbot. You had a rich life, a rich car, a mansion, a nice family. You had your own factory. We know your wife found out about the affair. We know you threatened to kill Karina because of it. We know you're guilty."

"Out!" Talbot said. "Now."

Talbot's cheeks flushed red with anger. Poppel got in his face again.

"We're coming back tomorrow with a search warrant from a judge and we're going to take a sample of your saliva by force," Poppel said. "You're going down for the murder of Karina Fuentes. You're going to spend the rest of your golden years in prison."

The shotguns were cheap at Wal-Mart and didn't require a waiting period. For $295 Talbot bought a single barrel, pump-action 12-gauge Remington with a carved wood grip and shoulder hoist. A pack of buckshot was $25.

It was 8 p.m., and Talbot's wife was out to dinner with their neighbors, the Yardley's, who were also their best friends. Talbot took a black felt-tip marker and a piece of paper from a drawer in the kitchen and scribbled a note:

"Please accept my apologies. I couldn't let my wife find me like this."

Talbot's cell phone vibrated. It was his wife.

"Hi George," Mrs. Talbot said. "How are you feeling? Has your diarrhea come back. We all miss you, dear."

"Hi honey," Talbot said. "I'm feeling a little better. But I feel a bit of a headache coming on. See you soon."

"Ok, darling. Love you."

"Love you," Talbot said, and turned off the phone.

Using the garage opener that the Yardleys had left at Talbot's house in case they were ever locked out accidentally, Talbot let himself into the Yardley's two-car garage. They had taken Mr. Yardley's Mercedes to dinner. His wife's Range Rover was unlocked and the alarm was off. The keys were in the ignition. Talbot left the note he had written pinned under a wiper on the back windshield.

The shotgun was still in the box. Talbot opened it, loaded a shell into the chamber, and pumped it. The tan-leather back seat of his best friend's Range Rover was spotless. Not a crumb or spat of mud in sight, not even on the floor-mats. Talbot sat in the middle of the seat, and nestled the shotgun between his legs. The time on the digital clock on the dashboard said 8:22.

Talbot' had sweated right through his blue Lacoste shirt. He opened his mouth wide. The shotgun's metal barrel clanked on his old molars and cavity fillings. The barrel rested on his tongue, giving him his last metallic taste of life.

His arm was just long enough to reach the trigger with his thumb.

EPILOGUE

Newstime, 1/21/2000

"Through DNA tests, Nassau detectives have confirmed that the unborn child of a woman whose body was hidden for decades underneath a Jericho mansion was that of George Talbot, a long time owner of the house.

Yesterday morning, Nassau police received a packet from a North Carolina lab with the results of the 10 tests that all pointed to Talbot as the father of Karina Fuentes's baby, which was entombed along with its mother in a 55-gallon drum beneath a house in Jericho for 30 years.

"This confirms it," Nassau Homicide Det. Sgt. said yesterday, explaining that the probability of paternity was 99.9 percent. "George Talbot was the father."

Nassau Homicide Detectives believe she was beaten over the head with a blunt object and crammed into the container by Talbot, her lover and boss at a Manhattan plastic flower company. Talbot, who lived in the house with his wife until moving to Florida in 1972, committed suicide in Boca Raton last September after admitting to Nassau detectives he had an affair with a worker in the 1960s.

CBS News, 48 Hours, Sept. 27, 2000

"We found a motive, we found a suspect and I think the case is closed at this time," said Det. Connery.

But exactly what happened that winter day three decades ago?

"I think he comes to the apartment, takes her out of there. I think he takes her to the factory. There's no doubt in my mind that he's the one who killed this woman," said Det. Connery.

"I don't think he knew what do do with her. I think he had a plan that he was going to package her up and perhaps get rid of her. But once the package was completed, it was just too heavy for one person to move, and I think at that time, he was stuck."

Newstime, 11/1/1999

Camila Fuentes left New York for El Salvador yesterday morning with the sister her family has missed for 30 years.

A month after detectives identified Karina Angelica Fuentes as the woman found in a drum beneath a house in Jericho, her remains were boarded onto TACA Airline Flight 571 at dawn to be flown to the land where she was born, where her family has lamented her disappearance since 1969.

Her sister's body will be taken to a funeral home in San Salvador, where her family will hold a traditional 24-hour vigil. Camila Maroquin said Karina will be buried in a Hillside cemetery in the village of La Fuente, next to her father.

The End

ABOUT THE AUTHOR

Oscar Corral is an award winning journalist, author and filmmaker who toggles between his pen and his video camera depending on the project at hand. Corral encountered the story of Reyna Angelica Marroquin, the Salvadoran immigrant discovered under a luxury home in Long Island, while he was a reporter for Newsday in New York. This novel was based on that case, which was featured in 48 Hours, Forensic Files, and an episode of Law and Order. After a successful career reporting for newspapers that include the Chicago Tribune, Newsday and The Miami Herald, Corral linked up with iconic American author Tom Wolfe in Miami while the master satirist researched his latest novel, Back to Blood. The result is Corral's first full-length documentary film, *Tom Wolfe Gets Back to Blood*, which enjoyed a run on PBS. Corral lives in Miami with his wife and fellow journalist Cecile, their two daughters, and their pound mutt Daisy Duke. Stay tuned for more of Corral's *"Keep Her"* series of books featuring the not-so-smooth but determined Journalist Michael Cervantes. For more information on the film, visit www.tomwolfemovie.com

www.ingramcontent.com/pod-product-compliance
Lightning Source LLC
Chambersburg PA
CBHW071141170626
46809CB00002B/721